W9-AVI-695

MOUNTAIN VIEW PUBLIC LIBRARY

1000591920

MOUNTAIN VIEW

PUBLIC LIBRARY

Mountain View, Calif.

THE CHELSEA GIRL MURDERS

Other Robin Hudson mysteries by Sparkle Hayter

THE LAST MANLY MAN
WHAT'S A GIRL GOTTA DO
NICE GIRLS FINISH LAST
REVENGE OF THE COOTIE GIRLS

THE CHELSEA GIRL
MURDERS

A Robin Hudson Mystery

SPARKLE HAYTER

MOUNTAIN VIEW
PUBLIC LIBRARY
Mountain View, Calif.

William Morrow
An Imprint of HarperCollinsPublishers

THE CHELSEA GIRL MURDERS. Copyright © 2000 by Sparkle Hayter.
All rights reserved. Printed in the United States of America.
No part of this book may be used or reproduced
in any manner whatsoever without written permission
except in the case of brief quotations embodied in critical articles and reviews.
For information address HarperCollins Publishers Inc.,
10 East 53rd Street, New York, NY 10022.

HarperCollins books may be purchased
for educational, business, or sales promotional use.
For information please write: Special Markets Department,
HarperCollins Publishers Inc., 10 East 53rd Street, New York, NY 10022.

FIRST EDITION

Designed by Oksana Kushnir

Printed on acid-free paper

Library of Congress Cataloging-in-Publication Data

Hayter, Sparkle, 1958–
    The Chelsea girl murders : a Robin Hudson mystery / Sparkle Hayter.
        p. cm.
    ISBN 0-688-15518-9
    1. Hudson, Robin (Fictitious character)—Fiction.   2. Women journalists—New
York (State)—New York—Fiction.   3. Chelsea (New York, N.Y.)—Fiction.
4. New York (N.Y.)—Fiction.   I. Title.
PR9199.3.H39 C48 2000
813'.54—dc21   99-086592

00 01 02 03 04 RRD 10 9 8 7 6 5 4 3 2 1

For my agent, Russ Galen,
and the Chelsea Hotel,
for keeping the wolves from the door

You meet people all over the world on this international Bohemian circuit, and they'll say, "See you at the Chelsea."
    —German writer Jakov Lind

She couldn't pay her rent so she moved somewhere more expensive. The Chelsea. Very artistic.
    —Candy Darling in *I Shot Andy Warhol*

It was said to be crazy but likable.
    —Florence Turner of the hotel in *At the Chelsea*

THE CHELSEA GIRL MURDERS

Thanks to Mrs. Dulcinia Ramirez and her pathological love of Jesus, and thanks also to the Holy Toledo Religious Novelty Company of Toledo, Ohio, and Shanghai, China, my neighbors and I found ourselves out on the street in our pajamas one spring night, watching our building burn. Of course, we didn't yet know what was to blame. It took several weeks for the fire department to trace the blaze to Mrs. Ramirez's electric Ascension of Jesus display, or what was left of it after the immolation.

My name is Robin Hudson and at the time of the fire I was the programming head for the Worldwide Women's Network, a subsidiary of Jackson Broadcasting. I was forty going on forty-one, divorced and childless. Since college I had lived in Manhattan's East Village in a prewar walk-up on East Tenth Street between avenues B and C, a clean, quiet block populated largely by Hispanic working people and their families. Through many eras and transformations, I stuck it out on the Lower East Side, from its days as an anarchist slum to the current haute-bohemian paradise enjoyed by yuppies and affluent twenty-somethings from elsewhere who had seen a road show of *Rent* and been inspired

to move here, dye their hair pink and blue, and taste *la vie boh-
eme*. It was this last incarnation that got me thinking it might be
time to leave the East Village and look for an apartment in a more
authentic, grown-up New York neighborhood, one that was less
at risk of being Disneyfied.

But it was just idle thinking, until Jesus short-circuited.

The fire alarm went off in the hallway with an unholy shriek
after midnight, as I was falling asleep and into a gauzy, half
dream, about Pierre, this French genius with whom I'd recently
had a mad fling. So appealing was this dream, I didn't react right
away to the alarm. Only when I smelled the smoke did I jump
out of bed, open the window, and kick away the poison ivy plant-
ers so my cat, Louise Bryant, could escape. Before I followed her,
I wildly grabbed stuff—my purse, my laptop, shopping bags full
of mementoes and personal papers, and an old Enfield rifle, a
present from a man I'd loved and lost. I threw a black coat over
my antique peach nightgown and shoved my feet into slippers.
Black smoke was starting to fill my apartment when I went clang-
ing down the fire escape.

After me on the fire escape came my neighbors, old Mr. O'Brien
and his latest "housekeeper," a widow he'd met through a mail-
order bride magazine he subscribed to. The way they went down
together, wrapped up in one big yellow blanket, made me think
they weren't wearing much underneath.

Most of my neighbors were already out of the building, standing
on the street in their pajamas. It's an odd thing to see your neighbors in their nightclothes. My neighbor Sally was standing in a
flowing, iridescent white nightgown, a bag under one arm and her
powder blue, circa 1962 Samsonite suitcase under the other, underwear and paper sticking out of it. Phil, our saintly super, a
tweed coat over his striped pajamas, was holding his scrapbook of
clippings and doing a head count with Helen Fitkis, unrepentant
Communist and widow of a longshoreman. She wore a quilted
orange-and-yellow housecoat over gray slippers, and was holding
my cat. Mr. Burpus, a subway motorman and enthusiastic philate-

list, wore green pajama bottoms and a brown houndstooth blazer, no shirt. He was clutching a stamp album. Three Japanese girls, NYU film students who were subletting the apartment above me, wore identical black leather jackets over flannel pajamas, in different pastel colors. Mr. O'Brien's bare, pale legs poked out from beneath the yellow blanket, next to the pale legs of the "housekeeper." He was barefoot, while she wore one red slipper.

At this point, only old Mrs. Ramirez was missing. Mrs. Ramirez's apartment, located conveniently below mine, was full of old wooden furniture, religious candles, scrapbooks, photographs, and other highly flammable stuff. As the biggest flames were coming from her window, we all assumed the worst: When that pile of tinder ignited, she went up like Joan of Arc.

"She was very dried out. She would have burned fast," said Mr. O'Brien, displaying the sensitivity of a man who orders his concubines from the backs of magazines and calls them "housekeepers."

"That's a great comfort," I said.

"It would have been a quick death," agreed his "housekeeper." "And now she's with Jesus."

"Who's with Jesus?" demanded a voice in the dark. "What's going on?"

Mrs. Ramirez stood there, in a trim black coat and matching hat, with her Chihuahua, Señor, just back from one of her one-woman Neighborhood Watch rounds.

"Who's with Jesus?" she demanded again. Maybe it was my imagination, but I thought I detected a note of jealousy.

"We thought you were, luv," Phil said. "Thank God you're okay. The building doesn't look very good though."

"A fire," Mrs. R. correctly identified. Mrs. Ramirez of course had a theory to share about the fire, that our neighbor Sally, "the witch," had caused the fire by burning herbs and had been inviting divine retribution for practicing "the black arts."

Sally began to weep, and protested: "I wasn't burning anything. I was asleep."

"Then who was it?" Mrs. R. asked, looking around for suspects.

Flashing lights from emergency vehicles strobed the street. It had rained earlier, leaving a wet, reflective sheen, making the darkness seem somehow brighter. Blurry ribbons of reflected light—red, white, yellow—bled into each other on the wet asphalt. Above us, burning pieces of paper and cloth came down in a rain of softly falling black ash, as though it were snowing in hell. More engines arrived. There was a lot of noise—the roar and crackle of the fire, firemen hollering to each other, the sound of the water hoses, and spectators chattering in various languages, but it quickly turned to white noise. I was stunned. How stunned? I only subconsciously noticed how incredibly manly and attractive the firefighters were. By now, the flames were coming out of my window and nearly two decades of my existence was going up in putrid black smoke.

"You're not going to be able to go back in there tonight," one of the fire guys said. "I don't know if or when you'll be going back. You'd better find other accommodation."

"Let's go have a drink," Phil the super suggested, taking control. In a motley procession of pajama-clad people and pets, we trooped down Avenue B to the Lucky 7 bar. After we took a couple of tables, we ordered a round of beverages. Even Mrs. Ramirez indulged, ordering a small sherry. The three of us with cell phones began making calls.

First we called the "management company" that ran our building, which is really just one miserly Greek guy, his indolent brother, and in the office a woman named Florence who couldn't find her ass with both her hands, and when they didn't respond to our page, we set about tracking down places for everyone to stay. Sally was going to stay with her friend Delia. Helen and Phil were going to stay with her sister and brother-in-law in Jersey, which did not seem to thrill Phil much. Mrs. Ramirez had no living relatives, and no friends, really, but she was a churchgoing Catholic and Phil was able to find an order of patient, long-suffering nuns on Long Island who could and would take her and Señor, no doubt earning themselves many indulgences in the kingdom of heaven.

As for me, my friend Tamayo Scheinman, a comedienne, keeps a place at the Chelsea Hotel. At the moment, she was traveling around the world with Buzzer, her new boyfriend. She could be anywhere from Outer Mongolia to Damascus, and was only reachable by native runner, high-psi telepathy, or irregular E-mail from an Internet cafe. But I had keys to the place in my purse and an open invitation to use the apartment whenever she was away—you know, for trysts and such, if my apartment was too messy or neutral ground was required. Until now, I'd had no need for it.

"Another round?" suggested Phil.

"Not for me. I have to work tomorrow," I said.

"I'll call you," he said to me, and we all said our good-byes.

Still in my nightclothes, I got a cab and rode uptown to Twenty-third Street between Seventh and Eighth avenues, and to the Chelsea Hotel. You may have heard of it. Maybe you've even stayed there, or walked past it on West Twenty-third Street. You can't miss it, a redbrick Victorian Gothic building, almost castle-like, looming over the staid, utilitarian buildings of Twenty-third. The front is lined with lacy, black wrought-iron balconies, the roof with turrets and pyramids. It looks like the kind of place the Addams family would check into when in New York. It is twelve stories high and was, when it was built in the 1880s, the tallest building in New York. Though it started out as cooperative apartments, it soon became a residential hotel for show people, artists, Negroes, homosexuals, and others who couldn't find lodging in more "respectable" hostelries. Over the years it has housed famous, infamous, and obscure artists, as well as nonartists and tourists drawn to its history or bohemian atmosphere.

Tamayo had put my name on her rental card at the Chelsea, giving me blanket permission to use her apartment. A bellman named Jerome helped me carry my few things up to Tamayo's floor. He smiled slightly when he saw me, in my bedclothes, carrying my cat and my haphazard belongings.

"Our apartment building burned down," I said, to explain, and he shrugged almost imperceptibly, completely unnonplussed. Probably not the first time someone in pajamas had moved into the Chelsea 'round midnight with nothing but a clutch of overflowing shopping bags, a rifle, and a cat.

The door of Tamayo's apartment, 711, opened into darkness. I turned on the light and looked around a largish studio partitioned by parchment screens into separate sleeping, eating, and sitting areas. One wall was curved. There were two sets of French doors onto the wrought iron–filigree balcony overlooking Twenty-third Street. The bed was a loft with a desk beneath it to save space. The decor was crazy Japanese minimalist. There wasn't a lot of it, but what was there was interesting. The paper screens, for example, were made of transparent parchment in disparate designs and colors—one was aqua-and-red checkerboard, another swirling green and purple, another concentric circles of alternating pink and orange. The walls were off-white. The asymmetrical furniture was shiny white and very simple, except for a coffee table Tamayo had made herself, white enamel inlaid with hundreds of small fragments of mirror that reflected the light through the screens into a spray of bright colors on the walls and the ceiling. It felt a little like being inside a *Laugh-In* sketch.

After fashioning a makeshift litter box for Louise Bryant using newspaper and a cardboard box, I fired up my laptop and sent an E-mail to Tamayo to let her know I was camping out in her apartment. Then I stripped to my underwear and flopped onto Tamayo's bed. I was pretty tired. I was still recovering from a long business trip for my company and what happens? My apartment burns down, and just one day before my much-needed vacation. My life is ruled by no law but Murphy's.

Why didn't I feel worse about this? I wondered. My home and almost all my belongings were gone. Under normal circumstances, this would have been cause for self-pity and an excuse to drink vodka, but for some reason I didn't feel too badly about it yet. Maybe it was because I was still in a state of shock. Maybe it was those two months on four continents, which made me harder to surprise, and made me realize that sanity and reality are relative concepts, relative to the patch of land you're standing on and the people you're with. What I was now in was just another alternate reality. Roll with the punches when you have to, right? And if that last trip had taught me nothing else, it was the value of traveling light, in every sense of the word, whenever possible.

Or maybe I was just too fucking tired for angst. I dropped off to sleep pretty quickly and slept until around four A.M., when I was roused by a terrible pounding and a hollering at the door.

"Hey! You in there?" a man called out.

Before I went to the door, I looked around for something to use to defend myself and that's when I felt the first twinge of real loss from the fire. I'd lost my entire arsenal of innocuous-looking self-defense weaponry—all my poison ivy, my various glue guns, my pepper spray, my cordless, gas-canister curling iron. I still had the nineteenth-century Enfield rifle, though, which I'd taken with me for its sentimental value. It had no bullets in it, probably didn't work anyway, but it was pretty scary looking.

"Hey, baby, let me in!" he said. "Baby, come on!"

As quietly as I could, I climbed down from the loft bed, picked up the rifle from the desk, and crept in the dark toward the kitchen, where I grabbed my cell phone and took it with me so I could call for help quickly if I needed to.

"You've got the wrong apartment," I shouted back, my eye to the peephole. Through the fish-eye lens, he looked like a white man/boy with a very small body and a very large head. He had brown hair, brown eyes, and a day or two's growth of peach fuzz.

"I know she's in there. Let me in!" He was surly and antagonistic.

"She's not here," I said. "Who lives here? Do you know?"

"Uh, I don't know. Or I forget. Nadia knows you."

"You've got the wrong apartment," I said. "Go away!"

"Let me in!"

"You've got the wrong apartment! Go away or I'll call the police."

He swore in some other language. I didn't speak that language but after you've traveled in enough countries and stepped on enough toes, you can recognize the curse words just by tone.

I watched until he was out of view, waited a moment longer, and went back to bed. Barely an hour had passed when, around five A.M. I was awakened by more racket.

"Hey! Who put the chain on?" a woman called out. "Hello? HELLO! Tamayo? Are you home already?"

The door was ajar, the chain on it. The woman kept pounding on the door. I stood in the shadows, away from the light coming in from the hall, so I could see her but so she couldn't see me. It was a young woman with bleached-blond hair and big, dark glasses, wearing jeans and a big T-shirt. She had a suitcase and a small backpack. Behind her across the hall and down a couple of doors, a bald man was standing in his doorway, watching us and lifting hand weights.

"I hear you in there, TaMAYo!"

"Who is it?" I asked, in a low, clear voice. "I've got a gun."

"Uh, er, uh. Is this TaMAYo Scheinman's apartment?"

"It is. How did you unlock the door?"

"TaMAYo sent me the keys. See?"

She stuck a padded envelope under the door chain.

I grabbed it and said, "Don't move," then slammed the door shut, and turned on the light.

"Dear Nadia," it said. "Here are the keys. Hope all goes well with your fiancé. Be very careful. E-mail me when you're grounded. If you need any help, call Maggie in 709. Good luck and good sex."

It was a note from Tamayo all right. I recognized the hand-writing and the style.

I opened the door.

"I'm sorry, I didn't know Tamayo had other guests coming. Come in," I said.

"Who the fuck are you?" she asked, with just a trace of an accent.

It sounded foreign, but I couldn't put my finger on what it was. In the kitchen light, she looked like a teenager, but that may have been because she had the kind of baby-face cutes that tend to make a woman look younger than her years all her life.

"Robin Hudson, a friend of Tamayo's."

"What are you doing here?" she demanded.

"My apartment burned down. I had keys, so I came to stay here. You were expecting Tamayo to be here?"

"No. But when I saw the chain was on the door I assumed she had come back to New York. How do I know you're a friend of Tamayo's?" she asked.

"Don't be paranoid. What is it with kids today? You're so suspicious," I said, but held back all sarcasm and hostility, a little trick I'd had to learn and use a lot while on the road.

"I need to know if you're telling the truth about being Tamayo's friend," she said imperiously. "Otherwise, you'll have to leave."

"I'll have to leave? My apartment burned down. It's after five in the morning. I was here first."

"I have a written invitation to be here," she said.

"I have a blanket invitation. Look, I am so tired I can't think straight—"

"How do I know you know Tamayo? I need to know."

"Oh hell. Let me prove it to you," I said.

In Tamayo's publicity library, several loose-leaf binders containing media coverage about her, I found an article from a women's magazine about "Girls' Nights Out" among women of all ages. Tamayo contributed with a story about our most legendary girls' night out, one Halloween. It was accompanied by a photograph showing me, Tamayo, another friend of ours, Claire Thibodeaux, and my former intern, Kathy Loblaws.

The girl looked at it and said, "All right, you can stay tonight. How long are you planning to be here?"

"I don't know how long I'll be here. My apartment burned down. How long are you planning to be here?"

"Not long. I'm meeting my boyfriend here, we have a little business, and then we're leaving."

"Oh right. He was by earlier," I said.

"He was here already? Where is he now?" she asked.

An awesome transformation occurred as her entire demeanor changed, from surly youth to gushy teenager. Her eyes lit from within, her face broke into a smile, a rosy glow flushed her cheeks.

"I don't know. I thought he was at the wrong apartment. I sent him away."

"YOU SENT HIM AWAY?!"

"Sorry, but a strange man pounds at the door at four A.M. and wants to come in? You'd do the same. Jesus. You'll find each other soon."

"You don't understand," she said, and slumped into a kitchen chair, her bag sliding off her to the floor. She started to cry. There was something about the way she cried that made me think of a terrier with its tail caught in a door. It was not a pretty sight.

I wasn't sure what my "human duty" was here—to leave her alone, or see if I could do anything. By now, I was dead tired, but I decided to give her a drink and sit with her. Tamayo had a whole cupboard full of expensive liquor in gift boxes, and Nadia took a glass of brandy. After a big glass of brandy, she was almost human. She was nineteen, she told me, her name was Nadia, "just Nadia," and she had been raised in New York, though the slight accent suggested otherwise. She'd met Tamayo about a year before and had stayed here at the Chelsea a few months earlier when in New York shopping.

"I'm only telling you because you're a friend of Tamayo's . . . My fiancé and I are planning to elope," she said. "It's tricky. We have to be careful."

"Why?" I had this sneaking suspicion that she and the boy were both underage, and somewhere there were very worried parents who wanted to keep their children from making a terrible mistake.

"We just do!" she said. "Why do you need to have so much information?"

"Okay, okay. I really don't give a damn, I was just trying to . . . Change of subject. If Mr. Right shows up tonight, are you going to want privacy? To have sex. . . ."

"We do not have sex. We'll have sex on our wedding night. We'll only be here a day or two, then we'll go get married. Oh my Godt, oh my Godt, where is he?" She began to cry again. "It's your fault."

"It's not my fault, and it's not the end of the world—" I began.

"If you had a boyfriend, you would understand."

Where did she get off assuming I didn't have a boyfriend? I mean, I didn't, not really, not officially. But just for the hell of it, I told her I did, and told her about Pierre, the French genius I'd had a fling with in Paris. It made for a good moral fable about the benefits of grown-up love, mature adults being so much calmer on the subject, but if Nadia caught the parable, she didn't appreciate it, sneering slightly at me instead.

"Look. Why don't we both get some sleep? You'll feel better if you do, I'm sure," I said.

She headed toward the loft bed, but I stopped her. "I'm sleeping there. The sofa bed is through there, in the living room."

"The sofa bed?" she said disdainfully.

"Yeah."

"I guess the sofa bed will do," she said.

I crawled back up into the loft bed and wondered what manner of stray this little princess was. She didn't look old enough to be out on her own. Not having sex until the wedding night? Kids today. What was it with the so-called New Modesty anyway, or the New False Modesty, as it were? Who knew so many children of former promiscuous pot-smoking hippies would rebel by embracing the sexual mores of the 1950s? After pondering this briefly, a nuclear apocalypse couldn't have kept me awake, and I fell into a deep, oblivious sleep.

chapter two

When the alarm went off a few short hours later, the morning light was shining through a crack in the curtains and through the pink-and-orange screen, lighting the room in those colors and giving the place a deep, warm cast. If it wasn't my last day before vacation and if I didn't need to tie up so many loose ends, I would have taken the day off. But there was a meeting and I had two reports to finish and turn in to my higher-ups.

Nadia was up already, or still up, sitting in Tamayo's kitchen, tapping on a laptop computer.

"I guess the fiancé didn't get here," I said.

"No, he didn't, thanks to you!" she snapped.

Rude child. I was about to say something when I remembered she was missing her boyfriend. That, and not being able to get a good night's sleep on account of the pea under her mattress, had no doubt made her a tad cranky. I cut her some slack.

"Are you going to be hanging around all day?" she asked.

"No, I'm going to work," I said as I poked around Tamayo's cupboards for something Louise Bryant could eat.

"When you come back, call first from the house phone in the lobby, in case my fiancé is here," Nadia said.

Tamayo's cupboards were stocked with canned goods and food presents from her various admirers—tins of caviar, European cookies in fancy boxes, all manner of delicacy from canned rattlesnake to a big jar of pickled whole squid, which looked like something from an old-time carnival freak show. There was a lot of fancy Japanese food too, with Japanese language labels, and it was hard to tell from the pictures what exactly was inside the cans. Even when the Japanese products were labeled in English, it was hard to know exactly what was inside. In the fridge, for instance, were two blue-and-white cans of frosty Pocari Sweat.

"What do you think a Pocari is?" I asked Nadia, showing her the can. She didn't even smile, and this worried me, that she had no visible sense of humor. Didn't bode well for an early marriage.

Finally, I settled on a can with a picture of a fish on the outside, which turned out to contain a premium salmon. Louise Bryant picked at her food, but finally gave in and ate it before slinking off for her hourly nap.

I was going to need clothes to go to work. In order to go out and buy clothes, I was going to have to borrow some clothes, since I had fled in nightgown, coat, and slippers. Though Tamayo is shorter than I am, we are the same size otherwise, right down to shoes. Her closet was full of clothes, but there wasn't a thing in there I could wear to work. Apparently, Tamayo had taken the one conservative outfit she owned with her on the road, leaving behind the wardrobe for *La Cage aux Folles*. It's all lovely stuff, if you're a drag queen, a free-spirited comedienne, or Marilyn Manson, but not if you're the head of programming for a major network. Amid the jumble of feather boas, sequins, see-through blouses, black leather, and silver go-go boots was one relatively conservative outfit, lime green capri pants and a periwinkle sweater-top. I put them on with matching periwinkle shoes, grabbed my purse and coat, and left.

In the elevator, I rode down with two tailored, proper-looking women in pale suits, their various colognes mingling in the closed space.

"This isn't at all what I expected," said one of the women, who had dark hair and bore more than a passing resemblance to Marilyn Quayle.

They were holding their purses close to them in the way wary tourists do, so I gathered they were here for a short stay and were not long-term residents. Each carried a pale pink folder with a red rose border and the words "Mary Sue Enterprises." They looked like they were here for either a gathering of Phyllis Schlafly's Eagle Forum or a cosmetics convention, but Mary Sue Enterprises is actually a women-run business that teaches people how to buy up foreclosed mortgages and resell the properties for enormous profits.

"Loosen up. I like this place. I have a lovely room," said one tourist woman. "Think of the history and the character. Dylan Thomas lived in the room you're in now . . ."

"Oh, I don't care how many artists live here. I was expecting it to be like the Marriott, with room service and little bottles of shampoo. And these elevators are so ancient and slow," said the miserable, dark-haired tourist. "Can't we move into a bland, modern place with no character?"

"I checked. There are no hotel rooms available anywhere in the city right now. There are five big conventions in New York," said another woman, who then changed the subject. "Are you going to the financing seminar this morning?"

I beat them to the street and grabbed a cab just ahead of them to take me to Macy's, where I have my own personal shopper, Blair. I share Blair with other harried professional women, but all the same, it's a nice luxury. She had all my sizes and designer tastes in her well-organized database, so all I had to do was pick out a few things to change into for work, and she'd get the rest and send them to the office later that day.

When I got to the WNN offices, on the twenty-second floor of the Jackson Broadcasting Building in east Midtown, our six executive producers were waiting around the oval glass table in the pastel conference room. Our president, Solange Stevenson, and our veep, Jerry Spurdle, were not there yet. All of our executive producers were women, with the exception of Dillon Flinder, who was in charge of our health and science programming, and Louis Levin, in charge of repackaging foreign entertainment programming. Jerry and Solange had hired the other four, and I'd brought Louis and Dillon onboard, albeit after a bitter fight with Solange over Dillon. Back in the late 1980s, Solange and Dillon had repeatedly made the "beast with two backs" (and on one occasion the beast with three backs, according to Dillon, though he refused to tell me who the third party was). Dillon's presence was a constant reminder of their sexual intercourse, but that wasn't why I'd brought him aboard. I didn't know about him and Solange at the time. Dillon had made quite a few strange beasts in his sexual prime, one involving a drilled watermelon, and it was hard to keep track of it all. The man had tried almost everything possible involving consenting adults and/or inanimate objects, though I knew for a fact he hadn't yet made it with a bearded lady or a native Texan, because he'd told me so one night at Keggers, our regular watering hole.

While I was filling everyone in on the fire the night before, Jerry walked in and interrupted.

"I hear you had a fire," he said to me, smirking his oily little smirk. He was stirring his coffee, which he drinks in a mug that says "Chief Melon Inspector, WTNA TV."

"Yes, there was a fire," I said.

"What happened? Some drunken sailor fall asleep in your bed with a lit cigarette?" Jerry asked.

"I don't know the cause of the fire yet," I said, ignoring the bait.

"Sounds like something you'd do, burn down your building," he said. "I mean, it fits the pattern. . . ."

"Well, I didn't."

"Methinks she doth protest too much," he said. "So how'd you do it?"

Jerry's ability to provoke didn't come from his cleverness, obviously. The secret lay in his persistence, the way he buzzed around you like a hungry mosquito. Jerry was always trying to get a rise out of me, get my goat, "make my monkey crazy," in the terminology of my friend, producer, and peasant-king Louis Levin. This was a constant quest of Jerry's. I don't know why. There are some vexing people you can't ever quite escape in life— they keep popping back up—and Jerry was one of those people in my life.

"Whatever you like, Jerry. Boozy sailor with a lit cigarette? Works for me," I said with a laugh.

He wasn't finished. "By the way, I just got some more reports about your last trip, sent by foreign affiliates," he said. "You really angered some people. Did you really defile the heads of the five children of the Thai TV president?"

Touché. It was true. I had completely alienated the very proper Thai TV president by patting his kids' heads—not just patting their heads, but mussing their hair. And when informed of my crime, it's true I laughed and said, "You're kidding me." But who knew that it was an offense to pat a child's head in Thailand? Okay, our protocol department knew, but somehow, I had missed the head-patting thing. You do twelve countries on four continents, each with its own intricate customs and etiquette, and try to keep it straight. I'll tell you, in the beginning I was diligent and alert about all this etiquette, but after the first five countries it becomes a blur, and you forget where you are, and which way you should or should not point your feet or bow, when you should and should not smile, or pour your tea, or whatever, in order not to give offense to the local potentate or six-armed god.

Somehow, I'd managed to offend people and minor deities in several countries without even trying. Far be it from me to ask where the "offense" is in hoisting my glass with the wrong hand to toast the vainglorious wife of the current dictator while outside the palace walls the ethnic majority is parading the heads of murdered minorities on pikes, or women are stoned to death for real or presumed adultery. An idiot like me just doesn't get this good-manners business, I guess.

But if being on the road taught me anything, it was to keep one's mouth shut as much as possible, lest someone take offense, or your words be misconstrued or misquoted, which could have a harmful effect on your company's business. So I kept all this to myself.

"What did you do in Singapore?" Jerry went on. "The liaison there says you insulted some people but he's too much of a gentleman to go into specifics."

"Singapore?" I didn't remember offending anyone in Singapore.

"You really offended people," Jerry said, pushing forward, a hint of desperation in his voice because he had been unable to provoke me all week. "I hear you were really on the rag in Beijing too."

The producers took a collective breath, and all eyes turned to me. It would have been so easy to say something wiseass to Jerry, Mr. Cultural Sensitivity. But I didn't.

"Enough squabbling, children," said Solange Stevenson, behind me. She had come in like an Apache without any of us hearing her. "I have lunch with Barbara Walters at one, so let's get down to work. Jerry, you've sent feelers out to some new sponsors?"

"It's preliminary with most of them, although Lose It Fast Diet Products is very close to making a worldwide deal," he said.

"Let's ask ourselves, do we want them as sponsors?" Solange said.

Before I could pipe in, Louis said, "I agree. Do we want to perpetrate western beauty ideals on the rest of the world? They have enough problems."

"Five million bucks," Jerry replied.

"On the other hand, being overweight is also a health issue," Solange said.

"Isn't there some question about whether those particular weight-loss products cause gallbladder disease?" asked Dillon.

"Is there?" Solange said, looking as if she was giving these pros and cons meaningful thought. She turned to Jerry. "Make sure the products are safe and fair to women. If they are, take the advertising."

This was akin to letting a tobacco lobbyist determine if cigarettes were safe for preschoolers. Jerry's pairing with Madame Solange would seem a fractious one. Solange, after all, is a card-carrying feminist on the board of a number of women's groups. Jerry is not what you'd call a real pro-woman guy, except when it comes to his sexual preference. At first Jerry was embarrassed as hell about working at the "chick network," and this made him even more of a macho braying ass than he already was. But Jerry knew how to get money out of sponsors, and Solange is a canny businesswoman first and foremost. She talked the good woman game, but would sacrifice her ideals in a New York minute for the sake of business. Perpetrating western beauty ideals? Bad. Five million bucks? Good. What was just as galling was that every one of the women they had hired had fallen in line with this philosophy. And the biggest feminists in the place were Louis and Dillon.

Me? I was the one upon whom both Jerry and Solange focused all their irritation and spite. Go figure. Was it just a coincidence I was sent on the road a lot to scout new programs, make deals, do public relations stuff? I'd come back from the road, work at the office for a week or two, and suddenly, another business trip would materialize. Jerry and Solange had run out of places to send me after the last trip, but then discovered I hadn't taken a vacation in a long time. My unused vacation at the All News Network had been transferred to WWN, but under company bylaws, I'd have to take my vacation before my anniversary date or lose it.

I decided to take it. I just had to get through this last day. . . .

The producers summarized their current productions. Our top-rated original-ish program was *World of Soap,* an hour that gave zippy synopses of our close-captioned soap operas from India, Iran, France, Bulgaria, and the USA. The soaps themselves were showing slow but consistent ratings' growth, as was *Jet Set Gourmet,* the international cooking show, and our reruns of sitcoms featuring women. Women's sports numbers were okay; the news and informational programming was lagging, in large part due to crappy time slots, usually wedged between paid programming for telephone psychics and personal-improvement messiahs. Reruns of Solange's old pop-psych talk show were doing well (no matter where you go, it seems, people can't get enough of reunited relatives and girls who date their mother's toothless boyfriends).

Overall, we were, in our first year, a modest ratings success, but were still bleeding money and making only incremental audience progress.

After we went over some budget stuff, Solange dismissed us so she could run to Le Cirque for lunch with Barbara. Before Jerry could snag me, I fled to my office, my perky assistant, Tim, right behind me.

"Here are the morning's memos, and your mail," he said. "I took the liberty of removing all the anthrax hoaxes and sending them to the police."

"Thanks. You busy?" I asked him. "I have a bunch of errands for you. Personal errands."

"I live to run errands."

"I'm staying at the Chelsea Hotel because of the fire, in my friend Tamayo's apartment." I gave him the room number and said, "Don't tell Jerry and Solange where I am. If there's an emergency and you need me, YOU call me."

I then gave him my account numbers for Con Ed, cable, insurance, and phone, so he could look after getting things cut off and forwarded and whatever. This was one of the great perks of an otherwise grueling executive gig, an assistant who sweats all the small stuff for you.

"I guess I'd better call the maid and tell her not to clean your apartment until further notice," Tim added.

"You're the best, Tim. How did I luck out and get you?"

"You made a deal with the devil but you were drunk at the time and don't remember it. Anything else I can do to make your life a more candy-colored place to be?"

"No, thanks."

When he left, Louis Levin rolled in. Louis is a paraplegic and motors around in an electric wheelchair. He's been known to use this for nefarious purposes, i.e., speeding toward a group of network censors in the narrow hallway, yelling, "She's outta control!"

"What is up with you, Robin? Why didn't you say more to Jerry?" he asked. "He gave you so many openings to zing him. You've let him get away with it all week. Dillon and I have had to promote your feminist point of view in meetings or it doesn't get said. Nothing against the sisterhood, Robin, but I feel funny having to be the biggest feminist in the place."

"I'm trying this new thing, being circumspect and turning the other cheek," I said.

"Right, sure you are," he said. "What's the deal, really? It's like Chinese water torture, isn't it? You're making him guess when the next drop will fall . . ."

"I swear, it's not a plot against Jerry. I'm trying to be, you know, mature about stuff."

"Oh, woman, you've gone soft!" Louis said. "Ever since you've come back . . . It's that man isn't it? He tamed you."

"What man?"

"The one in Paris you don't want anyone to know about," Louis said. "He called this morning and I happened to pick up. Evidently he had tried to call your apartment first and he got no answer. I think. It was very hard to understand him. He doesn't speak English very well."

"Oh. He called?" I said, very cool.

"God, you're blushing! And what's this?" He started pawing through a bunch of books and videotapes on my desk.

"*Virgin Queens and Lusty Consorts: Feminism and Romantic Love,*" he said, reading the title off a book. He turned to the back flap and read, " 'Can the modern woman reconcile the conflict between being a feminist and being a heterosexual?' "

"Someone sent that to me. I haven't even read it. Jesus. Don't jump to conclusions," I said. "Don't make connections where there aren't any. The man in Paris was a—"

"Fling," he said.

"A friend." As casually as possible, I added, "Did he leave a message?"

"Yeah, either he's going to his lib to work on an ex-parent, or he's off to the lab for his experiment. I'm not really sure. He's gone for a month. He'd try to E-mail when he had time."

"Thank you," I said.

"Lab? What's this guy do?"

"He's a physicist."

"You're blushing again."

"I'm tired and flushed," I said. "Jesus."

"Don't get me wrong. Nothing wrong with it. But why the secrecy? Is he married? Please tell me he isn't married . . ."

"No, of course not. We're just friends. No big deal. He's a friend of Tamayo's, actually. She told me to look him up while I was there and I did."

"What's wrong with him?"

"Nothing's wrong with him."

"Oh. I get it. It's unrequited. Your feelings aren't being re-turned the way you want," he said.

"I don't know." Louis had almost worn me down. I almost said, Look, this is the deal, Louis. Pierre and I live on two differ-ent continents, he reads English but doesn't speak it very well, and I have your basic bad-tourist French, which is amusing—for about a week. He's a French genius with excellent table manners, from a proud Gallic family descended from minor nobility, and I'm a crude American chick. These things only work out in Fran Drescher movies.

But though Louis is a good friend and an honorable colleague, he also runs the Jackson Broadcasting Rumor File, Radio Free Babylon, so I kept it to myself.

"He's just a friend," I said.

"If you say so," Louis said. "But whatever he is, he's made you soft. Jerry's going to run roughshod over you in absentia while you're on vacation. He thinks this is a trick, and he's going to try a preemptive strike. . . ."

"What can he do?"

"Don't underestimate him. He's up to something. I'm just not sure what yet," he said. "I'll keep my ears to the pipes and keep you posted. You might try disarming him with a few bitchy comments, just to reassure him."

Before Louis left, he filled me in on the many other plots swirling about the office. The politics of a medieval court had nothing on those of WWN, or as Louis called it, The Holy Woman Empire. It took every bit of self-control to resist being drawn into the various intrigues.

Being back in the office had been a challenge though. Every time I turned around, it seemed some plotting courtier was darting out of the shadows with a dram of poison about someone else. The executive producers were plotting against each other. The associate producers were plotting against each other. Even the interns were plotting against each other. Most of this plotting took place beneath a pleasant, pastel civility. This was the corporate culture Solange and Jerry had created. Before the day was through and I was freed, I'd have to dodge both the Evil Queen and her Cowardly Knave.

About an hour before quitting time, Jerry tried to provoke me by telling me we needed a younger, prettier cohost on our after-school program, a grab bag of dating issues, school, and adventures. He added that its focus should shift completely to makeup, fashion, and how to get a boyfriend. I promised to think about it.

I've never seen that guy look so miserable. If I'd known being mature and circumspect had this effect on him, I would have tried it long ago. What I told Louis Levin notwithstanding, I was doing this to Jerry on purpose. It hadn't started out that way. It started because I came back, jet-lagged from the road, too exhausted to fight, and forced to rely on the little bit of diplomacy I learned in my travels. But when I noticed how much it bugged Jerry when I didn't tongue-lash him, I started being mature and diplomatic just to, well, make his monkey crazy. It reminded me of one of my favorite old jokes: A masochist and a sadist are sitting on a bench. The masochist says, "Hurt me." The sadist says, "No."

Evidently, my new maturity was getting to Solange too. A half hour or so later, just as I was about to leave, Solange came into my office and said, "Get a lot of rest on your vacation. You look tired. I'm very concerned about you."

"Thanks."

"Relax. Don't worry about anything. I'll make sure Jerry doesn't make trouble for you," she said. "I'll make sure Paula and Lucille don't make trouble either. You just get lots of rest."

The last two were executive producers. We'd all gotten along okay in the brief times I was in the office, and it had never occurred to me that Paula and Lucille would want to make trouble for me—until now. I figured Solange was trying to pit me against them, and she was probably trying to pit them against me in a similar fashion. It was a favorite blood sport of hers, provoking people to attack each other, then stepping in after the bloodletting as the kindly voice of reason who would restore order.

I was tempted to use my favorite passive-aggressive weapon against her, telling her about someone she disliked who was now happy. That always burned her butt. But as with Jerry, it was even more vexing to her if I just took the high road and acted mature and kind of . . . what's the word . . . classy. Who knew? She hated people who took the high road over her even more than she hated people who were happy, which almost made taking the high road worth it. In any event, it was a good thing I was going on vacation, because torturing them was fun but that high-road thing is really hard to keep up for any extended period of time.

Finally, it was quitting time. At the end of the day, when I left the pink-and-black granite Jackson Broadcasting Building, I felt a great relief and freedom, as the giant fingers that had been squeezing my chest for the past five days peeled back and let me go. No intrigues, no gossip, no gender politics for two whole weeks. Just rest and relaxation. Heaven.

chapter three

When I got back to the Chelsea, loaded down with cat food, new clothes, and other essentials, I called Nadia from the lobby as she had requested.

"Who is it?" Nadia snapped.

"It's Robin, Tamayo's friend. I'm downstairs. Is it okay if I come up?"

"Give me half an hour." She slammed down the phone.

By now, I was really dragging my can. A half hour seemed an eternity—yet, ironically, not long enough to go somewhere and do something worthwhile.

I took a seat in the lobby. There were just three people sitting in the lobby—an old man who slept in an armchair, a hip-looking young man with a brush cut and black-rimmed glasses slouched in a chair, and me. The lobby was eclectically decorated, to say the least, with artwork of different, sometimes conflicting schools covering every available space. The walls were full of paintings, and there was sculpture scattered around the seating area. A papier-mâché woman in a swing hung from the middle of the ceiling. The black-iron fireplace was guarded by two snarling black griffins. Above the mantel was a carved wood tableaux depicting different artists at work. On the mantel were two strange silver filigree vases that looked like ancient Phoenician cremation urns, flanking a bust of Harry S Truman. Behind the lobby desk, where the mail was held in hundreds of tiny cubbyholes, there was more art—on the walls, even the ceiling. Some of the art was very good, by famous and nonfamous artists, some was very bad. The mix seemed democratic and nonjudgmental, like the hotel itself. It was otherworldly, yet warm and welcoming at the same time.

It was easy to imagine you were in another time because the lobby had only barely been modernized over the years, and the mix of furniture and styles gave it a timeless quality. I imagined the place around the turn of the century, when Mark Twain and Sarah Bernhardt took tea in this marble-walled lobby. In the 1950s, Robert Oppenheimer, father of the A-bomb, brooded over his creation here, and Dylan Thomas drank himself to death. In the 1960s, Janis Joplin gave Leonard Cohen a blow job on an unmade bed upstairs "while limousines [waited] in the street," inspiring him to write a song about it, and the delicate and doomed Edie Sedgwick, Warhol Superstar and Youthquaker, kept setting her room on fire. There is a famous picture of her sitting in the lobby with kohled eyes and bandaged hands, waiting for the management to find her a new room. Some of this I knew through Tamayo, and some just as a New Yorker who had long admired and been curious about the Chelsea.

While I was daydreaming about a young Edith Piaf taking refuge here with composer Virgil Thomson, a man with dyed apple-red hair came in with a black-and-white dog, who yapped at me and wrenched me back into the present. They were followed by a man with a horrible black toupee, who stopped just inside the glass doors and looked around.

After him came an elderly lady, elegantly dressed, accompanied by a solicitous young man who addressed her as Mrs. Grundy.

"I've been experimenting with new textures and surfaces, Mrs.

Grundy," said the young man. "A fine-weave bleached denim instead of canvas, also a shaved velour stretched over a frame, if I could have a half hour to show you, Mrs. Grundy . . ."

"I have to run now for a meeting. But call my assistant, Ben, and make an appointment to show me your portfolio," she said. "And please, call me Miriam."

It was Miriam Grundy, the widow of the late, great poet Oliver Grundy, a well-known patron of the arts and a genuine Chelsea legend. Miriam Grundy—that explained why, though a tiny lady, she had such a big presence. Miriam Grundy was larger than life, the darling of the avant garde as well as the Old Guard. The details of her life had grown mythic. When she was in her twenties, her family fled Europe and the Nazis for America, where young Miriam met Oliver Grundy, a poet, scion of a wealthy WASP family, and a married man. Their affair had caused a terrible scandal, and details of the divorce appeared in the penny papers along with some of the steamy love letters Miriam and Oliver exchanged, the filthy parts replaced with dashes. After she and Oliver married, they abandoned high society and ran around with beats, surrealists, and other bohemian artist types. High society welcomed them back in the 1960s.

Now, this rich widow's name showed up, boldface, in the gossip columns all the time, attending everything from high society Museum of Modern Art benefits to downtown performance art shows at avant joints like P.S. 22 and Here. What a life she had had. She'd escaped certain death in Europe, had a grand love story, had become a benefactor of the arts, and was now widely imitated by drag queens.

So distracted was I by Miriam Grundy, I almost missed the young man who came in behind her. When I did notice him, I had to look twice before I realized it was the manboy from the night before, walking determinedly to the elevator, which whisked him away before I could get my bearings.

I called Nadia from the house phone in the lobby.

"What?" she snapped.

"I just saw him, your fiancé!" I said. "He's on his way up. You can stop worrying."

"Oh, thank God," she said.

"You need some time alone with him now?" I asked.

"No, no, we have to go meet someone," she said.

"Then may I come up?"

"In about five or ten minutes," she said, hanging up without saying good-bye.

I gave her fifteen minutes before I hoisted my sorry carcass up and dragged it to the elevator. Just as the elevator doors were about to close, a man stuck his hand in, a very handsome man, fortyish, with a passing resemblance to Gregory Peck. At first, he didn't seem to notice there was anyone else in the elevator, but around the third floor he smiled, and looked at me in a very seductive way, with a combination of Christlike empathy and manly desire. I got a buzz off the eye contact, I admit.

"Hi," he said.

"Hi."

"You look familiar. Do you live here?"

"No. I'm staying at a friend's place."

"I'm Gerald," he said.

"Robin. Do you live here?"

"Not anymore, but I used to. How long will you be here?"

"I don't know. You see, my apartment burned down—"

I didn't get a chance to finish. The doors opened at seven to another woman, around my age, with masses of frizzy brown hair. As soon as she saw Gerald, she started screaming.

"You thieving bastard! Where have you been? I hope you brought my money," she yelled, her accent either Scottish or Irish.

"Maggie, I was delayed. I have to meet someone . . ." Gerald said.

"Who?"

"It's confidential. I'll be back with the money later tonight or tomorrow."

"I'll be out tonight."

"Tomorrow then."

"You'd better not be lying, you bastard!" she shouted. "Or I'll feed you to the dogs."

Mercifully, I was able to push past them and escape the fray. Gerald tried to escape too, but the woman with the frizzy brown hair got on the elevator and wouldn't let him out. The doors to the elevator closed, shutting out their argument behind me.

The seventh floor was pretty lively. The man in the horrible toupee was in the hallway, talking to a bald, tattooed bodybuilder who was standing in his doorway, lifting hand weights. The bodybuilder didn't even seem to see the guy in the bad toupee, and just stared, stone-faced, past him. Down the hall, a door next to Tamayo's opened and a pile of men's clothes flew into the hallway, followed by a short, compact man with a leonine mane of white hair, wearing boxers and an undershirt. The door slammed shut. The man began to put on his trousers, and had them half on when the door opened again and a blond woman in a dressing gown came out and threw a pair of shoes at him, one after the other. The poor guy tried to duck the shoes while pulling on his trousers, and fell over. From the floor, he said something in Spanish to the woman that sounded very sweet and apologetic to me, but it didn't move the blowsy blond woman. She swore in Spanish, went back inside, and slammed the door again.

What a nuthouse, I thought. There was a reason residents referred to this place as "The Mothership." Not that I was judging, mind you. The whole world is nuts.

As a courtesy, because Nadia was a friend of Tamayo's, I knocked on the door instead of using my key. The door opened with the chain on.

"Oh, it's you," Nadia said.

"Yeah, it's me."

She slipped the chain off, quickly, pulled me in, and shut the door.

"I thought it was my fiancé," she said.

"Manboy's not here yet?"

"Manboy? No, he's not here yet."

"He got on the elevator more than fifteen minutes ago."

"He didn't arrive," she said. "Oh my Godt."

"Maybe he got lost. Does he know this was the right apartment after all?"

"I don't know. I haven't spoken to him. Oh my Godt."

"Don't push the panic button," I said. "Maybe this is a blessing in disguise. You know, a chance to think about things before you rush into something."

"You don't understand. We must get married."

"Why? You're not pregnant, right? You said you haven't had sex yet . . ."

"Swear you won't tell anyone this," she said.

"Uh-huh."

"My people come from a country where marriages are arranged. My parents wanted me to marry someone I do not love. So I had to run away."

"Oh. Okay, but why do you also have to get married to another man? Marriage is a big step . . ."

"Why? Don't be an idiot. Because I'm in love," she said.

"Where are your people from?" I asked her.

"Plotzonia," she said.

"Plotzonia?"

"That's what I call it," she said.

"What's it really called?"

"It's better if you don't know," she said.

I pressed her, but she wouldn't tell me the real name of the place. She said her family had moved back there from America a year or so before. It was apparently a pretty backward place with arranged marriages, lots of hostage-taking, no decent malls, bagels, or discos, and the whole country smelled as if dirty socks were burning all the time. Her parents were very controlling, and while in Plotzonia she spent most of her time in her room watching satellite TV with her cousins and chatting on the Internet. She'd met Tamayo on the Net.

Then, six months earlier, while on a shopping trip to New York with her "family chaperone," she'd ditched the chaperone and come to stay here at the Chelsea with Tamayo for a week. It was after that escapade, she said, that her family decided to marry her off sooner rather than later.

"You understand now?" she said.

"I understand the part about choosing your own life. Getting married, though . . . You seem awfully young to be getting married, if you don't mind me saying so."

"I do mind. What difference does age make, when you've met your soul mate?" she said.

"Oh yeah, soul mates. I've had a couple dozen of those."

"If you knew him as I do . . . ," she said, and went into a paean to her man.

You'd think this guy was God the Father, Jesus, and the Holy Ghost rolled up with Leonardo DiCaprio and Alan Greenspan from the way she talked, the way her eyelashes fluttered, her face glowed, and her breath kept catching in her throat. Clearly, this girl was in the grip of The Madness, that biologically induced hallucination designed to make young people mate, breed, and buy a lot of consumer goods to salve the misery of an early marriage. It was probably no good pointing this out to her. People in the grip of that madness can't see reason.

"He's The One," she said, in summation, sitting down at the kitchen table.

"Does he have a job? How will you live? Where will you live?"

"Why do you need to know so much?" she snapped, and grew suspicious again.

"I don't. Whatever. It's your life. Blessings, et cetera. I'm going to take a shower now and then crash if you don't mind."

While I was showering, the phone rang. Nadia must have jumped on it because it only rang once. She hollered something, but I couldn't make it out over the sound of the water. The next thing I heard was the door slamming, and when I came out, she was gone.

A book she'd been reading, *Man Trap,* was on the table. I took it to bed with me, figuring it would either be good for a few laughs or put me to sleep. It was frankly hard to resist the testimonials on the back from women who had almost lost hope, then found the men of their dreams thanks to the *Man Trap* Way. It wasn't Nadia's book. According to the note inside, it had been loaned to her by someone named Maggie M., who wrote, "When your man is starting to drift away, use this book to bring him back."

Louise Bryant jumped up and parked her carcass next to mine on the loft bed as I opened *Man Trap.* A matchbook Nadia had used as a bookmark fell out. Thinking it might provide a clue about where she was from, I picked it up and looked at it. But it was local, from a place called Bus Stop Bar & Grill, and it showed a black silhouette of a building on a red background. The matchbook was either really outdated or really retro and cool. I couldn't decide.

Inside, in Tamayo's handwriting, were the words, "Say hey to Stinky for me. T." I had to laugh. It was just like Tamayo to know a guy named Stinky.

Man Trap was a very Machiavellian program of tyranny tempered with indulgence, with chapter headings like "Choosing Your Prey," "The Right Bait," "Setting the Man Trap," "It's Kind to Be Cruel," "Pulling the Strings," "When to Use Tears" (and other weapons God gave us), and "Playing Hard to Get." This book was the latest in a whole industry of books telling women how to plot against men to get commitment without sex, and books telling men how to plot against women to get sex without commitment.

Two pages into chapter two, as I was learning how to feign a combination of simmering sexuality, sexual innocence, and moral superiority (because men are supposed to find this irresistible), my eyelids grew heavy. I was almost asleep when I thought I heard the front door slam.

"Hello?" I called out.

There was no answer.

"Hello?" I said again, then got up, grabbed my rifle, and went to the door. I couldn't see through the peephole and figured some jokester had his or her finger over it. Very quietly, I slipped the chain off, planning to open the door really fast so whoever it was would lose their balance and stumble into the apartment.

But when I jerked the door open, a body fell forward onto me, landing on me with such force that I almost lost my footing and fell flat on my ass. I was face-to-face with Gerald, the man who kind of looked like Gregory Peck. I pushed him off me, and he fell backward, onto the hallway floor.

He was bleeding. He opened his mouth and said something that sounded like, "Bye," and then he died.

chapter four

You have a curse on your head?" NYPD detective Barry Burns asked me, not making any effort to suppress his skeptical smirk.

Burns, a portly black man with a very wrinkled forehead, had asked what my connection was to the dead guy, and I'd had to explain that I had no known connection beyond some curse that had me stumbling over murder victims about once a year, though this was a new one—it had stumbled on me this time, and while I was inconveniently holding a firearm. He then wanted to know about the previous victims, making a lot of notes and looking at me with narrowed eyes of suspicion while I told him. You can't blame him, really.

Burns turned to a uniformed cop and said, "Get me the arrest record on this woman, PLEASE."

I was sitting at the Formica kitchen table in bloody clothes staring out into the hallway. A cop was drawing an outline around the body, which was still on the floor, the feet in Tamayo's apartment, the rest of the body outside the door in the hallway. Another cop was trying to keep the neighbors away from it. A couple of the pastel-suited Mary Sue women came out of their room, skirting around the neighbors and the cops.

Pushing past them came the man who worked the front desk at night.

"Mr. Bard is going to hate to hear this!" he said, referring to the eccentric businessman and art lover who runs the hotel. "We haven't had a speck of trouble in years. We haven't had a murder here in two decades."

Another detective arrived, pushing his way through the spectators and stepping carefully over the corpse.

"You must be the good cop," I said to him hopefully.

But I was wrong. Instead of getting your standard good cop–bad cop team, I got bad cop–worse cop, though they were both observing the city's new politeness guidelines for police, adding please and thank you every now and then. Maybe I was being too sensitive, but there seemed to be some sarcasm in their pleases and thank-yous.

Burns gave the second detective, Corcoran, a synopsis of my explanation, and went to consult with a cop out in the hallway.

"A curse, huh?" said Corcoran. "Do you hear voices? Please, tell me, did a voice tell you to kill this guy?"

"I didn't kill him and I don't hear voices. I just have bad luck."

"This guy break your heart or something?"

"I don't even know this guy. I met him for five minutes in the elevator today. That's it."

"PLEASE tell me, why did you open the door then? You open your door to strangers as a rule?" Corcoran asked. He pulled a piece of nicotine gum out of his pocket, peeled off the foiled backing, and put it in his mouth.

"I thought it might be the other houseguest, or her boyfriend . . ."

"Where are they now?"

"I don't know." I looked around and realized Nadia's stuff was gone. "I guess they hooked up and went off to elope."

"What is her name?"

"Nadia something."

"She was staying here, but you don't know her name?"

"Nadia didn't tell me her last name. I don't know anything about her except she came to New York to elope with her boyfriend and she's from a country with no Benettons and no bagels," I said. "I don't live here, I'm a guest of the woman who rents this apartment. She's traveling around the world. You see, my apartment burned down . . ."

"Yeah? How did that happen?" Corcoran asked.

"I don't know. I didn't cause the fire," I said.

"And you didn't kill anyone."

"Exactly!"

"What about the gun you had? Please, tell me about it," said Corcoran.

"Forensics will find it hasn't been fired. I don't even have bullets for it. I just keep it around because it's scary looking and has sentimental value," I said. "You won't find the gun that killed him around here."

"Did an accomplice take it away?"

"Look, I don't even know the dead guy. If I killed him, would I have signed that consent form to let you search the place? If you don't believe me, call June Fairchild in the NYPD public affairs department, she'll vouch for me. I've helped solve a few homicides."

There's nothing a hardened New York cop likes more than amateur crime fighter such as me. My situation wouldn't be helped once the head of homicide, Richard Bigger, got wind of this. Bigger thought I was a very clever serial killer who had somehow committed all these murders myself and had constructed elaborate frame-ups to conceal my crimes.

Around us, two cops wearing surgical gloves were dusting for prints, picking up bits of lint and things with tweezers and putting them into little plastic evidence bags. Another took photographs of the scene from the hallway.

"You see anyone in the hallway when you found the body?" Corcoran asked.

"No. But I wasn't looking. I did see the dead guy arguing with a woman with frizzy brown hair and an Irish accent earlier," I said. "I think her name is Maggie."

One of the other cops said, "From the way blood dripped in the hallway, it looks like he was shot down the hallway, about ten feet away, then he staggered to the door, and died."

"See?" I said. "It was a random act that he picked this door."

One of the uniformed cops came over and said to Corcoran, "The victim's name is Gerald Woznik. He's an art dealer. Apparently a real bastard and a gopher with a lot of enemies."

"A gopher?" I repeated.

"In one hole and out another," said Corcoran. "See what you can find out about a woman in her thirties or forties with frizzy brown hair and an Irish accent, possibly named Maggie."

Probably, I should have called my lawyer, Spencer Roo, before speaking to the cops, but in the excitement, and my exhaustion, I figured it was better just to tell the truth. Besides, Roo was a major publicity hound, and I hoped to keep my name out of the papers if possible.

It took another hour of exhausting back-and-forth before I was vouched for by June Fairchild, though Burns and Corcoran were not quite sold. They weren't taking me downtown to book me, but they were still suspicious, what with the gun and the dead man's blood on me. They didn't let me go until one of the uniforms came in and told them that some other woman was seen climbing down one of the side fire escapes around the time the dead man was shot and killed. Only then did they let me change out of my bloody clothes, shower, and collapse on the loft bed, which had been scoured for fiber and DNA evidence.

Naturally, I felt bad, in a generic way, for this dead art dealer, Gerald Woznik, because he had lived and loved and died too soon; nobody should have to meet a violent end in a bright, white, perfect world, and every man's death diminishes me because the bell tolls for me, etc. I knew from previous homicides that his face in that last moment would haunt my nightmares for years to come, sometimes in sick ways that would make Freud blush so hard he'd lose the circulation in his legs. But it was a relief, in a way, to learn that the victim was a "bastard" with enemies, because that indicated the killer was someone out to get him, and him alone, and was not, hopefully, a serial killer on the loose.

The cops would be there all night, looking for tiny bits of evidence, measuring things, taking pictures, and the last of them, Burns, was just leaving when I woke up late the next morning. They had taken my rifle with them. The body was gone, but the chalk outline and a splattering of blood remained on Tamayo's floor.

"Did you get a suspect?" I asked.

"We're investigating," he said. "But you'll be glad to hear we're not sealing the crime scene, and the hotel is sending a maid up to wash the floor."

"I'm in the clear, right?"

"We haven't officially cleared you yet," he said, but he was no longer looking at me as if I was a killer.

In all the commotion, I'd somehow lost track of my cat, who was nowhere to be seen after the cops left. After I called down to the front desk to ask them to keep an eye peeled for an old gray cat with a glow-in-the-dark collar, I took a walk down the hallway to see if I could find her. Louise always roamed pretty freely when we lived in the East Village, and always found her way home, but this wasn't our home, and I was worried she might wander all the way back to our burned-out building. She was nowhere to be seen on the seventh floor. I asked the tattooed bodybuilder, who stood in his doorway lifting hand weights, if he'd seen her, but he didn't answer. He just stared ahead, stone-faced.

When I got back to Tamayo's apartment, Louise was scratching at the balcony doors.

"How did you get out there?" I asked as she ran inside to the kitchen, howling for breakfast. After I started the coffee maker, I made Louise the special meal she likes—prescription cat food sautéed with bok choy and low-salt, low-fat oyster sauce, then let the poor maid in to clean up the blood.

"You must have drawn the short straw," I said to her.

"I don't understand," she said to me.

"To get the job of cleaning a crime scene."

"Oh, I got the job because I've cleaned bloodstains before," she said and told me she used to work at a fancy-schmancy four-star hotel uptown that was a popular spot for socialite suicides, "people who check in to check out," she said, in a soft voice and with the sad acceptance that comes from seeing into people's bedrooms for three decades.

"You might want to open the windows. I'm going to apply the bleach solution and the fumes can be powerful," she said.

I took her advice, poured myself a big European-size cup of coffee, and went out on the balcony with Louise. Ever since the homicide, the giant fingers had been squeezing my chest again. Homicide used to energize me, fill me with a sense that the guilty must be found and justice must be served. But I was getting older, and crime-fighting is a young girl's game. Relax, relax, relax, I told myself as I sat down in a molded white chair outside. You're on vacation. The cops are on the job. You don't have to get any more involved in this than the average good citizen doing their duty. Let it go, let it go, let it go.

A light breeze blew. The smell of hot fat and sugar wafted down the street from Krispy Kreme doughnuts. I closed my eyes and tried to block thoughts of the murder with a daydream about the day I met Pierre, the French genius, while I was in Paris for a Women in Media conference. When Tamayo heard I was going to Paris, she insisted I call him. Tamayo knows some pretty interesting people, so I did, arranging to meet him at his favorite cafe on rue Jacob.

Pierre was there when I arrived, reading a magazine called the

Journal of Recreational Mathematics. *I recognized him from a photograph of Tamayo's. He hadn't seen me.*

I sat down at the next table, leaned over, and said, "That's a much more fun magazine since Tina Brown took it over."

He smiled. Later I learned he didn't get the joke. Though he read and wrote English perfectly, he didn't speak it very well.

I closed my eyes, did some deep breathing. A guitar wailed somewhere, a siren somewhere else. The wind changed, and the smell of hot sugar was blown away by the smell of hot soap and bleach in a bracing blast of air from the hotel laundry. At my feet, Louise was asleep and purring in a sliver of sunlight.

The balcony doors to the east of me opened, and the Hispanic woman I'd seen throwing shoes down the hallway came out, dragging a phone with her. She was dressed in a transparent blue-and-pink flowered dress, the buttons of the bodice undone to reveal the top of a white slip. She was smoking a Gauloise, exhaling twists of dark, tarry smoke into the air, looking very blowsy and louche, as if she had stepped right out of a Tennessee Williams play, or off the cover of one of those sex-and-crime pulp paperbacks of the 1940s and '50s.

"There are so many people who had motive to kill the bastard," she said into the telephone.

On the other side of me, the balcony doors of the west apartment opened, and Maggie, the woman with masses of frizzy brown hair came out to water her flower boxes while talking into her telephone. She was wearing pale orange pedal pushers and a pink half T-shirt.

"Too many people had motive to kill him," the Irish woman said into her phone.

"Maggie, did you kill him?" the blowsy blond woman asked, and laughed. "You had such good revenge plans for him last week."

"I'd never kill anyone who owes me money, Lucia," the frizzy-haired Maggie said into her telephone. "I have an alibi. And now I don't have to get revenge.".

I was caught in a crossfire. The two women were talking on the phone to each other on either side of me, but looking out into the street, not at each other.

Maggie went on. "A lot of people may have wanted him dead."

"Oh, Carlos is awake," blowsy Lucia said, going back into her apartment with the phone.

"Call me later," Maggie said, hanging up.

She looked over at me.

"Hello," she said.

"Hello."

"You found the body, did you?"

"The body kinda found me . . ."

"I'm Maggie Mason," she said. "Who are you?"

"A friend of Tamayo's, Robin—"

Before I could finish introducing myself, her phone rang in her hand and she said, "Excuse me," and answered it. "Hello? Oh, hi. Can't. Busy that night. I have an art action. What? I can't tell you that."

Maggie Mason. That sound familiar.

"Roger's the dealer who handles Blair's work? Yes, I've met him and I didn't like him. Something about him just sends a rat running up my trouser leg," Maggie said into the phone.

Involuntarily, I jerked upright. My ex-boyfriend Mad Mike O'Reilly used to say that "it sent a rat running up my trouser leg."

"I've got to find some money. Have you ever had a day when you had to choose between food and cigarettes? Yeah? Well, have you ever had a day when you had to choose between cigarettes and Tampax? Ah, I'm not going to worry yet. I've been on the bones of me bum before," Maggie said. "What? No, the police know I didn't kill Gerald. I have an alibi, thank God. You know Grace Rouse would love to hang it on me."

Rats running up trouser legs, bum bones . . . I suddenly knew where I'd heard of Maggie Mason, aka Mary Margaret Mason, the "scourge of Kilmerry, the only dry county in all of Ireland," as my ex-boyfriend Mike put it. Don't bother looking Kilmerry up on a map. You can't find it. That was one of Mike's whimsical nicknames. It was a tiny county, naturally, in Ulster, populated by an ascetic Protestant sect, industrious like Mormons. Maggie was the local angry rebel bent on corrupting every male in her village before she left at age seventeen for Belfast. There she met Mike, who was shooting a story for ANN foreign correspondent Reb Ryan. Mike is a cameraman.

Mike was married at the time, but that didn't stop either him or Maggie from dating. They dated off and on for years before they finally split up, after his marriage ended and before he took up with me. He had told a lot of stories about her over the years, not all of them very flattering.

Maggie, according to Mad Michael O'Reilly, was a wild woman of extreme passions with a legendary bad temper, especially when it came to the men in her life and the other women in her men's lives. Mike and I had been nonmonogamous, EX-CEPT while we were both in New York, so it wouldn't have been kosher for him to be carrying on with Margaret at the Chelsea Hotel and me in the East Village. Possible, even likely, come to think of it, but not kosher.

After what I'd heard about Maggie, she'd be a lot more upset about it than I would though. As I recall, when she caught Mike with another woman, she threw the woman's clothes out of the window, sprayed her and Mike with red paint, and broke a lot of glassware. She and Mike were "off" at the time, so she wasn't in a position to be jealous. Come to think of it, wasn't Maggie Mason the woman who forwarded an ex-lover's mail to NAMBLA, the North American Man-Boy Love Association? Granted, that was years ago, but you get my point. She was a vindictive woman, and not in a fun way.

What sick-humored twist of fate had brought me here, right next door to Maggie Mason? But of course, there was a logical explanation. Tamayo had found this place at the Chelsea Hotel through a friend of Mike's, though she'd declined to name that friend, who had to be Maggie Mason.

Maybe she did have an alibi in the Gerald Woznik death, but even if she did, she was someone to avoid, clearly. While Maggie was distracted on the phone, I went back inside.

The maid was still scrubbing. Watching her scrub a dead man's bloodstains wasn't very appealing either, so I went out to get newspapers and check out the neighborhood. Just in case my mug and my name were in the morning papers, I put on sunglasses and a scarf so I wouldn't be recognized. Funny, when I was a young reporter I couldn't wait to become famous. But unfortunately, most of the recognition I got as a reporter had come mainly because of homicide, and fame brought unwanted attention for a while from a fervent coterie of hard-core masochists, all of whom had since moved on to worship more powerful women. In fact, some of my masochistic former fans were more famous than me now. Remember a story a year or so ago about a man arrested in England for stalking Margaret Thatcher? He had her face tattooed over his heart. He was my fan for a while, though I never inspired him to a tattoo. And that guy who pulled out his toenails and sent them to the perky blond cohost of a popular entertainment TV show? That guy is Elroy Vern, who stalked and kidnapped me several years ago, begging me to beat him. He's in a maximum-security psychiatric hospital now for murder and attempted murder; his correspondence is being more closely monitored.

Down at the front desk, the dark-haired, well-tailored tourist lady I'd seen before was asking questions while another of her flock stood nearby. There were still cops about and I saw one of the detectives from the night before coming out of the office of the manager, Stanley Bard.

"There could be a murderer running around this place," the tourist lady said, alarmed.

"Madam, we'll do our utmost to ensure your security," said

the desk clerk. "These things happen everywhere, but they rarely happen here."

The woman turned in a huff, pushing past me. Her friend followed. "A man shot in our hotel, the horrible insane man outside the convention center, and those frightening teenagers fighting in Times Square last night? I don't know if I can make it through a week of this," she said. "On the news this morning, they said there was a slasher on the subway, on the E train, the same subway we took two days ago."

I thought, How easy it is to tune into the things that confirm our prejudices, and tune out those things that challenge them. New York City was safer than most big cities these days. The odds of being killed by a stranger were way down; the odds of being killed by someone who was supposed to love you, however, were way up. Statistically, she was more likely to be harmed by the women she was keeping company with than by a subway slasher or a homicidal maniac.

The city was cleaner than it used to be too, but this woman, who no doubt came from a gentle, sweet-smelling place where people only die from natural causes and gun-cleaning accidents, saw just the slashers and the murderers, the lack of small amenities. I felt bad for her, that she'd seen the dead guy on the floor. Probably, she'd never seen a murder victim before, and it can be quite a shock the first time, even if you've seen it a thousand times on TV shows or on the news. I felt bad in a more general way too, that she wasn't enjoying New York, a city I came to as a tourist and fell deeply in love with.

It seemed a shame that she couldn't see everything that this city, or even just this particular street, had to offer. Twenty-third Street between Seventh and Eighth avenues is one of the city's more eclectic blocks and I walked slowly down it, trying to chill out, looking in the windows of the stores. There were two hotels—the Chelsea and the Chelsea Savoy—a YMCA, a library, a fishing-tackle store, a synagogue, a secondhand guitar store, a comic-book store, S&M cafe, two banks, a Radio Shack, three hairdressers, three holistic healers, a record store, a tax attorney, an art-supply store, a health-food store, two delis, two boutiques, an optometrist, a dentist, a stationery store, a movieplex, two subway stations, the headquarters of the Communist Party of the United States of America (CPUSA), plus its bookstore. There was a place called The 99 Cent Palace ("A Kingdom for Under a Buck"), where cheap sundry items were sold—brands of cereal and cleaning products I'd never heard of, Mexican toothpaste, cheap plastic bowls.

There were eight or nine eating places, two of them in the Chelsea Hotel, and two doughnut places, a Krispy Kreme and a place on the corner of Eighth and Twenty-Third known simply as "Donuts," which had two horseshoe-shaped lunch counters and looked like something right out of an old *Life* magazine, as if it hadn't changed since 1945, except for the ten different flavors of Snapple in the cooler. I went inside Donuts. It was a funny little place. Its motto was proudly emblazoned on the menu signs on the wall: "Open 24 Hours. We stay open to serve you when you need us, not when we need you."

There was just one other customer in the place, a white guy with a gray ponytail, wearing a red flannel shirt and some sort of New Age rainbow medallion around his neck. I imagined he fancied himself some kind of cross between Hemingway and Timothy Leary. An old waiter in a big white apron approached me timidly and said, in a voice barely above a whisper, "What can I get for you?"

"A chocolate chunk muffin," I said. "And coffee, light, please."

He mumbled something and backed away from me.

The murder had happened late, and only one paper, the *News-Journal,* had the story in time to make its deadline. To my great relief, the *News-Journal* reported the body had fallen on "an unidentified tenant." Thank you, June Fairchild, I thought. She'd kept my name out of it . . . for the moment.

"Who Shot Controversial Art Dealer?" The *News-Journal* asked. "Troubled art dealer Gerald Woznik was found dead in the notorious Chelsea Hotel last night. Police say he'd been shot in the back."

It went on to say that in recent months, Woznik reportedly had had financial and personal troubles, and quoted Woznik's ex-wife, Naomi Wise Woznik, who issued a brief statement from the surrealist commune in Tuscany where she was living: "The world has lost a great art connoisseur and a real bastard."

That word, "bastard," came up a lot in quotes from "friends," fellow art dealers, and artists who claimed the dead had ripped them off. Gerald Woznik was also "arrogant," "manipulative," and "a liar and a thief."

Only heiress and art dealer Grace Rouse, the woman Woznik had been living with, defended him.

"He was a misunderstood genius," she said.

My cell phone rang, startling the timid waiter and drawing looks from the short-order cook and the guy who looked like Timothy Leary. I felt like a traveler from the future, whipping out the phone in this anachronistic joint.

"Robin, it's June Fairchild," said the caller. "I wanted you to know, one of your neighbors at the Chelsea had been watching through the peephole, and saw the man slam, bleeding, against the door, before you opened it."

"Great, so I'm completely in the clear then."

"You haven't been cleared officially, but I wouldn't worry. Richard Bigger won't officially clear you until they've arrested someone else. You know how he hates you, Robin."

"Who was this neighbor? Was it the bodybuilder?" I asked, and described him. "He seems to spend a lot of time in the hall-way."

"He told us he didn't know anything. The neighbor who saw you was a man named Cleves, a tourist from San Diego. Didn't see the actual crime, didn't see anything else and was flying back west today. Robin, I'm beginning to believe you really do have a curse on your head," she said, with her tony, uptown, Dalton School accent. June Fairchild of the NYPD was once known as

"The Debutante Detective" because of her flawless social pedigree. I knew her from a previous unfortunate incident.

"What about the frizzy-haired brunette, Maggie Mason?"

"The police weren't able to interview her until this morning, but, she apparently has an alibi. She was on AOL in a comic-book chat at the time of the murder. I'll try to keep you informed, as much as I can, Robin, but I'm taking a few days off to look after my daughter. She's having her tonsils pulled. I have to go, Robin. I'll talk to you later."

What a serene vacation it had been so far, I thought—an apartment building burns down and a dead man falls into my face. I was having dinner with Phil, from my old building, that evening. Phil's philosophy was not to complain about bad things that happen, they might just prevent something worse. I'd have to ask him what horrible event could possibly be prevented by these disasters to make them somehow justifiable in the cosmic scheme of things. It would have to be a pretty bad event, like a sarin gas attack on the subway or a Pat Buchanan presidency.

chapter five

The fire, it's a shame, luv, but who knows? If it hadn't happened, a week from now a gas pipe might have ruptured, blown up the building, and killed us all," said Phil, lifting his big Thai beer in a salute to our good luck. We were sitting at a corner table at Regional Thai Taste, a restaurant on Seventh Avenue and Twenty-second Street.

"Except you. Somehow, you'd survive," I said.

Phil has survived an extraordinary number of disasters in his lifetime. This all began during World War Two, when Phil was a young British soldier in North Africa and the only survivor of an attack by Rommel. Since then, he'd pulled widows and babies out of fires, crawled out of the wreckage of plane crashes and ferry sinkings, and eluded a cobra that came up a Calcutta toilet. The stories he told about these things were really unbelievable—I thought he was completely full of crap until he showed me his scrapbook of news clippings about his various adventures. He didn't show it to me to be boastful, although he had a healthy ego and was not a falsely modest saint kind of guy. He showed it to me to prove he wasn't full of crap and to get me to buy into his wacky philosophical tricks.

Tricks like: When something inconvenient happens to you, something beyond your control, you have to try to look at it as maybe preventing something worse. This kind of washes out when facing famine, war, or epidemic disease, but it can really help with day-to-day coping. In my life, there seems to be no completely reliable law but Murphy's—whatever can go wrong will—and the idea that what goes wrong might in fact prevent something far more terrible is more reassuring than that old morose "things could be worse" digestive.

The first time Phil told me this little trick, he had just fixed my front door, which had jammed, locking me inside and making me late for a very important business meeting. "Robin, if you'd been able to get out sooner, you might have wandered into the path of a car or a killer," he said at the time.

"You think this murder prevented something worse from happening, Phil?" I now asked. Phil chewed on his pad thai and washed it down with more beer before saying, "What's the quote you like from *Twelfth Night*?"

" 'Many a good hanging prevents a bad marriage.' "

"You never know what might have been averted. Everything in the universe is connected. Drink some of the beer and let's talk about something else. You haven't told me yet how your trip was."

I took a swig and said, "It didn't go that well. It's hard traveling from country to country. Every country has new rules you have to memorize and follow or risk offending people. I don't know how you do it, Phil, with all the traveling you've done. On this patch of land, you can't eat pork. Jump over to this patch, you can't eat beef. Move sideways a half step and you're among people who don't eat any meat, who wear special shoes on their feet and screens over their mouths so they don't accidentally step on or swallow an insect. It's confusing."

"Did you offend some people?"

"To put it mildly. Among other things, I brought a curse upon the heads of the five children of the Thai TV president, or some damn thing. I liked those kids too, Phil, we took to each other. Now, they all think they're cursed and I'm the big red-headed bogeyman who did it to them."

"Every place has its own traditions, superstitions, etiquette. . . ."

"How do you manage to travel to all those refugee camps in all those places and not offend people without meaning to?" Phil spent part of each year volunteering in refugee camps.

"I do offend people. That can't be prevented. When I do, I apologize sincerely, explain my ignorance, and ask where that honorable tradition I've offended came from. That way I learn, and they see that I have no harmful intent."

Phil was so smart. That was much better than bursting out laughing and saying, "You're kidding me," for example.

"But sometimes people don't even know how something got started," I said. "They do it because it's always been done that way, and everybody else is doing it too. And sometimes they don't tell you that you've offended them. They're too polite. You continue having what you think is a lovely time with them, and think all went well, until you get back to the office and there's an angry fax about your rudeness and lack of respect."

"Not everyone takes offense so easily. Don't worry about the ones who do. They're a minority." He took another swallow and said, "I have more bad news, I'm afraid. The building looks bad, luv, six apartments completely destroyed, including yours. There's smoke damage, water damage. But you've seen it, I suppose."

"No, I haven't been back to the neighborhood yet. Not ready to face it."

"It looks bad. The management company wants a couple of weeks to assess the damage, decide whether to restore the damaged building or tear it down and start over," Phil said.

"Tear it down and start over? How long will that take?"

"Whatever they decide, it is going to take time. We're planning to have a tenants' meeting later this week or next, when we can get everyone together. Your brow is furrowing again. Drink some more beer. It's good for you," he said, and smiled.

Phil had this theory that for every person who drinks too much in this world, there are two who don't drink nearly enough. As I drank, he filled me in on the news about our other neighbors. Sally was doing some three-day meditation thing that involved a vow of silence, so Phil hadn't spoken to her but to her chatty friend Delia instead. Reportedly, Sally was viewing the fire as a kind of cosmic purification, a message that it was time for a fresh start. Now she was meditating and waiting for a sign to point her to the next "phase."

"Mr. O'Brien and his housekeeper are staying at a motel in Brighton Beach," he said.

"Watching porno and taking advantage of his Viagra prescription?"

"Watching game shows and soaps and arguing. The Japanese film students have been squeezed into NYU dorms. Mr. Burpus is at the Y."

"And Dulcinia Ramirez?"

"I saw her yesterday. She's fine," he said.

"How is she enjoying convent life? I hope the nuns aren't too radical for her."

"It's not one of those hip, modern-dress left-wing feminist convents," he said. "It's the old-fashioned kind, on a wooded lot surrounded by high walls. The sisters wear traditional black-and-white penguin habits."

"Mrs. R. must be happy out there with a lot of other old-fashioned, celibate women who love Jesus," I said.

"She is ecstatic," Phil said. "They pray a lot, they sing, they read from the New Testament, they bake cakes, they have different activities every night. Monday night is video night. Wednesday night is whist night. Saturday afternoons they go on an outing to a museum or a park. The nuns love Señor. One of them made him a little habit, and now they call him Sister Señor."

"And the nuns love Mrs. Ramirez?"

"Well, Robin, they love her in that good, Christian way. Those nuns love everyone. There's a little friction there though. I can't put my finger on it, but it's there."

"How do you know these nuns?"

"I did some handyman work for them, installed their security system and fixed the cistern. When I was in India, I rewired their mission. In return, they send me free cakes. They bake cakes, you know. Immaculate Confection . . ."

"Immaculate Confection? THOSE nuns?"

"Yes, you've heard of them?"

"I saw a report about them on ANNFN after they went public, or the bakery operation went public anyway. Those are great cakes. Piety and cake, it's Ramirez heaven. Think she'll stay on out there?"

"Oh, I think she may want to come back to the neighborhood when she can. She was quite concerned that, in her absence, crime was going to skyrocket because there'd be nobody to patrol and call in reports to the police the way she does."

"Public urinators are probably running rampant."

"Take another swallow," Phil said. "She may be calling you too. I let it slip out you were at the Chelsea . . ."

"Oh, great."

For years, Mrs. R. and I had been mortal enemies, on account of her thinking I was a transvestite-madam-drug dealer, and always trying to rap me with her cane. Once the misunderstanding cleared up, she decided we were friends, which was worse. She'd corner me, call me, follow me sometimes wanting to tell me about her ideas for TV shows, her conspiracy theories, to complain about her new favorite whipping boys, baby boomers, or just to show me the new electrified Ascension of Jesus display she'd bought for Easter.

"They're keeping her pretty busy out there," he said. "I don't think she'll be bothering you much. I'll be visiting her again tomorrow. Want to send a message?"

"Just my fond regards."

I turned to wave for our check, and saw the man in the bad toupee at a nearby table, talking into a telephone. Our eyes met for a moment, and then he looked away. He waved for his check too. I had to force myself to look away from the toupee. It was so bad it kept drawing my eye. By far, this was the worst toupee I'd ever seen in my life, and I've seen some bad ones, having once done a report on the shady side of the hairpiece industry and interviewed six bald guys with brain abscesses from a faulty hair-replacement system. But this wig took the cake and begged the obvious question: Why would anyone wear such a terrible and obvious toupee? Did he know how bad it looked? Of course, I was just assuming it was a toupee from the false look of it and the uncomfortable way it sat on his head. If it was his real hair, it was even more horrifying. It answered that age-old question: Can space monsters mate with earth women?

Phil had borrowed a car to come in from Jersey, and had parked it down Seventh Avenue near Twenty-first Street. I walked him back to it. Before he got in, I said, "What about you? Are you going to stick around, move back into the building if they rebuild?"

I'd waited until the last moment, not sure if I was going to ask at all, afraid I might hear an answer I didn't want.

"I don't know, luv," he said. "Have to see what Helen wants to do. She's undecided."

Like a little kid, I watched him as he drove off until I couldn't see the car anymore. I got this weird chill watching the car vanish into a blur of taillights—I don't know if it was déjà vu or *sera vu*, but it wasn't a good feeling. After it passed, I turned and walked back to the Chelsea.

Rounding the corner to Twenty-third Street, I noticed that the man in the bad toupee was behind me. I speeded up because I was getting a vaguely menacing vibe from him, and not just because I've been menaced by wig-wearing people more than once. Something else about him spooked me.

Speed-walking, and half-looking behind me as I did, I headed toward the hotel, and ran smack dab into a young man who was lurking in the grainy shadows between streetlights, next to the Capitol Fishing Tackle Store.

It was the manboy. He had looked more impressive through the distorted fish-eye peephole than he did now. He looked about sixteen and kind of pathetic.

"Where have you been?" I asked. "Where's Nadia? I thought she met up with you and you two had eloped."

"We didn't meet up. Do you know where she is?" He had the same accent as Nadia, which sounded kind of Slavic and kind of Central Asian. Couldn't put my finger on it, but it landed somewhere between Pakistan and Germany.

Meanwhile, the man in the bad toupee had walked past and vanished.

"Well, obviously I haven't heard from her, if I thought she was with you. You'd better come upstairs," I said.

He came in with me, looking around himself in a fearful manner. He was a nervous young man.

"You didn't hook up with Nadia at all?" I asked.

"No," he snarled.

"Well, she's gone. No sign of her anywhere. Where would she go?"

"I don't know. I thought you might know," he said. He was acting very resentful and suspicious of me for some reason.

"I don't know her at all and we didn't talk much," I said. "I've had my own shit to look after. Someone was killed here last night."

He didn't seem to hear this. "When did she leave?"

"Early evening, six, seven P.M. What happened to you? I saw you come into the hotel yesterday, but you never showed at the apartment."

"I didn't know this was the right apartment, because you told me the night before it was the wrong apartment ... ."

"So you just wandered the hotel hoping to run into her?"

He looked at me angrily.

"Look, I'm sorry I sent you away the other night," I said. "I didn't know who you were or why you were here," I said.

"Yes, and you made a lot of trouble for me and for Nadia," he said. "You have no idea."

"Well, as I said, I'm sorry I sent you away. But no one in their right mind would let a strange man into their apartment, especially at four A.M. Don't lay a guilt trip on me."

In Tamayo's apartment, I offered him a seat at the kitchen table and a beer. I got one for me too, and sat down across from him.

"You got a name?"

"Nadia may have given you my code name . . ."

"She didn't give you any name."

"Rocky."

"Rocky, would you feel better if we called the cops? You could file a missing persons report . . ."

"Not yet."

"Why?"

"It'll ruin everything," he said. He took a Marlboro out of a slightly crumpled soft pack and said, "Do you have a match?"

"No," I said. "And yes, I mind if you smoke."

"No matches?" he said.

"No."

"Oh damn," he said, and muttered something, low, in some other language as he patted his pockets looking for a match. He was so nervous and fidgety. I had a feeling that his nic fit would end up being more annoying than his smoking, so I relented and said, "Wait . . . Nadia left some behind."

"Nadia left matches? Nadia doesn't smoke."

"She was using them as a bookmark."

I found the book, *Man Trap,* on the loft bed and brought the matches to Rocky.

As he lit the cigarette, I said, "Why will the cops ruin everything?"

He exhaled his smoke but said nothing.

"Because of the arranged marriage thing, and her family making trouble?" I asked.

"It is a dangerous situation."

"Yeah, I understand. I've heard about things like this, girls from closed cultures who marry against the family's wishes and bring dishonor on the clan, et cetera, and their families hunt them down. Is this the case here?"

"Something like that."

That was a problem. There'd been a lot of stories in the last few years about women running away to western countries, seeking asylum to avoid arranged marriages or charming cultural practices like genital mutilation, only to be deported and returned to their homelands. There, they were either married off against their will or, on occasion, killed by their responsible male relatives for bringing dishonor on them. The cops might just give Nadia away to Immigration, and I didn't want to be responsible for that. On the other hand, a man was dead.

"I still think you should call the cops. I can give you the name of a very understanding woman who will do her best to keep it on the QT," I said. "A man has been murdered already. Murdered. There could be a connection. Maybe Nadia saw something and the killer or killers know that. I . . . I don't want to alarm you, but what if they kidnapped her? Even if they didn't, what if her family found her and grabbed her? The police might be able to help."

"Too much risk. I know in my heart Nadia is okay. She may have seen the police here after this person was killed, and decided to stay away until things calmed down," he said.

"Maybe you're right," I said. "She's probably just hiding out until things cool down."

"But where?" he asked. "You are quite sure you don't know where she has gone?"

"We didn't talk much. It's an accident that we both ended up in Tamayo's apartment at the same time. You see, my apartment burned down—"

"Did she talk about me?"

"Not much, but what she said was very flattering."

Love isn't just blind, I thought, it's been sniffing glue! Nadia saw him as a poetic, romantic, yearning, soulful man, whereas I saw a low-wattage half man with all the physical charm of John Gotti, Jr. Obviously, Nadia had projected some false romantic illusions onto this boy while in the grip of her hormones.

"Where were you while Nadia was here? Maybe she's gone there, and you're just missing each other."

"I slept in . . . a park."

"A park? In New York City? At night? Rocky, that's dangerous," I said.

"I can look after myself. I'm tough," he shot back.

"Don't get me wrong. I'm impressed you'd take that risk for a girl. You really love this girl?" I asked.

"Yes."

Because he smiled bashfully and looked at the floor when he said that, I decided to cut him some slack. He was surly and dim, but he was just a kid in love. His attitude was probably just macho bluster and youthful suspicion of a member of an older generation, me.

"She's the one for you, is she?"

"The only one," he said.

"How can you be sure?" I asked.

Now it was his turn to sing the praises of his Juliet, as she had sung his praises.

"She is so beautiful, with such a sunny disposition and a sweet nature," he told me. "A good girl, but easily led and too trusting."

"Nadia? Sunny and sweet?"

"Yes."

"Are we talking about the same girl?" The vulnerable waif he described was not the same girl I'd met. "Do you have a photograph of her?"

He pulled out a billfold and several pictures of him and Nadia. At first, I thought we were speaking of a different girl, because the girl in the first few pictures was a brunette. One photo looked like it was taken in New York, in front of a brownstone, when they were a couple years younger than they were now. Another showed him and the same girl dressed up as a gangster and his moll, surrounded by other teenagers in costumes. But in a more recent photo, a head shot of her, she had blond hair, and I saw that we were indeed speaking of the same Nadia.

"Who are these other kids in the costume picture? Maybe Nadia is with them?"

"I don't know where they are. I don't remember their names."

"Does she have any other friends in New York? Or New Jersey? Connecticut?"

"I don't know."

"Well, I don't know what else to do. Maybe she'll come back here. Or she'll call," I said.

"I'll stay here until she does."

"Oh. Good," I said. "While we're waiting, you wanna tell me about this country you come from?"

"I do not think I will," he said. "You might tell the police, or you might tell someone, and they might tell the police. Nadia could get deported. Her family could do something terrible to me or my family."

I tried to guess, but it was hard to pin down his ethnicity. He was pale with dark hair, soft features, small eyes a little too close together, and a hint of dark fuzz on his face.

"Aw, come on, Rocky," I said. "I won't tell anyone."

"What did Nadia tell you?"

"She calls it Plotzonia," I said. "I only ask because maybe it will provide some clue to where she is."

"It won't!" He was surly again, and changed the subject, demanding in a princely way, "I need to eat. Do you have anything to eat?"

"Yes, but first can you give me a little more information—"

"I need to eat now. I'm hypoglycemic."

"Keep it in your pants, kid. I'll feed you," I said.

I gave him some cold cuts and potato salad, and he ate like he still had a growth spurt ahead of him. They were so obviously doomed, these two bad-tempered brats, heading down lust-slicked rails to a shattering heartbreak, the kind of disillusionment that scars you for life. There was so much I wanted to tell him. I could have quoted some insightful poetry and homespun wisdom, told him about good hangings and bad marriages. I could have provided a few vivid real-life examples of young love gone wrong, crimes of passion and other homicides that involved people stuffing the dismembered bits of their "true" lovers into trash bags.

Instead, I said, "You want dessert?"

"Do you have any ice cream?"

"There's some Ben and Jerry's in the freezer," I said.

He looked around the room, seemingly baffled.

"It's the compartment on top of the refrigerator."

He still looked baffled, so I got the ice cream for him. He ate straight out of the tub, digging his way to China through a half-gallon of Ben & Jerry's Wavy Gravy.

"What's the other guy like?" I asked. "The man you're stealing her from?"

"He's an old man," he said. "An ugly, disgusting old man."

"That's a shame. Well, let me take this head shot of Nadia, show it to some of the neighbors tomorrow," I said. "Maybe you can track down some of her old friends, see if they've heard from her."

"How would I do that?" he asked.

I couldn't decide if he was a complete moron, an only child, or an eldest son accustomed to being waited upon, who played dumb in order to get others to do his bidding.

"Have you heard of the telephone? It's this newfangled invention . . ." I said, and stopped myself. I sounded like every snarky grown-up who'd ever burned my butt when I was a teenager. "Make some calls. You must know someone who knows something."

I showed him where to sleep, and pointed him to the bathroom so he could shower and wash up. When he thought I wasn't looking, he took a copy of *Cosmo* into the bathroom.

I logged on to my laptop to see if Tamayo had E-mailed. She hadn't, nor had Pierre, not that I expected him to. The only E-mail was from someone E-named MrsKisses. Turned out it was from Phil, using his sister-in-law's E-mail address. He was sending along a wire story he'd pulled off Drudge about the Woznik murder.

DEAD ART DEALER'S LOVER ARRESTED

Socialite art patron Grace Rouse was arrested tonight on suspicion of murder in the death of bad-boy art dealer Gerald Woznik, police sources say. Woznik, 44, was shot and killed Friday night in the notorious Chelsea Hotel on West Twenty-third Street. An eyewitness claims to have seen Rouse, 43, escaping down a fire escape on the west side of the hotel around the time of the murder. Rouse claims she was at home meditating when Woznik was killed. Woznik and Rouse, who is heiress to the Rouse shipping and securities fortunes, had been an item on the New York art scene for about a year, and had been living together for almost as long. Friends say they had a tempestuous relationship and often fought over Woznik's womanizing ways.

There was a sidebar story about some of Rouse's previous dalliances with bad boys, something I can identify with in concept, though not on the same level. Rouse had been involved with a paranoid film auteur, had "canoodled" at Moomba with an aging actor before he went into rehab for sex addiction, and was named as a corespondent in the divorce cases of an elderly, desiccated rock star and an obscenely wealthy European art dealer whose horse-loving wife had had massive plastic surgery to make herself look more equine. After Rouse was dumped by an evil New Zealand media mogul for a leggy Indian film star, she rebounded with Woznik. Said a "friend," "She developed an unhealthy obsession with Gerald, was insanely jealous, and tried to control him with money."

Love. Ain't it grand?

chapter six

It's a small world. It turned out that Grace Rouse was being represented by the famous Spencer Roo. This might even seem a tad cosmic to me, if Roo wasn't the obvious legal choice in a high-profile murder case. The man was known for taking on famous open-and-shut cases, and somehow getting his clients off. When I called him the next morning, he was out "conferring with a client"—Rouse, I figured. But no sweat. He was a pal, would call me back as soon as he could, and do everything he could to get me a meeting with the accused heiress, just in case she knew something about Nadia's whereabouts.

After I called Roo and fed the manboy a healthy breakfast, I went out to talk to the neighbors within the hotel. As much as I wanted to avoid Maggie, I wanted to get rid of Rocky much, much more. Maggie's name had been in the note Tamayo wrote to Nadia and in the *Man Trap* book, so she was likely to know something about the girl. When I called I got her voice mail, and there was no answer when I knocked on her door. I wrote a note and shoved it under the door, asking her to call because I needed to talk to her about "a sensitive matter."

Across the hall, the bodybuilder was watching me. What was his story? I wondered. He never seemed to go out, and I'd already seen him several times, standing in his doorway, looking into the hallway. He'd told the cops he knew nothing about the murder, but maybe he knew something about Nadia's disappearance.

I stood in front of him, but he barely acknowledged me—just a flicker of the eye as he continued lifting hand weights, one after the other. He had the kind of face you'd expect to see in news footage of soccer hooligans or skinheads, pretty beat up, with a number of scars, and his nose looked like it had been broken a few times. His eyes were a bit off, not quite crossed but leaning in that direction. Up and down his arms were a lot of tattoos of what looked like eastern mystical symbols. Behind him, what I could see of the apartment was all black. Scary guy.

"Excuse me," I said. He didn't respond. I waved my hand in front of his face and said again, "Excuse me."

He stared at me for a moment, and finally said, "Yes?"

"Hi. I wondered if I could ask you some questions."

He was silent.

"Did you see anything strange or hear anything the night Gerald Woznik was killed?"

He said nothing.

"They found his body right there, across the hall from you. Maybe you saw something through the peephole, or you heard something?"

He lifted the right, hand weight. Then he lifted the left one.

"Did you see a young woman, eighteen-ish, curly blond hair?" I said. "She went missing the night the art dealer was killed. Do you know anything about that?"

"Everything worth knowing is unknowable," he said evenly.

"Well, not everything. Knowing where this girl is, that's worth it to me."

"The ultimate goal in life is to pass through the world and have no effect at all," he said.

"Excuse me?"

"The ultimate goal in life is to pass through the world and have no effect at all," he said, each word squeezed out through some dense filter of fear or madness or both.

"No effect at all? Excuse me, but what would be the point of going through life then? Listen to me. Someone was killed—"

He stepped backward, two steps, into his dark room and shut the door in my face.

"Hey, that affected me!" I called out as I stomped off.

The seventh-floor neighbors either weren't home or claimed to know nothing, so I headed downstairs to the front desk. Someone in this hotel had to know something about Nadia, but I was either asking the wrong people, or the right people weren't talking. The staff was notoriously discreet and protective of its guests and tenants. Though very pleasant when they heard I was a friend of the legendary Tamayo, they knew nothing about Nadia or the murder, or so they claimed. The inscrutable Sikh manning the front desk just smiled. The assistant manager, Jerry Weinstein, had been off with the flu and had missed the mayhem. The head switchboard operator, Edna, who had piles and piles of shiny silver hair, said simply, "If I knew anything, and I don't, it would be a secret, and my secrets die with me, hon."

If I wanted more information, they said, politely and in a variety of New York and foreign accents, I'd have to speak to Stanley Bard, the devilishly handsome man who owns and manages the hotel on behalf of the stockholders.

Bard's a legend in his own right, having seen quite a lot of luminaries who lived and worked here, and kept a lot of them alive by cajoling them to work, taking art in lieu of rent, or letting them slide on the rent for months at a time until checks came in. He has bailed artists out of jail, coaxed them into rehab, mediated their lovers' quarrels, and viewed their moods and eccentricities with an art lover's indulgence.

Mr. Bard's office was just off the lobby.

"Come in," he barked when I knocked.

I did. Bard looked up from behind a cluttered desk in a cav-

ernous office done up in dark wood with carved detailing and a
fading fresco on the ceiling of what looked like Cupid and Psyche.

After I introduced myself, I told him about the star-crossed
lovers who were supposed to meet in Tamayo's apartment, and
how the murder of Gerald Woznik had interfered with their plans.

"It's a terrible thing. I've know Gerald for years," Bard said.
"First murder we've had here in twenty years. How is Tamayo?"

"She's fine, as far as I know."

"When you speak with her, tell her we miss her here."

"I shall. Do you know anything about this young woman, Nadia?" I asked, showing him the photograph.

"I don't; I'm sorry," he said. "So many people come through
here."

It was hard to tell if he was being straight with me. He didn't
know me, after all, except as a friend of Tamayo's, and I knew
from her stories that he was very protective of his tenants.

"If you learn anything—" I began, but before I could finish,
the door opened, and a young black man with a bleached-blond
buzz cut stormed in.

"Stanley, you've got to do something about Old Frank," he
said in a weird way, emphatic and blasé at the same time. "Miriam had a dinner party last night and the son of a bitch stood
outside Miriam's door pissing on the hallway wall and cursing at
the guests. Luckily, Miriam's friends thought it was some kind of
performance art."

"No harm done then."

"But it upsets Miriam because of her history with Frank," Ben
said. "It upsets the neighbors as well."

"I'll talk to him, Ben."

"Talking hasn't helped in the past."

Mr. Bard took this opportunity to turn to me and say, "Could
you excuse us? I'll call you if I find any information on . . . what
did you say her name was?"

"Nadia," I said.

As I closed the door, I heard Mr. Bard shouting, "What can I do? He's eighty-nine years old, he's a great painter. You want me to throw him out into the street? An eighty-nine-year-old man? I'll talk to him, Ben, I'll talk to him."

For the next few hours, I stopped people around the hotel and asked them if they'd seen the girl in the photograph I was holding. A couple of people thought they'd maybe seen her, but weren't sure where or when.

In the course of my investigation, I met a bunch of people from the hotel: a long-haired drummer half my age; a middle-aged married couple, with a small daughter, who looked like they had money; a secretary who worked at the U.N.; a woman from Eastern Europe who worked as an engineer; a plucky filmmaker named Jan and her daughter, Chelsea, named after the hotel; and an actor who had been wandering about with a Do Not Disturb sign around his neck, muttering, trying to stay in character and evidently doing it until I disturbed him. I also talked to some tourists staying in the hotel, one from Japan, one from Hungary, and several from Ohio, who told me they always stayed at the Chelsea when they came to New York. Nobody knew anything about Nadia.

The first break I got came when I got back to the seventh floor, where I ran into Lucia, the blowsy Hispanic girl who lived on one side of Tamayo. She ushered me gleefully into her apartment and had me take a seat in the combined living room–kitchen.

Her small apartment was haphazard, but brightly so. The studio apartment was divided by a garment rack, which had colorful dresses, most of them retro postwar dresses, hanging on hangers and flung carelessly over the top of the rack. The furniture was what I would come to know as standard Chelsea Hotel issue, oak dressers and chairs, a double bed with a flowered bedspread, a beige lamp. Nothing matched of the things Lucia had added, knickknacks, objets d'art, paintings.

"Would you like a drink?" she asked.

"No thanks. Actually, I wanted to ask you about the girl staying at Tamayo's this past week, Nadia—"

There was a knock on the door.

"That's my man," she said. "Excuse me."

In walked a small, muscular man with a leonine mane of white hair, brushed back, the man I'd seen her yelling and throwing shoes at the day before. They embraced passionately.

"This is Carlos. He's a retired bullfighter," she said, and introduced me to him in Spanish.

He kissed my hand, then sat down on a sofa in the combined living room–kitchen.

Lucia handed him a drink, and then handed me one, a tumbler full of whiskey, despite my protests. I took it just to make her happy.

After Lucia got herself a tumbler of whiskey, Carlos grabbed her and they cooed to each other in Spanish. He was an odd-looking character but he had a certain earthy, Castillian peasant kind of appeal. His mass of white hair was completely out of proportion to his smallish body. When Lucia laughed, his morose, jowly face lit up. Lucia was very happy. I don't think I've ever seen anyone that happy before. She was happy to a fault. She was insanely happy.

I pushed Nadia's picture across the coffee table at her.

"Have you seen this girl?"

"No, I don't think so," Lucia said. The bullfighter said something in Spanish and Lucia translated. "He says he saw her, but not on this floor. He doesn't remember which floor."

"Ask him to think about it."

"Oh, he has a problem with his memory," Lucia said. "From being a bullfighter. I'll ask him again in five minutes, after his brain rests a little."

The bullfighter spoke English badly, so Lucia translated as we conversed. I'm not sure how good her translation was, and how much of it was her own opinion. I asked Carlos if he'd been a successful bullfighter, and he said something in Spanish, very grand sounding in a braying way, and Lucia said, shaking her head ever so slightly, "He was not a big star. He was in the middle. He's been gored twelve times! Once in the head! Poor baby. That's what damaged his memory."

"How did a retired bullfighter end up in the Chelsea?" I asked.

"His brother, a musician, lived here. Carlos came to stay with him after the last goring. And after the brother died, Carlos stayed on," Lucia said.

"And you?" I asked.

"My father's family pays me to stay out of Argentina," she said brightly. "So as not to cause a scandal and harm his political ambitions. I was born out of wedlock."

"Really? But why the Chelsea?"

"I don't know. The wind blew me to New York, and into the Chelsea one day, and I stayed. And you?"

"I came to stay at Tamayo's place because my apartment burned down—"

Carlos interrupted to say something in Spanish. He and Lucia talked back and forth and then she said to me, "He saw her when he was posing for Miriam Grundy. She paints a little. He doesn't remember what day, but I do. It was the day Gerald Woznik was killed."

"What time was he posing for Miriam Grundy?"

"Early evening."

"Did he see Nadia before or after his session?" Lucia asked Carlos this in Spanish.

"He doesn't remember," she said, and smiled apologetically.

"Did you know Gerald Woznik?" I asked her.

"Oh yes. He used to live here," she said.

"Where were you when he was killed?"

"At El Quijote, at the bar, with Edna the switchboard operator," she answered.

"Have you heard anyone else in this place talk about the murder? Any of the neighbors?"

"Yes, everyone, but nobody knows who did it."

"Do you know Grace Rouse?"

"Not well. She used to visit Gerald when he lived here," Lucia said, jumping up to put a record—an LP—on her turntable. Crackling, tinny music came from the speakers. It was the kind of falsely cheerful singsongy music you hear at old-timey carnivals and carousels, and for some reason it flashed me back for a moment to Paris.

"What's the deal with the bodybuilder who stands in his doorway a lot?" I asked.

"We call him the Zenmaster," Lucia said, settling back into Carlos's lap.

"He's scary. Doesn't talk much."

"He's very sweet, deep down. I haven't spoken to him in weeks. The last time he spoke to me, he told me his invisible eye had been opened."

She started to translate this to Carlos, and he kissed her, for a long time. There seemed no point asking her any more questions, what with the bullfighter's tongue down her throat.

"If you see or speak to Maggie Mason, tell her I'm looking for her," I said, and saw myself out.

THE YOUNG BLACK MAN with the blond buzz cut whom I'd seen in Mr. Bard's office turned out to be Miriam Grundy's assistant.

He welcomed me into her tenth-floor apartment with a blasé nod, an aquamarine earring in one ear sparkling as his head moved.

"Mrs. Grundy is upstairs in her studio. Follow me," he said.

The apartment was a duplex, with a red spiral staircase leading up to a large, sunlit studio on the unofficial eleventh floor. The walls were dingy white, and the high ceilings sloped up into gabled windows facing south, to bring in the sunlight.

I didn't see tiny Mrs. Grundy, who was sitting on a stool in front of a large canvas, until she hopped off her stool and came out from behind the painting. She was dressed in a white men's shirt over slacks, her hair in a turban. Her makeup had been done and her eyebrows were penciled in, a little too darkly, making her look angry despite the slight smile on her face. I half-expected Erich Von Stroheim to appear and whisper that he was madam's second husband. Every once in a while, I still have a small-town-girl glamour moment, when the small-town girl I used to be pipes up and says, "Holy cow! I'm talking to [insert name of awesome celebrity here]." I was having one now. Here in front of me was the woman who inspired the Pulitzer prize–winning Mimi poems. Those poems would never have been written if it hadn't been for her, if years before that she hadn't inspired a young, married investment banker to ditch his society wife, reject his family's ways and wishes, give up his hated career, and follow his dream of being a writer.

"Hello, Miss Hudson," she said graciously, sitting back down on a stool in front of a half-finished half-abstract painting of what vaguely looked like Carlos the retired bullfighter. She was a good distance away from the canvas. She could only just reach it with her brush.

"Would you like a beverage?" Ben asked me. I declined.

"Ben, did the caterers call about the party today?" Miriam asked.

"No, they said they'd call tomorrow."

"The cleaning crew is lined up to clear out the studio?"

"Yes, Mrs. Grundy."

"Are the Living Statues lined up?"

"Yes, the last one is coming by today, and the florist wants to know—"

"All white. I want the flowers to be all white, and the vases to be set in frothy nests of silver tulle," she said.

"White roses, white freesia, white carnations, white hyacinth, white daisies."

"Good," she said. "I will need the schedule by the end of the day, Ben. I don't want the guy who walks backward to be there at the same time as the Chinese midget acrobats or the fighting mimes."

"The fighting mimes can't make it, Mrs. Grundy. They're shooting a movie."

"Oh. Well, thank you. That will be all for now."

After she dismissed him, she said, "What was it you wanted? You didn't make it clear when you called."

"This girl"—I held up Nadia's picture—"came to visit you the evening before last, around the time Gerald Woznik died. Someone saw her," I said. I did not tell Miriam it was Carlos, whose memory left much to be desired.

"Hold the picture back a bit, dear," she said. "Oh yes. I remember her."

"Why was she here?"

"She is a great admirer of my late husband, the great American poet Oliver Grundy, and she wanted to meet me. She is also a friend of Tamayo's, and so I met with her. Tell me, when did you see Tamayo last?"

"In Tokyo, about six, seven weeks ago."

"And what was she up to?"

"She was holed up in the Okura Hotel, finishing a book on her adventures with the Americans for a publisher over there."

"Did she have her monkey with her?" Miriam asked.

"Yes, but I understand he was sent to live with her grandmother in Osaka before she left Japan," I said. "About Nadia—"

"Which grandmother?"

"Her grandma Rei. Her grandma Ruth lives on Long Island."

"And what is her monkey's name? I've forgotten," Miriam said.

I got the feeling she was quizzing me to make sure I really was a friend of Tamayo's. You couldn't blame her. When you're a famous patron of the arts, people probably go to great lengths to get your ear.

"Ernie Kovacs. About Nadia . . . when was she here?"

"Early evening," she said. "She had just left when I heard the news about Gerald Woznik. I was absolutely speechless."

"What time did you hear about the murder?"

"Oh, dear. It was after Carlos was here, after Nadia was here, before dinner with John Wells, around eight P.M."

"Do you know where Nadia went afterward?"

We were interrupted. Ben came in with a young woman and said, "One of the Living Statues, Mrs. Grundy."

"Oh, good. Show me what you do, young lady," Miriam said.

The young woman posed, very still, for what seemed a long time.

"Another pose, please," Miriam said, and then requested yet another pose before saying, "That'll do. You're hired. Ben, I just had an idea. I want one very tall man, the tallest man you can find, and one very tall woman, to just mingle. Oh, oh, and those drag queens who do me in that cabaret act, the Swinging Miriams."

"Of course, Mrs. Grundy. That's inspired," said Ben, still blasé.

After the living statue and Ben left, I asked again, "Do you know where Nadia went after she saw you?"

Before she could answer, Ben came in again, this time with a contortionist, twisted like a pretzel but somehow managing to walk.

"No," Miriam said, sending the pretzel on his way. "I don't think so."

"We're having a party later this week," she explained to me. "And we're still putting the entertainment together."

"It sounds like some party."

"Oliver's birthday party," she said. "It's always an event."

"For your late husband?"

"Well, for his ghost," she said. "And the other ghosts of the Chelsea, and our living friends. You were asking about Nadia?"

"Do you know where Nadia is from?"

"Oh, she had a funny name for it. Plotzonia." She studied me for a moment, and said, "I hope I'm not violating a trust by telling you this. She was eloping, I believe."

"I know," I said. "But she didn't meet up with her young man."

"That's a shame."

"Where was she going to elope?"

"I don't know where she was going to elope. You might ask Maggie Mason. I believe she's involved. I must excuse myself, I have—"

"Do you have any idea who might have killed Gerald Woznik?"

"My dear, who knows what sets people off?" she said. "He was a ladies' man, he was a less than scrupulous businessman. But in cases like these, I tend to think passion is a more likely motive than money."

As Ben escorted me out, I asked him about Old Frank, the guy who peed on the wall and cursed out Miriam's dinner guests the night before.

"Frank Gozzomi, the surrealist painter. You've probably seen him. He often sleeps in the red armchair in the lobby."

"He had some history with Mrs. Grundy?"

"He's in love with her. He met her here in the Chelsea, just after her family fled Europe."

"She left him for Oliver Grundy."

"Yes."

"And Old Frank has just hung around being jealous all that time?"

"No. He moved to Italy and lived there until ten or so years ago, when he moved back to the Chelsea. He's essentially harmless, but very annoying. I do wish he wouldn't urinate on the walls, especially without using his hands."

"You mean . . ."

"He must be taking Viagra. The man is eighty-nine years old," Ben said.

As far as Nadia info went, my visit with Mrs. Grundy was fruitless, though it was a genuine kick in the ass to meet her. What a dame, I thought as I walked down the wrought-iron circular staircase that runs through the middle of the Chelsea. Miriam was the kind of old lady I wanted to become—rich, mischievous, an eccentric role model for future drag queens.

But Maggie Mason remained my best lead. This gave me a sharp pain. Maybe she was over the whole Mike O'Reilly thing, I reasoned, though Mike had said she held a grudge for a long, long time. Didn't he say for over ten years she sent a velvet heart with a wooden stake in it to her first lover every Valentine's Day?

As long as I remained very circumspect, didn't spill any give-away information, maybe she wouldn't know about my tempes-tuous relationship with Mad Mike.

Nadia and Rocky ... that gave me knots too. Crazy kids. There was no way to feel good about this one. If Nadia got nabbed by the feds and was sent back to her homeland, she'd be forced into a marriage to a man she didn't love in a country she utterly despised. If she and her equally belligerent beau Rocky got together and eloped, they'd hate each other in two years and be in divorce court in three, unless they found some applied-physics way to turn two negatives into a positive and stay together bonded by mutual loathing and seething resentment. But that was a far better scenario than the worst-case one—that something had happened to her because she witnessed the murder of Gerald Woznik.

Here was where Phil's little equation went wonky, because the only thing that could clearly prevent the first two scenarios was the last.

I did know this much: Nadia didn't kill Gerald Woznik, be-cause she was with Miriam Grundy at the time of death, unless Miriam was lying, and why would she lie? Lucia had an alibi too. According to the cops, Maggie Mason, who had threatened Woz-nik right in front of me in the elevator, had an alibi too.

As I was coming up the seventh-floor landing, Maggie Mason scurried past.

"Maggie!" I called after her. "May I speak with you?"

Quickly, she turned and said, "What?"

"I'm Robin, I'm staying at Tamayo's."

"I remember . . ."

"Did you meet Nadia? I know that Tamayo told her to call you if she needed any help, and I saw that she had a book of yours."

"Yes, *Man Trap*. Great book. It got me my current boyfriend. Have you read it?" she asked.

"Not really. You talked to Nadia when?"

"The day she arrived. The day of the murder."

"She called you."

"Yes, and I went over, we had coffee, chatted for a while, but she hasn't called me back for any help."

"That's because she's gone. She has disappeared," I said. "I'm worried. . . ."

"Oh, I think you're overreacting," she said. "She was planning to elope, after all."

"The groom-to-be is at Tamayo's place now, so they didn't elope. I don't think I'm overreacting."

"The groom is at Tamayo's? *Quel dommage*."

"Yes, and Nadia left Tamayo's with her things not long before Gerald Woznik was murdered, dying in Tamayo's doorway. The timing bothers me. Where were you around that time?"

"On AOL, E-mailing my boyfriend and some friends, chatting in a comic-book chat room. Why?"

"I saw you in the elevator arguing with the dead guy, Woznik, before he was killed," I said.

"The bastard owed me money for some paintings I gave him to sell. He was supposed to bring me some money and he was late, so I was angry," she said. "The police checked it out. As far as Nadia goes, I just can't believe Nadia would be connected to the murder."

"She might have been in the wrong place, wrong time," I said. "Think. She must have said something that could give us a lead to her."

"I really can't think of anything, and I'm late for a meeting.

I'm sure Nadia is just hiding out until the heat's off. I'll call you as soon as I have a free moment. Sorry."

Without waiting for me to respond, she disappeared through the swinging door to the east wing of the seventh floor. I followed, but when I got there, she had vanished.

Meanwhile, Rocky had found out exactly SQUAT. He was in the bathroom when I got back to Tamayo's, and hollered at me through the door. He claimed to have made some calls, but when quizzed couldn't say whom he had called or where they were. He was useless.

Maggie was the only lead. Nadia had left no clues behind; the only thing she'd left was that stupid book, *Man Trap* . . . and the matchbook inside, from the Bus Stop Bar & Grill.

"Rocky," I said, knocking on the bathroom door.

"Huh? What?" he asked.

"You know those matches I gave you? Where are they?"

"I don't know. I found a lighter. Do you need the lighter?"

"No."

Tamayo had written something inside that matchbook, something about saying hi to Stinky. That sure sounded like some kind of code.

chapter seven

Bus Stop Bar & Grill was a name that could indicate either understated whimsy or complete lack of imagination, as there was a bus stop right outside the bar. It's on Bowery, south of Bleecker, a distinctly ungentrified stretch of Manhattan real estate where grass and weeds grow in the cracks of the buckled sidewalks and the air smells of gasoline from nearby taxicab garages and gas stations.

The front of the Bus Stop Bar was tilted slightly, as if the building was sinking on the west side, but it was just the fronting that was affected. Inside, the bar was level. Except for one miserable male loner at the bar, chain-smoking and drinking, and a woman, maybe in her late sixties, flipping through a magazine, the place looked empty. There are few things as depressing as a not-quite-empty bar just after it opens in the late morning, the sunlight coming through the windows in a filtered way that makes the interior of a shady place shadier.

I asked the woman by the jukebox if she could point me to whoever ran the joint. After looking me up and down, she told me that would be her husband, Stinky, and called for him loudly.

A few minutes later, an old guy came out of a back room. He was easily seventy, with thinning white hair, a gold tooth, and a big beer belly reined in by the strings of his white apron.

"Irene, get back to work. We could have a rush in an hour," Stinky said to his wife, who got up, scowled at me, and went behind the bar.

Stinky and I sat down and I told him briefly about my romantic mission to help lovers elope. He snorted and said, in a coarse, deep voice, "Don't do 'em any favors!"

By now I understood where his nickname came from. He had a powerful body odor with a sharp, individual edge to it, like onions boiled in beer, with just a soupçon of ripe game.

Stinky leaned over the table, bringing his ripe aura closer, raised one eyebrow in a way I imagined he thought was very devilish, and said, "Marriage is the death of love."

Well, that—and that powerful force field of yours, Stinky, I thought.

"You might be right," I said. "Oh, Tamayo says hey."

"Tamayo! She's a friend of Tamayo's," Stinky called out to his wife. "How is Tamayo?"

"She's traveling around the world with her boyfriend, Buzzer. I'm actually here about another friend of Tamayo's."

I pulled out the photo of Nadia and showed it to him.

"Have you seen this girl?"

"She doesn't look familiar," he said. "What's your name again?"

"Robin."

"Stinky and Robin, that sounds good together," he said without any hint of irony at all. Maybe I was flattering myself, but it seemed like the bastard was flirting with me.

"You're sure you haven't seen this girl in here?"

"Sure I'm sure," he said. "Are you married?"

"Divorced actually, but . . ."

"Then you know what it is like. Don't be in such a hurry to help others make that mistake. You want a drink?"

"No, thanks."

"Irene, bring me a boilermaker," he yelled.

When Irene brought his boilermaker, I asked her about Nadia. She looked at the picture and handed it back with a frown, shooting darts at me with her eyes.

"That's enough, Irene. Back to work," Stinky said, slapping her ass.

Irene couldn't help smiling when he did this. She stood there, blushing, for a moment, until a new customer, a security guard, came in and sat down at the bar, well away from the miserable loner.

Stinky said to me, "Men and women should be coconspirators, doncha think?"

"What do you mean?"

"Coconspirators," Stinky said. "They should plot together against the government, the churches, the institutions, the husbands, the wives, all of 'em that are trying to keep 'em apart."

"Well, in a way, my young lovers are doing just that," I said, trying to get back on the topic.

"What can you tell me about you?" he asked.

In the background, I saw his wife, glaring at me while sharpening a big knife.

"I'm boring, Stinky," I said.

He did the eyebrow thing again. He had an endearing, lopsided grin, marred now by the gold tooth, and with a little imagination one could see the face of a handsome, cocky young man. It was kind of cute that he didn't realize he'd lost that old magic. But did this guy really think he could pick me up . . . right in front of his wife? What balls. Did his wife really think there was any threat at all of this happening? And why was she chopping that corned beef with such fury?

"How come you haven't been by before? Listen," he said, his voice lowered to a rough whisper. "Irene goes to see her sister Daisy on Thursdays. Why don't you come back then?"

"I'm busy on Thursdays, Stinky, but thanks," I said. "You've got a nice wife there. Have you been married long?"

"Twenty years."

"Kids?"

"I hoped to have children, but Irene, she was in an industrial accident at her old job in a pesticide plant. It made her barren and cost her her sense of smell. But the settlement bought us this bar."

"You ought to look after her, be nice to her," I said. "Pretty lady like that. You two are meant for each other."

He grinned at my chastisement like a naughty boy who just couldn't help himself, light reflecting off his gold tooth. I hesitated before giving the hound my card, then decided he was harmless and handed it to him with the Chelsea number written on the back.

"Call me if this girl comes in here. And keep this on the QT."

"Always on the QT. I'm a discreet guy," he said, with a lewd emphasis on the word "discreet."

Irene yelled at him to take a call, and Stinky left me with a clammy grope of a handshake.

Well, it had been a long shot. The matchbook was probably put in the book by Maggie Mason before she loaned it to Nadia, and the message inside was not code at all, as there really was a guy named Stinky at the Bus Stop Bar & Grill, a friend of Tamayo's. (Her affection for people of all kinds was almost as embracing as that of the good, Christian nuns Mrs. Ramirez was staying with. Maybe more so.)

Not sure where to go next, I ambled toward Canal Street and Chinatown. How quiet the city had become. At the moment, I could hear no honking horns, no sirens, no boom boxes, no hollering workmen, no screaming teenagers. The people weren't talking, to each other or to themselves, they were just walking forward, silently, steadily. It was so quiet you could hear the electricity humming inside office buildings, the wind blowing, the eerie tinkle of wind chimes somewhere. It was spooky, it was *Twilight Zone*. In my absence, someone had replaced the old city with this impostor. Through all the changes the city had undergone it had heretofore retained that energy and attitude that propelled eight million dreams and/or nightmares. But both those things were lagging now.

This was what really bugged me about the new New York. It wasn't just the gentrification of the Lower East Side, or that Times Square had gone from a steamy sleaze pot to the equivalent of Las Vegas's Glitter Gulch, cold and shiny, or the erosion of small personal freedoms. It was kind of low-energy, low-grade passivity that seemed to be everywhere. People were more polite, but not nearly as friendly. The whole city was becoming circumspect.

Chinatown, with its blaring Taiwanese music and merchants calling out to each other, was a welcome relief. I had to get food for the manboy—it was freakish how much food disappeared into that fuzzy young maw—and I was thinking a healthy stir-fry might be just the ticket. The food he had asked me to get was all crap—beer, Coca-Cola, chocolate, potato chips. What he needed was fruit and vegetables and protein, milk for strong bones, and some canned things he could prepare for himself while I was out finding his girlfriend.

When I got back, my arms were full of bulging bags of groceries—in paper, not plastic. I knocked on the door with my foot, hoping Rocky would answer and help me out. But he didn't. I had to put the bags down, unlock the door, pick up the bags, bumble in, and try, unsuccessfully, to slam the door shut with my foot so Louise Bryant wouldn't get out.

Before I could put the groceries down and close the door, I heard a man in the "living room," beyond the colored parchment partition, talking in an agitated fashion in another language.

I peeked into the living room. Rocky was standing, faced-off with the man in the bad toupee. When the guy in the bad toupee saw me, he made a sharp, surprised noise, and ran toward me.

I couldn't swear to it, but I thought he had a gun. Without

even thinking, I threw the groceries at the man in the bad toupee and unleashed my brain-freezing shriek. Cans rolled and spun on the floor. The guy in the bad toupee was stunned for a moment, but not long enough for me to jump him. He ran past me, stomping on a box of Granola.

"Call the front desk," I said to Rocky. "Tell them to stop the man in the bad toupee and call the cops."

When I turned to run after him, I tripped on a can of chili. To his credit, Rocky came to help me up, but just made me lose my balance again.

"Don't help me, call the desk," I said, and took off down the hallway.

The man in the bad toupee had taken the stairs circling down to the first floor. I could see him two floors below me. As I ran down after him, I screamed, "Stop him! Stop the man in the bad toupee!"

I was screaming at no one.

Luckily, the man in the bad toupee was older and more sluggish than I, and I was gaining on him, with just one floor between us by the time I got to the third-floor landing. By the time he got to the ground floor, I was a mere half flight behind him. He tore through the lobby, where I ran into, literally, two of the Mary Sue convention women in pastel suits by the elevator.

"Stop the man in the bad toupee," I screamed, pushing past them and accidentally knocking over the dark-haired, uptight one who looked like a younger, meaner Marilyn Quayle.

When I got to the street, at first the man was nowhere to be seen. Then I saw him, down the block, in front of the Aristocrat Deli, getting into a cab. It pulled away before I could reach it, but not before I'd made a note of the hack number on the top of the taxi, BF62. I looked for a cab, ready to jump in and demand that the driver "Follow that cab!" But the first available cab I saw was half a block back, behind a delivery truck and a city bus.

"BF62," I said, reciting the hack number on the cab. I didn't have a pen on me. So I wouldn't forget it, I repeated it aloud as

I went inside the Chelsea Hotel. With the help of a source in the taxi industry, I could track that hack and find out where the guy in the bad toupee had gone.

"BF62," I said, getting on the elevator as the doors were about to close.

The uptight, dark-haired tourist lady in the pink suit and her shorter friend were on the elevator.

"BF62, BF62," I said. "I have to remember those numbers, they're very important. BF62. Do you have a pen?"

The tourist lady in the pink suit was against the wall of the elevator, looking at me with alarm. She reached into her purse, maybe for a pen or maybe for a gun.

"BF62. I'm not nuts, I just have to remember BF62, BF62, BF62."

"Here," said the uptight one suddenly, pulling a pen out and handing it to me while holding her body back. It was the way someone gives their wallet to a mugger: Take it, but spare my life! She must have had another bad day in the Big Apple.

"BF62," I wrote on the back of a receipt in my pocket. "Thanks."

We were all getting off on seven, but they held back until I was gone. As I went into Tamayo's, I looked back and saw them poking their heads out of the elevator to make sure I was well down the hallway before getting off.

"She's the one who found the body," one of them said.

"She's crazy. Did she kill him?" asked the other.

At Tamayo's, Rocky was smoking and pacing nervously in the living room.

"Did you call the desk?"

"Yes, but they put me on hold," he said.

"Who was that guy?"

"The man Nadia is supposed to marry," he said. "I didn't recognize him with the toupee, and he said he had news of Nadia, so I opened the door. . . ."

"Rocky, don't let anyone in here but me. Okay? Jesus. If someone has real information on Nadia, have them call you from the house phone in the lobby. Did he have a gun?"

"Yes, a big one."

"Fuck. Okay, I'm calling the cops," I said.

"NO! You think the police will find Nadia before he does? Or her family does? If you call the police, you are putting Nadia's life, and my life, at risk."

Those people who always seem to know the right thing to do, instinctively, who don't have to weigh all the pros and cons, are really lucky. It just seems that too often, the right thing turns out to be the wrong thing, causing some worse thing to happen.

"I have to think. You have to think too," I said.

Rocky, with some coaxing, helped me shove an armoire in front of the door, in case the man in the bad toupee came back with a gang of wig-wearing friends. I called a guy I knew who owned a cab company and left a message asking him to find out where BF62 dropped a man in a bad toupee. It would take a day or two, he figured, to find the driver.

Rocky picked up groceries off the floor—not all of them, just the things he felt like eating at that particular moment. He wasn't happy with the food choices and made a face.

"Did you find out anything today?" I asked him.

"No! I couldn't find any of Nadia's American friends. One girl, Amanda, moved to Washington. I can't remember her last name," he said, putting the can of chili into the microwave.

"You can't microwave it that way," I said. "You have to open the can and put the chili into a microwave-safe container."

"What's a microwave-safe container?"

"It's . . . I'll do it," I said. I had to microwave Louise's special cat food and bok choy dinner anyway. "Do you know Miriam Grundy?"

"Who?"

"Weren't you supposed to meet Miriam Grundy with Nadia?"

"I don't know. We were supposed to meet someone. I don't remember names."

"Nadia left here with her suitcase and stuff, and went up to see Miriam Grundy instead of waiting for you."

"I was supposed to meet her after her meeting," he said. "I got lost . . ."

The microwave dinged. He sat down at the table while I retrieved his chow and put it in front of him with a spoon and a fork.

"You're going to have just that for lunch? Chili?"

"Do you have beer?" he asked.

"It's in the fridge."

"I drank what was there."

"All of it? Well, I didn't buy more beer," I said. I poured him a glass of milk and put some salad-in-a-bag and fresh fruit salad on a plate for him.

"I'll try to track the cabbie who picked up the man in the bad toupee, see where that goes. In the meantime, I don't think it's safe for you to stay here, Rocky," I said.

"But I must, in case Nadia comes back."

"Well, I think we know why Nadia hasn't come back, don't we? Someone is definitely after her. Is there somewhere else you can go, someplace I can contact you and we can keep up-to-date on this?"

"No. There is no such place. I stay here," he said.

The phone rang and I picked up, hoping it was Nadia, or at the very least, Maggie Mason.

"Hello," I said.

"Robin, this is Dulcinia," I heard.

Before she finished saying her name, I started talking again. "You have reached Tamayo Scheinman's answering machine. Nobody is here right now. Leave a message after the beep, and someone will get back to you as soon as possible."

Then I hit the nine on the phone to approximate an answering-machine beep.

That was a close call. Mrs. Ramirez would keep me on the

phone for hours if she could. Instead, she dictated her message into my ear.

"I am sorry I missed you, Robin. I'm just calling to see how you're doing. Señor and I are fine. We are at the Sisters of the Wretched Souls, and it's a lovely place, an oasis of virtue, although there's no public transportation anywhere close, and some of the nuns . . . a few of them seem to be more interested in cakes and pastry than prayers. Yesterday, I caught a bit of a news story during TV hour, about a mugging on East Eleventh Street. Did you see that? The police sketch looked a lot like that man—you know the one? The Russian boy who lived with the old man in the red building on Ninth Street who sat on his stoop and swore at children until he had that stroke and couldn't swear anymore and he just spit at them?"

Until he couldn't spit anymore, then he just opened his mouth and wheezed loudly instead, à la the bad guy in David Lynch's *Blue Velvet*.

Mrs. Ramirez continued. "I tried calling Richard Bigger but that home number you gave me for him doesn't work anymore, and June Fairchild isn't returning my calls. Will you please call me?"

She left the number for the convent, adding that Phil had been coming by every day to visit her. "You should come by," she said.

I didn't call her back. But she had given me an idea. I called Phil and asked if he could do me a favor and install one of his superb security systems at Tamayo's. If I'd had the time, I'd have set up my own system, which is cheap, easy, and yet innocent looking. But it takes time to grow the poison ivy. It takes time to fill the tin cans with marbles and string them together. It takes time to record the loud, insane laughter that greets an intruder who doesn't know to pull the little wire sticking out under the door that disables the system.

"Luv, you don't know how much I would like to leave New Jersey and come in to see you," he said. In the background, I could hear Helen and her kin arguing politics, which is a subject Phil tries to avoid as much as possible.

After I hung up, I asked Rocky again where Plotzonia was.

"It won't help find Nadia if you know. It will only lead to trouble."

"How?"

"You might tell someone."

"You have to trust me," I said. "I'm trying to help, goddammit."

Unyielding, he responded by spooning another large ladle of chili into his mouth. He was trying to do it in a cool, defiant way, but some of the red-bean goo dribbled down the side of his mouth and onto his chin. He wiped it away angrily. I found this oddly endearing.

"Okay, okay," I said. "Let's just relax awhile. Clear our heads. There's no beer, but we have some wine."

Over goblets of a nice burgundy, I asked him a few questions— what kind of music did he like, what was the last movie he saw, coaxing him into more specific territory that might reveal the name of his homeland or some pertinent information. But it's a global village. His favorite music was hip hop and rock, the last movie he saw was *The Blair Witch Project*. We talked for a good hour, but I learned little.

"You grew up here in America?" I asked.

"Here and in my homeland."

"Where did you meet Nadia?"

"At a party."

"In America?"

"Yes."

"Jeez, slow down, Rocky, I'm being buried under this blizzard of information," I said, getting up to let Phil in.

Phil was good with the kid. When I'd told Rocky I wanted to bring a friend in to secure the joint, he had protested. But Phil disarmed him with his self-effacing charm and a few funny stories of Mrs. Ramirez among the Good Sisters. At the same time,

Phil armed me, giving me Mrs. Ramirez's pearl-handled pistol and some bullets, which he'd insisted on taking from Mrs. R. before she went into the convent. I hate guns, especially illegal, unregistered weapons. But it wasn't the first time I'd had to break the law for a higher purpose, i.e., to prevent me from becoming a headless torso buried upside down in the Arthur Kill landfill. I calculated the risk this way: This was the age of *Titanic* and *Shakespeare in Love,* and no jury in the land would convict a woman for aiding and abetting so-called romance once this story came out (and was properly spun). As far as my professional reputation was concerned, I programmed a network aimed at women and girls and this kind of publicity couldn't hurt us, provided the story had a happy ending. That was the trick.

While Phil installed the security system with the help of the manboy, I called every friend of Tamayo's in New York who I could remember meeting. Most of these were comedians and none were home. I got a series of "disconnected number" recordings and answering machines, some with "funny" outgoing messages, and some with very quick, straightforward messages. It seemed the funnier the comic, the more straight the answering-machine message.

When I exhausted the New York friends, I started dialing the out-of-town Americans. After more answering machines, I got my friend Claire, a White House correspondent in Washington.

"Oh, you're talking about Tamayo's underground railroad," Claire said.

"Underground railroad?"

"For runaway lovers."

"Underground railroad for runaway lovers. Are you a part of it?"

"I haven't participated yet except financially," Claire said. "But yes, I knew about it. You know, these young girls—and boys—from restricted cultures are attracted to her freedom and attitude. She's a magnet for them."

"Yeah, I've seen that in Tokyo and New York too, the kids who come up to her with their tales of woe," I said.

"She has been helping some of these kids she meets, here and there, for about a year."

"Helping them how?"

"With money, contacts, and inspiration too I guess. She has helped a few escape with their lovers before arranged marriages could take place. She finagled college tuition for a girl she met in a refugee camp who wanted to go to school against her family's wishes," Claire said. "In Thailand, she bought a young girl and her brother out of prostitution. Those are just the ones I know about, because I helped finance them."

"Jeez, Tamayo never told me about an underground railroad. But then, we've both been traveling a lot," I said. Still, I was miffed at being left out of this. Did Tamayo not trust me?

"She probably forgot or didn't want to bother you. She has this railroad organized very loosely," Claire said. "Information is given out on a need-to-know basis because of the danger these kids could be in. It was kind of inspired by those anarchist econuts you were mixed up with last year."

"Do you know this girl named Nadia? I think she's from a former Soviet republic or eastern bloc country? She came through on this 'railroad.'"

"No," Claire said.

"Do you know who else is on this railroad?"

"No. I don't know much. I just write the checks. And I haven't heard from Tamayo in weeks. If I hear from her, I'll have her call you. I haven't heard from you in a while either. How are you?"

We chitchatted for a bit. Claire was just back from the road herself, having gone with the President to California for a fund-raiser followed by a Pacific Rim economic summit in Vancouver, Canada. She was still seeing her guy, an attaché at the Chilean embassy.

"And you? Really sorry about the fire. But when God closes a door—"

"My foot is in it at the time," I finished. "It's okay, actually. I haven't really had time to think about the fire because of the murder and the missing girl . . ."

"Are you seeing anyone?"

"Well, I met this guy in Paris, a friend of Tamayo's . . ."

"Pierre?" Claire said.

"Yes. You know him?"

"He's a dreamboat, isn't he? I met him there last year. If I wasn't so in love with Salvatore, I would have jumped him," she said. "Did you?"

"None of your business."

"Since when?"

"Someone is at the door, Claire. I've got to go," I lied, and hung up. It made me so uncomfortable that she knew Pierre too, for some reason.

"Take a look at this, Robin," Phil said. "This is a dandy system. I ran the wire around the balcony doors, right under the baseboards. You can't even see them. You'll have to punch in a code on the keyboard outside to get in, but it'll make you feel secure."

He demonstrated how it worked, and how to program in the entry code. I picked my birthday, 0818, and made Rocky memorize it too.

I wanted to get Phil alone to find out what he had learned from Rocky, but it was almost suppertime. Rocky was hungry—again—and so was Phil. Phil offered to cook for us, but I owed him. I put on Tamayo's Escher print apron, hanging from a white mannequin hand on the wall by the refrigerator, and cooked for the menfolk. At Rocky's age, it wouldn't be long before he went back into the bathroom with *Cosmo,* leaving Phil and me alone to talk about him.

While I cooked, Phil talked about out East Village neighbors. Phil was worried about Mrs. Ramirez at the convent. Without her crime watch to keep her occupied, she was turning more and more to prayer and penance, and things were getting a bit competitive with some of the other nuns, vis-à-vis, "Who loves Jesus best?" Mrs. Ramirez had sniped a bit about one of the nuns in particular, Sister Teresa, who ran the convent bakery marketing department and spent four times as much time watching financial news on cable as she did on her knees in prayer. Mrs. Ramirez had kindly pointed this out to Sister Teresa at breakfast, prompting Sister Teresa to thank Mrs. Ramirez for her record-keeping and concern, and to point out kindly that she, Sister Teresa, had been in this nun business for sixteen years. Her devotion to the Savior was total, she assured Mrs. R., and her interest in financial matters was purely in service to the mission of the convent. At that point, the Mother Superior changed the subject to the work of an overseas mission, thereby preventing a really ugly slap-fight between an old, blue-haired lady and a nun.

"I was hoping you'd be able to go out and visit her, luv," Phil said. "Tell her some news, get her mind on other things. But it looks like you're tied up."

"Yeah, but give her my best when you see her," I said. "Et cetera, et cetera."

"I shall. Have they arrested anyone in that murder?"

"Not yet. But the consensus among people in the hotel is that it was a crime of passion," I said. "What a shame. That happens all too often; people think they're in love, end up killing each other."

If Rocky picked up the cleverly hidden moral of the story, he didn't show it.

"I hope they get the guilty party," Phil said.

"Me too. Dinner's ready."

While we ate, Phil and I tried to wheedle something out of Rocky about his homeland, about Nadia's friends, where they were planning to be married and honeymoon, in case Nadia had gone there. He assured me she had not. It was hopeless. The boy would not talk. After two plates of food, a beer, and a big bowl of ice cream, he excused himself, saying he wanted to take a bath, and left me and Phil alone.

"Let's take our coffee out to the balcony," Phil said, acting as though he was the host and I was the guest.

It was just nightfall. The pale pink streetlights gave a surreal, romantic cast to the street, a kind of noirish elegance that reminded me of Paris. The Chelsea Hotel sign, an old-fashioned neon sign suspended vertically from the middle of the building, started to buzz, flickered, and then lit up. Some of the letters were orange neon, some pink, all mixed up together. Across the street, the orange YMCA sign was on too. The moon hung in the sky exactly between these two signs. From Lucia's apartment came the strains of that spooky, sad carnival music she liked so much.

"So where's Rocky from?" I asked.

"I'd say somewhere between Central Asia and Eastern Europe. I haven't spent much time in that part of the world and I wasn't able to pinpoint it any better than that. He doesn't speak Arabic, so he probably isn't a Muslim, and he isn't Turkish—I've been to Turkey and he doesn't have a Turkish accent," he said. "How did these kids end up here to begin with? I'm not clear on that," Phil said.

"Tamayo is apparently running, or part of, some underground railroad for runaway brides and/or star-crossed lovers," I said.

"Star-crossed lovers. Nadia and Rocky came all this way, with all this subterfuge, all for love," Phil said admiringly, though he really should have known better, having been married "twice in the Church of England and once in the church of Dolly and Phil."

"The fools," I said.

"Oh, you're so cynical. And why? Didn't you meet a man during your travels?"

"Who? Pierre? That was just a fling," I said.

"Flings can lead to real things."

"Not in this case. We're wildly incompatible. He's classy, I'm rough; he speaks French, I speak English; I work in television, he doesn't even watch television unless one of his pals from the Sorbonne is on some egghead program. The Sorbonne—is that class or what, Phil? This guy has class out the wazoo."

"Look at me and Helen. I'm a libertarian. She's a Communist. She's a homebody. I'm a traveling man. We worked it out."

"Yeah, but you both speak the same language," I said, then corrected it to "languages," as Phil and Helen both spoke Esperanto, in addition to English.

"You should be spending your vacation in Paris," he said.

"It was just a fling, Phil," I said. "Besides, he's off with his Sorbonne scientist pals conducting some big particle experiment for the next month. He's busy."

"Well, keep the faith, luv. Now, I'd better get back to Helen before her right-wing relatives tear her apart," he said. "Or tear each other apart. There's an object lesson. Helen's brother and sister-in-law speak the same language, value the same things, vote the same way, pray to the same God, and they're as mean as starving dogs to each other."

"Go figure."

"You call me if you need anything else."

"Thanks, Phil," I said.

When we turned to go back into the apartment, I noticed that Maggie's balcony door was slightly ajar. Figuring she was home, I gave her a call as soon as Phil left. Her machine answered. I parked myself in the kitchen, by the front door, so when Maggie Mason came home, I'd be able to corner her. To pass the time, I read from *Man Trap,* chapter three. Chapters one and two had dealt with how to bait the trap to lure the man in. Chapter three dealt with ways to cripple the man so he wouldn't run away before the trap snapped fully shut, somewhere around chapter ten: These were tricks to undermine his self-esteem. Whatever his vulnerability, one was to go for it. Did he worry about his weight or his looks? Don't reassure him that he looks great to you. Too easy. A missed opportunity! Instead, the book advised, comment that while you've never found "chubby" men attractive in the past, you like him. When you go for dinner, suggest he try the heart-healthy low-cal entrée instead of the steak. Comment favorably but obliquely on other men's physiques—"Joe is looking very trim these days, isn't he?"

And so on, culminating with this last, brutal tactic to under-mine a man and make him want you even more: Refer to the man as a "friend," as in, "I like you. You're a real friend," even though by chapter three you've gone out with him at least several times.

This was inhumane. I had half a mind to do a special on this underground classic, "out" it to the world, let men know what millions of women were up to. But at the moment, I wasn't too enamored of men as a demographic, either. Maybe the body-builder, the Zenmaster as Lucia called him, was partly right. Sometimes it is better to have no effect. Any man stupid enough to fall for this crap probably deserved it.

At the end of this chapter, I fell asleep. I never did hear Maggie Mason come home that night.

chapter eight

Grace Rouse was happy to speak with me—in person, with her attorney present—especially when she learned I was the woman Gerald had died on. She was out on bail by noon the next day and agreed to meet me at her gallery "after the paparazzi leave."

Paparazzi were no problem. All I had to do was call up this paparazzo I knew from the *News-Journal,* David Fowler, and tell him I'd heard a hot rumor that Courtney Love was holed up at the Metro Grand Hotel with Ben Affleck. Later, I'd have to apologize for being wrong and send him a case of Black Bush whiskey, but that was a small price to pay for privacy, and in any event, I'd just expense it as "miscellaneous promotion."

It worked, and when I got to Rouse's gallery, the photogs had taken all their shots and fled uptown.

In the weirdly lit office of her gallery in Soho, Spencer Roo introduced me to Grace Rouse.

"Did you see who killed him?" she asked. "Or hear anything?"

"No. I mean, I heard a thump at the door, and then he fell on me. He said, 'Bye,' and then he died. I didn't see you. . . ."

"I didn't kill Gerald—" she began, stopping to weep a little, blowing her nose gracefully and quickly composing herself.

Roo gratuitously patted her arm sympathetically.

She appeared to be grieving. She was dressed in proper black—a black sweater, black sunglasses, black denim jeans, and black boots. But her auburn hair was neatly slicked back, her makeup was immaculate, her nails had been done in the last few days. This was remarkable to me, because me and my friends, when we're grieving, tend to be red-nosed, rat-haired messes. Her weeping produced no tears or mascara stains and was over quickly. It seemed a tad cold-hearted, though that may have had something to do with the swimming pool–blue light coming through the glass brick wall of the office, which made her natural paleness seem somewhere between ethereal and embalmed and made me feel as if I was inside a very quiet aquarium.

At this point, I did a quick sexism check, asking, Would I find this lack of messy grief as disturbing in a man? Deciding that I wouldn't, that I would have seen it as strength and emotional restraint, I cut her some slack.

"I believe Gerald was at the Chelsea to meet with Maggie Mason when he was killed," she told me.

"When they met in the elevator I was riding in, it looked like an accidental meeting to me," I said.

"Maybe they were faking that for your benefit."

"Back up a second," I said. "Why did you lie to the police about your alibi if you didn't kill him?"

"I lied to the police because I knew it would look bad—his murder, my having been there. I didn't think they could check it out, but someone saw me leaving down the fire escape," she said.

She looked at Roo. He nodded slightly. He was letting her do the talking, which was unusual for Roo. Either he believed she was innocent or wanted it to appear he did. To emphasize his casual attitude, he picked up a copy of *aRt Magazine* with a cover article on Scandinavian surrealist Odd Nerdrum and read it as Grace and I talked.

"The police tricked me," she said. "They let me lie to them about where I was at the time before they told me someone had seen me leaving."

"Who saw you?"

"There's a wino who panhandles the stretch between the S&M restaurant and the synagogue on Twenty-third Street. He saw me, but I didn't see him. They didn't tell me the witness was the wino until after I admitted I was there. If they had, I would have said the man was a drunken fool. They tricked me, and now I'm in all this trouble."

"Why were you at the Chelsea?"

"Gerald told me he was going out to meet a collector about an art deal. I followed him there because I thought he was going to meet a lover. Not just a lover. A pregnant lover. I thought it was Maggie Mason."

"Is Maggie pregnant?"

"I don't know," she said. "That's what I was trying to find out."

About a week before the murder, Rouse claimed, she'd "happened to see" an E-mail on Woznik's computer while he was away from his desk. It had been sent by chelgal@hotmail.com. Grace Rouse had only been able to read one line before Woznik returned: "The baby is on its way. Is money arranged?"

The day before the murder, she'd just "happened to pick up the extension" while Woznik was on the phone, talking to Maggie Mason. All she managed to hear was Maggie saying, "Bring the money tomorrow and don't be late."

It was creepy talking about Woznik because there were big pictures of him staring down at us in the office, big photos of Gerald Woznik, and Grace Rouse with him, along with a large oil painting of the dead man alone. That look I'd seen in the elevator, that incongruous mixture of Christlike empathy and manly desire emanated from each one. I'd gotten such a buzz off that look in the elevator, but seeing it now made me realize it was a generic look, not specific to me, and it gave me a creepy chill.

"The cops say Maggie Mason has an alibi," I said.

"It's a false alibi. I'd bet my gallery on it," Rouse said. "She had an affair with him, but she wasn't in love with him. She got pregnant to get his money and his name. She's fooling you. She's devious and vindictive. And her work is crass and derivative."

"Has she done anything to you before?"

"I think she's the one who put a personal ad with the gallery number in the back of a *Star Trek* fan magazine—'Luscious heiress seeks mild-mannered loner who's a dominant Klingon behind closed doors.' The ad was paid for with my credit card info. I filed a complaint about that but the police couldn't find the guilty party. We had to change the gallery number, and the occasional Klingon still wanders in."

"But murder is a much bigger kind of vindictiveness. You think Maggie killed Gerald, the father of her alleged baby?"

"Why not? She's a psycho, and she holds a grudge longer than the Balkans. Perhaps Gerald went there to talk to her, but not to tell her what she wanted to hear. I didn't think she was a threat to me. She was just a fling to him, but she schemed to get pregnant and use that to bring him to her, or else she made up a pregnancy."

"What happened at the Chelsea? Did you see Gerald there? Or Maggie?"

"No, when I got there, I hid on the fire escape," she said matter-of-factly, as if listening in on a man's phone calls, reading his E-mail, following him, and hiding out on a fire escape to spy on him were perfectly normal things for a woman in love to do. "I didn't want to be seen entering the building, so I climbed up the side fire escape. I thought it was the seventh floor, but I forgot that the Chelsea's floor-numbering system starts with ground, European style, not one, American style. I was on the eighth-floor fire escape."

"How long were you there?"

"Until I overheard some of the eighth-floor residents talking about Gerald being killed on the floor below, and I took off."

"You told the cops all this stuff about Maggie?"

"Yes. But I can't prove any of it. Yet. Gerald always deleted his private E-mail the day after he got it. I've been through his personal papers and can't find anything incriminating to give the police. I thought maybe you could try to coax some information out of Maggie, seeing as you're staying next door to her, in Tamayo's apartment. Maggie is very friendly with Tamayo."

"I'm sure the police would do a better job of getting information out of Maggie."

"Well, you might hear things the police won't," she said.

She started to weep in her controlled, no-drip way. "It's insane to think I'd kill him. I loved him. I miss him."

"Why?" I asked.

"Why? Well . . . it's one of those things you can't understand unless you're in it. We were soul mates, underneath all the—"

"Cheating, lying, emotional abuse, suspicion?" I filled in helpfully.

"I know how it looks. The man could not control his penis. But he couldn't help it. It was like trying to wrestle an out-of-control fire hose. Poor guy." She sounded angry, but angry at me for asking, not so much at him for doing it, it seemed.

I must have had a skeptical look on my face, because she said, "Are you one of those dreamers who think men and women can be friends, and open up to each other, have equality in a relationship? Forget it, sister. Men have to be trained and kept on a short leash. Sorry to say it, but that's the way it is."

"And Gerald Woznik was worth all this?"

"Beneath that sick man was a special man, a misunderstood genius," she said. "Haven't you ever loved a man in spite of yourself? You knew all his faults, but you just couldn't help loving him?"

At this, she flashed a few frames of what appeared to be genuine sadness. It moved me.

"I get your drift," I said, dodging the question. I've loved men who played around a little and had the usual minor faults. I had loved a man who had the blood of twenty-seven Pakistani dogs on his soul, who had broken hearts from Hoboken to Hong Kong. But not one of those guys used women, or screwed around so cavalierly, or (allegedly) ripped off artists.

"What about all these artists he screwed over?" I asked.

"According to his books, he didn't rip off anyone."

The books could be cooked.

"Were you supporting him?" I asked.

"No. Is that what you think? He loved me for my money?" The words shot out of her red-lipsticked mouth like bullets.

"No, I was just asking if—"

"He lived with me, I picked up a few bills, that's all," she said.

The phone rang and she said, "Excuse me," and picked up.

"Grace Rouse. WHAT? What do you mean he isn't going to have that painting done in time? I'm flying in collectors from Europe for that! What? Oh, his boyfriend left him, boo hoo hoo. My lover was murdered! And I was arrested for it! Look, get hold of his shrink, his drug counselor, and find his boyfriend! His what? His psychic? A case of Dr Pepper? Get him Dr Pepper then. Get hold of whatever and whomever he needs, call his bloody masseuse and manicurist. If that doesn't work, threaten to call his mother. I know he hates his mother; don't call her, just threaten to. And call me when you have better news."

She hung up and said, "Painters!" She clenched her fists and her jaw for a moment, took a deep breath, and quickly composed herself. It no longer looked like strength and emotional restraint. "I have some other business to attend to, you'll have to excuse me."

It was then I pulled out the photo of Nadia. I wanted to be kind of casual about it. If Rouse had killed Gerald and bumped

off Nadia because the girl saw something, I didn't want to tip her
off that I was suspicious. I also didn't want Grace Rouse making
a big deal out of it or blabbing about this to the cops.

"Do you know this girl?"

"No . . . wait. She looks familiar," she said. "I may have met
her."

"When?"

"I don't know. Not recently. Sometime in the last year. How
would I know her?"

"She's a friend of Tamayo's."

"Should I know this girl?"

"Not necessarily. I was supposed to meet her, and we missed
each other," I explained. "I'm asking all Tamayo's friends about
her."

"I hope you find her. Tell Tamayo hello for me," Grace Rouse
said. "And check into Maggie's alibi. It isn't legitimate."

"I shall."

Her lip quivered ever so slightly and she choked out another
sob, just one, with no inadvertent spitting or any mess at all.

Spencer Roo walked me out.

"Did she do it?" I asked him.

"Of course not."

"Yeah, that's what you said about the guy who killed his wife
with thirty or so blows to the head with a hammer."

"That was a suicide," Roo said with a straight face. "I got him
off."

"On a technicality."

Roo shrugged. I hated that he got people like that off, but at
the same time, if I am ever arrested, he's the man I want in my
corner.

What a piece of work Grace Rouse was. On paper, she was
the number one suspect. But she'd met with me and spoken so
openly that despite her bizarre way of expressing her grief and
despite her bitchiness, I was inclined to believe she was innocent

of the murder. On the other hand, she could be a master manipulator, faking openness to win trust and cooperation. That she loved Gerald Woznik, or thought she did, was no defense. It never ceases to amaze, how often sex and love lead to murder and hatred.

What a shame Woznik hadn't said something grander before he died, instead of just "Bye." Rouse, I bet, wanted to hear something validating, i.e., "Tell Grace I loved her and only her." Her interest in that seemed legit, her motive romantic. But maybe I was wrong. Maybe she wanted to know if he'd said anything that might lead to her, if she was the killer.

Before I left, I turned my reversible coat—dark rose on one side, pale lime green on the other—inside out, and tucked my hair under a scarf, then poked my head out and looked both ways, to make sure I wasn't being followed.

At Houston Street, I grabbed a cab back to the Chelsea, where I hoped to corner Maggie Mason.

As I passed the bodybuilder, the Zenmaster, in the seventh-floor hallway, I stopped in front of him and said, "You know, you could save me a lot of trouble by just telling me if you know anything, anything at all, about that murder, or about the girl who was staying in my apartment."

He did not respond.

"I hear you have a third eye," I said. "Did it see anything the night of the murder?"

When he didn't answer, I tried a looser approach.

"You know what would be even more fun and more useful than an invisible third eye? An invisible third hand. Think of the trouble you could start with that on the subway during rush hour," I said. "Or in church. Or with a juggler."

He was not amused.

"I know you told the cops that you don't know anything. But did you mean you really don't know anything about this, or did you mean that in the 'everything worth knowing is unknowable' sense?" I asked. "Just tell me if you do NOT know anything. That will give me one milligram of peace and I could use it right about now. Then I'll leave you alone."

He twitched a little, but just kept lifting those fucking hand weights. It only served to make me angrier and I had an involuntary cartoonish vision of grabbing those fucking hand weights out of his hands, breaking them in two, and hammering him into the ground like a big spike.

"I don't know who fed you that Classic Comix Buddhism, BUD, but it's bullshit," I snarled.

Politeness hadn't worked, humor hadn't worked, and anger didn't work either, although at least this time I elicited a reaction. He looked terrified as he stepped backward and slammed the door in my face. I got to him, but got diddly out of him. Did he not say anything because he DID know something? Or because he was still maintaining his silent noninvolvement?

"Yeah, leave me wondering, just like every other human being in my life. Why can't people just play it straight with each other! Why does everyone have to be finessed and schmoozed?" I screamed just as the uptight Mary Sue lady who looked like Marilyn Quayle was leaving her room. After a split second frozen in panic, she withdrew into her room and slammed the door.

"I'm not nuts, lady! I'm just pissed off," I screamed at her door.

Preoccupied, I punched in the wrong code on the security buzzer. When I unlocked and opened Tamayo's door, the alarm let out a wail that opened doors up and down the hallway, all except those of the bodybuilder, the Mary Sue lady, and Maggie Mason. Took a couple of fumbling moments to shut the damn thing off.

Rocky was at the table, his hands over his ears, a large spoon stuck in his mouth, milk dribbling down his chin back into a cereal bowl.

"Sorry," I said. "You're eating cereal at this hour?"

"It doesn't have to be cooked," he said.

"There are cold cuts in the fridge and Bag O' Salad. You should eat that."

"Did you get my CDs and my videos?" he asked.

"What? Am I made of money?"

The kid hadn't offered me any cash—he claimed he had spent everything he had feeding himself while he was wandering around New York after I turned him away the night he'd arrived, though I half-suspected this was a cheapskate con of his.

"I did have my personal shopper at Macy's send you over some things. They should be here later today. Other than that, I've been busy," I said. "I'm trying to find your fiancée. Why hasn't she called here?"

"She maybe doesn't know I'm here."

"Granted, she doesn't know you're here but common courtesy . . . Doesn't she know how worried I am? What if she's been kidnapped or something?"

"Oh no. I know her. She's hiding out," Rocky said.

"Who would they deliver the ransom demand to if she was kidnapped? Her family?" I asked. "Tell me her parents' names. Tell me how to contact them."

He shook his head. "They'll kill you. You know too much," he said matter-of-factly.

"I hardly know anything," I said. "I don't know nearly enough—"

"The light is flashing on the phone, for messages," Rocky said.

"Thanks, you're so helpful."

On the voice mail was a message from Maggie Mason: "Hi, Robin, sorry I haven't been back to you. I've been incredibly busy running around. Can we talk tomorrow? À bientôt."

Okay, this was suspicious. My one lead and she was avoiding me.

There was a second message, from my assistant, Tim, saying he really needed to talk to me. When Maggie didn't answer her phone, I called Tim back.

"I'm glad you called, Robin. Things are happening here," he said.

"What's happening?"

"Jerry's assistant requested some programming files. I saw her in the copy room photocopying some of the documents in it."

"What kind of stuff?"

"Your idea for Tranquil TV," Tim said.

Tranquil TV was a proposal for two hours of soothing, beautiful television programs, one hour for adults and one for children, which overstimulated viewers could tape and watch when they needed something that's intelligent, visual, and calming. The demo reel we'd done consisted of songs by "girl singers" like Jewel, Victoria Williams, Nana Mouskouri, Bjork, and a tiny Taiwanese singer whose name I could never pronounce, lovely ballads and folk songs with smart lyrics and soul-enriching scenes of natural beauty, interesting faces, art, ballet, animation, philosophical snippets, and a lot of little "smell the flowers" moments. Jerry had scorned it as "video Prozac."

"He's also been photocopying old news stories about you, the bad ones, and reviews, the bad ones, and asking the staff about you, gathering complaints," Tim said.

"So what? I have a contract and Jack Jackson likes me. I'm not worried."

"Did you once belch on live TV?" Tim asked.

"Oh that was so long ago. He's using that too?"

"Yeah, and some stuff about the time you pushed the mayor's face into a bowl of soup."

"Tim, for the record, I was getting up to receive an award at a big diner, and on my way to the head table, I tripped on the hem of my dress and *accidentally* pushed the mayor's face in his soup. I didn't do it on purpose."

"He has a letter from a New Jersey widow . . ."

"Okay, someone should have warned me ahead of time that if you attend an airborne ash scattering, keep your mouth shut and beware the updraft. These aren't things people are born knowing, you know? I learned from all these things."

"He also has all the reports on your recent worldwide trip. There was a new one came in today. Apparently you ate with your left hand at a dinner with a newspaper publisher in—"

"Hey, the guy I offended beats his servants, with both hands, and I have a sneaking suspicion his newspaper empire is funded with heroin trafficking. But I must say, he has exquisite table manners."

"—and kept calling one of his wives his 'lovely young daughter.' "

"She's seventeen! He's gotta be sixty. He had a wife with him there already. It was a natural assumption. Tim, photocopy my triumphs file so we have something to counter with," I said.

Admittedly, that triumphs file isn't a very thick one, but it had some good things in it. Man, you can save the world, you can solve a few homicides, you can win a few awards, but what everyone remembers is the time you accidentally pushed the mayor's face into his soup, or asked that plane crash survivor a cannibalism question. What good were my triumphs going to be, anyway? In a rare, generous moment, I had attributed all my successes to others during an interview for a newspaper piece the year before, which undercut my triumphs a bit. I was trying to be fair, since I hadn't done those things alone. Other people had saved me— my aunt Mo, a bunch of animal rights guys, my cat—and I decided to clear a little extra karma and give a little extra credit where it was due. It would look really jerky for me to now lay personal claim to all those triumphs.

"I just think you should be aware," Tim said. "Solange and Jerry have both been stabbing you in the back, and they've been talking to Jack Jackson on the phone a lot. Maybe you should give him a call."

"Jack is not going to fire me," I said. "Trust me. But all the same, try to get some positive stuff together about me."

I needed to worry about the machinations of the Holy Woman Empire on top of everything else? Jesus. Those giant fingers were squeezing harder and harder. I felt like I was going to pop right out my skin.

This called for a drink, a healthy shot of vodka from Tamayo's liquor cabinet, and another for the attempt to bond with the man-boy, who eluded conversation by going back into the bathroom and taking yet another bath. He took Tamayo's *Cosmo* in with him.

Dinner had to be made—a seafood stir-fry served with brown rice and microgreens. It had been a long time since I'd actually cooked for anyone other than my cat. I rarely did it for myself. I was quite proud of the results, but when Rocky emerged from the bathroom he took one look and made a face.

"Why can't you get me the food I want?" he asked.

"Just eat and be grateful you're not a starving refugee . . ." I began, and stopped.

He was holding a photo of Nadia, and his eyes were red-rimmed. He'd been weeping about his girlfriend, I thought. Poor kid. Why did I have to be such a bitch?

"I did get you some beer and some more ice cream," I said. "Beer's in the fridge, that big appliance in the corner there. Can't miss it. All you have to do is open the door and take the beer out."

He shot me an angry look. What did I say?

While he chowed down, I logged on to AOL to check out Maggie Mason's alibi. She'd said she'd been in the comic-books chat room at the time of the murder. Under the comic-books listing, I saw an archive for logged chats. The chat for that date and time was a moderated chat for underground comic-book artist Martha Rodriguez and had just been uploaded.

I downloaded it and read.

Maggie Mason, aka, Eire8, entered the chat shortly after it began, about fifteen minutes before Woznik died. Early in the chat, she submitted a question to the moderator. After it was answered, she did not "speak" up in the chat again. Fairchild had told me the cops checked with the server and she was indeed online that whole time. But even if she was, it wasn't an alibi. She could have stepped away from the computer, left herself logged on, perhaps with anti-logoff software, and come back whenever she felt like it.

And if she was home, and logged on, why didn't she respond to the police when they knocked on her door? Why were they not able to interview her the night of the murder? There were some big holes in this alibi. Without Fairchild's assistance, I wasn't going to be able to get info from the cops on Maggie or anyone else.

Outside, Maggie's door slammed. Without even thinking, I grabbed Mrs. Ramirez's pearl-handled pistol, threw it in my purse, and went out to try to catch Maggie Mason before she ran away again.

chapter nine

Maggie Mason was walking down the hallway, carrying a huge black garbage bag.

"Maggie, wait up!" I called.

"Oh. Robin, hi," she said. "I'm in a dreadful hurry. . . ."

"I need to talk to you. I spoke to Grace Rouse . . ."

"That spoiled, homicidal harridan? You do know she was arrested?"

"She got out on bail. I don't think she did it."

"What load of shite did she feed you?" Maggie asked.

"She says she didn't kill Woznik. She says you did it."

"She's insane. I have an alibi."

"You were on an AOL chat, right? Eire8."

"Yes. How did you—"

"A police source told me," I said. "But you only spoke once in the chat, before Woznik died, and didn't speak again. And when the police went to your door to interview you that night, they got no answer."

"I was listening to music on a headset," she said.

"But in the elevator, when you confronted Woznik, you told him you were going out later."

She shot me a dirty look, then said, "I didn't kill Gerald. The guy owed me money. If I was planning to kill him, I would have waited until AFTER he paid me. Look, I have to meet someone in exactly half an hour. I have to run . . ."

"Grace Rouse says you called him about a baby. . . ."

"Baby? What baby? She is insane. You're a friend of Tamayo's, so I suppose I can trust you. You want to meet my real alibi? I'm on my way over there now."

"This is important."

"Yes, but people are waiting for me," she said. "You can come along."

She began walking toward the swinging doors to the east wing. She might be a killer, I thought, but my curiosity was piqued. I followed her.

"You must swear you won't reveal what happens on this trip," she said.

"Why?"

"Swear."

"Okay, I swear," I said.

"Do you have Rollerblades?"

"No." Me on wheels. What a good idea.

"We'll have to hoof it when we get there then. Do you have any money?"

"Yes."

"Good. We can take a cab," she said.

"Where are we going?"

"Central Park."

"What's in the bag?" I asked her. It didn't look like it was too heavy so it probably wasn't a body, I figured. She scared me, but her hands were full so she didn't pose a threat, and besides, I had Mrs. R.'s gun. I hate to say this, as I am antigun, but having a real gun on my person gave me a new sense of confidence that was kind of worrisome.

"You'll see. Let's take the service elevator," she said, leading the way to an unmarked door past the trash room. "We'll go out the back way. I'm a bit behind on the rent and I don't like to walk by the front desk if I can avoid it."

"I didn't even know this elevator was here."

"The tenants are not supposed to use it," she said. "We all do, but we're not supposed to."

"It smells like garbage," I said as we got on.

"This is the elevator our rubbish rides down in," she said, pushing the letter B on the old control panel. Just as the doors closed, a couple of guys who looked like workmen tried to get on. I went for the door open button but got there too late.

"Damn. They looked like staff, didn't they? I hope they don't tell Mr. Bard I was using the service elevator again. Bloody hell," Maggie said. "Nadia hasn't shown up yet?"

"No. And she hasn't called."

"That is very peculiar."

"How well do you know Nadia?"

"Not well," Maggie said. "I met her last year when she was staying with Tamayo. She'd come to New York to shop, with a chaperone, a big brute."

"The guy she's supposed to marry, a man with a bad toupee, showed up at the hotel, threatened Rocky with a gun."

"Well, that may be why Nadia is steering clear of the Chelsea. I liked Nadia."

"You liked her?"

"Yes, what little I knew of her I liked. Any friend of Tamayo's is a friend of mine. Well, almost any friend. There are a couple of exceptions."

"Are you part of Tamayo's underground railroad?"

"Yes, when she needs me to be."

"Who might know the next stop on this railroad? Your contact?"

"My contact was out of town. I couldn't reach her. I know Nadia isn't there."

Maggie seemed civil enough, but her voice had a serrated edge

to it—despite the residue of an Irish accent that normally makes
the most heinous people sound somehow charming—and she was
dodgy, looking away when she talked instead of looking me in
the eye.

"Nadia is probably just hiding out somewhere until things cool
off, or she's looking for her fiancé in all the wrong places." Maggie said. "She obviously doesn't know he's at Tamayo's or she
would have called."

"I hope you're right."

The service elevator was slower than the regular elevators,
which were themselves slower than most elevators, and it was
much noisier, creaking its way down and grinding to a stop with
a lurch. We got out in a small lobbylike space leading to two
other corridors, a dim, narrow hallway and a bright plastered one
lit by fluorescent lights. Even here, there was art everywhere,
hanging on all the walls. For a moment, I worried that she was
the killer, that I'd been lured down here so she could murder me
for knowing too much. I opened my purse slightly so the gun
would be accessible.

"The unvarnished heart of the Chelsea," Maggie said. "The
basement. Over here is the housekeeping room. The maids hang
out here. I came down here one day and I heard loud, loud laughter coming from the maids' room. Tamayo was in the maids'
room. . . .." Maggie started to laugh. "She was in pajamas and
slippers, sitting with the maids, watching *Green Acres* on TV. She
was helping them fold towels. They were all laughing. Tamayo
kept folding the towels wrong, and another maid was beside her
refolding them. Tamayo didn't even notice."

"Her mind is on loftier things," I said. "Where are we going?"

"To the secret exit. This is the engineer's room, there's the
telephone room. Storage, storage, storage; this is the art room,
where Mr. Bard keeps art that tenants have given him that he
hasn't found a place for yet. This is going to be the dinner club,
it has an entrance to the street which is left open sometimes so

workmen can come and go, or so supplies can be brought into the hotel or the El Quijote restaurant," Maggie said. "Leaving this way, we avoid an uncomfortable scene between me and the front desk over my back rent."

We went through another little basement tunnel and a gated door leading to steps that led up to Twenty-second Street, where we snagged a cab.

The sun was setting over New Jersey as we cruised uptown on Eighth Avenue.

"It's funny that you and I never met, Robin, both of us being such good friends of Tamayo's," she said.

"Isn't it?"

"I've heard a bit about you from Tamayo, but our paths never crossed before."

"Tamayo has a lot of friends, all over the place. You meet them in the strangest places," I said. "Grace Rouse is a friend of Tamayo's too."

"I don't understand why Tamayo likes Grace. What did Grace have to say?"

"She says Gerald Woznik paid you all the money he owed you, according to his books. She also says—"

"First of all, Gerald keeps double books. He claims he sells the work for a lower price than he actually sells it for, and he deals with a lot of sub-rosa buyers who don't necessarily want to reveal how much they spend, or have, so they go along with it. But I happen to know he sold my paintings for five thousand and he only paid me fifteen hundred. I'm not the only one. I can give you a list of promising artists he's screwed over this way."

"Grace Rouse says she overheard you speaking to Woznik on the phone the day before his murder . . ."

"Yes, because he called me to say he'd be by the next day, early, to pay me the money he owed me. He pacified me with that. He didn't show up until later, and didn't call me the next day the way he was supposed to, so when I saw him in the ele-

vator I was furious. I thought he was trying to slip past me without paying me. It would be just like him to do that."

"She says you and Gerald had an affair."

"We did, briefly. He was dating her and me at the same time,
but he dumped me for her, moved in with her. Unceremoniously.
He was such a coward, he had her assistant call me to tell me it
was over."

"She also intercepted an E-mail about a baby. . . ."

"Well, that I don't know anything about," she said. "I didn't
have his E-mail address. But I wouldn't be surprised if he spawned
a few on the wrong side of the blanket. Do you know who Ruck
Urkfisk is? The painter? I always thought his youngest daughter
bore a striking resemblance to Gerald, between you and me."

"That would explain it. Maybe someone is having his baby,"
I said. "What did Gerald tell you when you cornered him in the
elevator?"

"That he was at the Chelsea to broker a deal and he'd come
by my apartment later that evening or the next day at the latest
to pay me. The sad thing is, the bastard was probably on his way
to pay me when he got killed. *Tant pis pour moi.*"

"The cops didn't find any money on him though."

"Whoever killed him robbed him I suppose. That's my luck,
that I'd be so close to getting paid, and then the payer would die
just feet from my door."

I kind of believed her, as I kind of believed Grace Rouse. On
a gut level, I was almost certain neither of them was the killer,
but I've found that gut level is about as reliable as the rhythm
method.

"You really think there's a connection between Nadia and the
murder?" Maggie said.

"I don't know. I can't find a solid one yet beyond the Chelsea
Hotel and Tamayo Scheinman."

"Who have you spoken with at the Chelsea?"

"The staff, you, Lucia, Carlos, the Zenmaster, Miriam
Grundy."

"You met Miriam Grundy?"

"Yes."

"Does she know Nadia?"

"Yeah. She told me Nadia was interested in her love story with Oliver Grundy. Their are some similarities between their tales, I guess. I can't get through to the Zenmaster. Scary guy."

"You have to understand him," Maggie said. "He used to be the sweetest person. He doesn't look it, I know. He's got a lazy eye, so he looks cross-eyed, and has fearsome features. People were always beating up on him for looking at some guy or some guy's girlfriend 'the wrong way.' He can't help looking at people that way, that's just how he looks!"

He'd also had his heart broken a few times by women who just used and abused him, Maggie went on. Now, he stayed in the hotel, cashed a disability check, ordered his groceries in, and avoided all trouble. It seemed a wise policy.

"You can drop us here, driver," Maggie said.

I paid the driver and got out after her at Seventieth Street and Central Park West.

"Your purse is open. You'd better close it. Don't want to attract muggers."

The purse was open so I'd have quick access to Mrs. Ramirez's pistol if the need for it arose, but I closed it now.

"Where are we going?" I asked.

"A big rock in the triangle between the Ramble and the boathouse and Belvedere Castle," she said. "We'll meet the others there."

"The others?"

"The guerrilla artists. You are along on a guerrilla art operation," she said. "Very handy you showed up, because my usual partner, Tommy Mathis, had to cancel at the last minute."

"It's not going to hurt anyone, is it?" I asked.

"No. You'll like it," she said. "I went to a guerrilla art meeting after I logged on to AOL the night Gerald died. I always log on to the chat before an operation, so if the cops come after me for a guerrilla art action, I can deny I was involved, as I was online."

"You weren't in love with Gerald still, or in passionate hate?" I asked.

"No. I just wanted my money. That's all. In fact, I believe my affair with Mr. Woznik cured me forever of men like that."

"Men like what? Hounds?"

"That's a polite way of putting it. 'Hounds.' I like that. My relationship before Gerald was with a hound, this mad Irishman. The bastard went back to his ex-wife, of all things."

That would be Mad Mike O'Reilly, and I thought he'd dumped ME for his ex-wife. That meant he and Maggie were having an affair in New York while he and I were having an affair in New York. Even though I was well over Mike, this irritated me and made me feel some sort of retroactive jealousy or something. Which one of us had he dumped first, I wondered.

"Look out!" Maggie said, suddenly pulling me off the stone path. Ahead of us was a huge brown coil of what looked like shit from either an enormous dog or a cloned dinosaur running loose in the park.

"Jesus H. . . ."

"Damn. Art Break is in the park tonight," she said.

"Art Break?"

"Another guerrilla group. They're so tacky and scatological. They mix up this foaming plastic with brown dye, and leave huge coils of fake doggie doo on big wax paper circles."

"Wax paper circles?"

"So when it sets, it can be removed easily by park cleaners. Otherwise, it's defacement and vandalism, which carries a stiffer penalty than littering. Art Break gets the press, but my group has more imagination. Don't step in that stuff, in case it hasn't set yet. It hardens like a rock. You'll never get that dog shit off your shoe."

"Speaking of hounds," I said.

" 'Hound' implies something kind of goofy and lovable," she went on. "My ex was a hound. Gerald was worse than a hound, he was a vampire. He was one of those dazzling, gorgeous, brilliant, cruel men who can shut down women's brains with a look, the kind of man otherwise reasonable women climb all over each other to get to, as a friend of mine put it. You met him. Did you feel that buzz effect?"

"Briefly," I admitted.

"These men look at all women the same way. You think you've clicked in a special way, but the spell they cast is a generic, universal sort of spell."

"Like some form of mass hypnosis," I said. (Note to self: Study and master mass hypnosis so when looks go, it won't matter.)

"Exactly right," she said. "I got over Gerald very quickly, and then met a man who isn't a hound or a brain stopper. He's not flashy, glamorous, or temperamental. He's cerebral, calm, caring, and sweet. It took Gerald to finally show me what I wanted and didn't want in a man, and then I found it."

"Sounds great. Is the new guy an artist too?"

"No."

"Does he live in the hotel? Did he know Gerald . . . or Nadia. . . ."

"No, and actually, I prefer not to talk about him until the relationship has really gelled—and then some. I always get in trouble when I discuss my men with other women. No offense intended."

"Why is that?" I asked.

"Because the most well-intentioned friend can feed your insecurities and doubts and slowly poison a relationship, and the ill-intentioned might make a play for him. This is all in *Man Trap*. You should read it," she said. "My experience backs it up. I'm thirty-seven. I've seen it all in the love stakes. It's best to keep it between you and the man as much as possible."

"That makes sense," I said.

"If I hadn't gone through that nightmare affair with Gerald, I wouldn't have been able to recognize real love when it came along. There they are, my fellow Erisians," she said.

"Erisians?"

"After Eris, the goddess of mischief and hilarity," she said.

We approached a group of eight people sitting behind a large rock in the shadows of some big old trees. Some of them were in camouflage makeup. Maggie said hi, and introduced me as a "trusted friend" who'd be her partner.

"She doesn't have blades, so we'll go on foot," she said.

"Okay, just be careful," said the head "guerrilla." "Listen up. Maggie brought the clothes. Stan has the lighting fluid. Missy brought old wallets. And I have the torches and fire extinguishers."

"Excuse me. Fire extinguishers? Torches?" I said.

"Mini-blowtorches," the head guy said.

"This sounds dangerous. What are we—"

Maggie shook her head at me sternly, while the head guy handed out maps, showing the areas to be avoided, where the police precinct in the park was (north of the Great Lawn), and where the other security details were situated. Each map had an area circled for each pair of guerrillas to cover.

"It's not dangerous if you only use green wet grass. If you need to wet the area thoroughly first, do so and keep the extinguisher handy. We don't want to start a forest fire in Central Park," the head guy said. If the fire looks like it's not going to go out, or spreads, extinguish immediately."

This did not sound promising.

"And watch out for Art Break. I hear they're doing something in the park tonight too."

"We saw their fresh spoor on the trail in," Maggie said. "They're already here. It's as if they're following us. This is the third time we've been on an operation and Art Break has been here."

"Keep an eye out," the head guy said again. "Watch where you step."

After we assembled our equipment, Maggie and I walked off toward the obelisk, just north of Turtle Pond. It was dark now, and the Victorian-style standing street lamps along the path flickered on with a foggy golden glow. Central Park is a very dark park at night. The big black rocks that jut out of the ground make it seem darker somehow, as do the trees and the gloomy tunnels under the footbridges.

"So Nadia met with Miriam to do what?" Maggie asked, picking up the thread of our conversation.

"Get her blessing, I guess. It's weird though, because she left Tamayo's apartment, said she was going to meet her guy, and she arrived at Miriam's alone."

"That is strange. The boy got lost on the way?" she asked.

"He's a pretty dim bulb, and spoiled rotten."

"And Nadia took off when she heard of the murder?"

"Evidently. I hope. The guy with the bad toupee, the man she was supposed to marry, showed up and is after her too. I scared him off and secured the apartment, but it is still very risky having that boy there."

When we got to the obelisk, we scoped out the area to make sure nobody was watching us. There were a couple of people who had been on the path behind us. Once they walked out of our sight, Maggie squirted the lighting solution in a large circle about six feet in diameter.

"What are we doing?" I asked, suddenly realizing how it would look if I, a respectable-seeming TV executive, was caught starting a fire in Central Park just a few days after my apartment building burns down. It's always in the back of my mind how easy it would be for people to build a totally wrong, circumstantial case against me because of the curse on my head.

"Patience. You'll see. Stand by with the little fire extinguisher," she said. "Just in case."

Squatting low to the earth, she took the mini-torch and ignited the fluid. It flared up, then burned out quickly, leaving a sooty, black ring.

"Hand me the clothes, shoes and sock first," she said.

When I pulled out a shoe, it stuck to one of her Roller-blades. It took me a moment to untangle it and get everything in place.

"Quickly," she said.

The shoes and socks went down first, followed by trousers with the underwear inside, a shirt, a jacket, and an empty wallet, all in a carefully messed pile. When it was done, Maggie took a moment to admire it, then stepped out and brushed away her footprints in the grass.

"This is the first time we've used the blowtorch," she said. "We used to just drop full suits of clothes in front of buildings and in elevators. But the torching is just such a nice touch."

"I've seen that before, a full suit of clothes on the sidewalk! It never occurred to me it was guerrilla art."

"What did you think when you saw it?"

"Someone was beamed up by the mothership from where he stood," I said.

"Good, it worked, then. But not everyone gets it."

This changed the way I looked at her. Anyone who would go to the trouble to do something so devilishly brilliant and meaningless gets major points.

"You're just doing the park?" I asked.

"For tonight. We've already done it this year out in Flushing, Queens, and Madison Park in the Flatiron district. Next time we want to hit Wall Street."

"You could torch the clothes too, and then people would think it was a case of spontaneous human combustion," I suggested.

"Hmmm. I like the way you think," she said with an edgy admiration. "It's so odd that Tamayo has never introduced us."

"Yes, isn't it," I said. "But I'm on the road a lot and so is she. I haven't seen her in New York in ages."

"I have heard about you, I think. Are you the friend of hers in television who once baked her cheating husband's lucky shirt into a pie and made him eat it?"

"I didn't make him eat it," I said. "I was pissed off. That was the day I found out he was having an affair."

"It's a bloody good bit of revenge, all the same," she said. "Let's get out of here. We have to hit the Alice in Wonderland statue at seventy-fifth next."

So we wouldn't be seen and give ourselves away to Art Break, we took the lesser-used footpaths to get there. Taking this route after dark in Central Park is none too wise, but hey, I figured, who was going to bother one woman with a blowtorch and another with a pearl-handled pistol and a fire extinguisher?

"I'm a big believer in revenge," Maggie continued.

"Nonviolent, nonlethal, in-your-face revenge is the best revenge, I think. Don't you?" I wanted her to consider this possibility, lest she find out about me and Michael O'Reilly and try to sign me up for the American Nazi Party or forward all my mail to a cult in Texas. "It's honest and harmless."

"Oh, eye for an eye, I say."

"Oh, but something that's irritating to the object, and really funny to everyone else is so much better, karmically," I said. "The punishment should not be as bad as the crime. Not even close. You can't spread malicious lies, or call some guy's wife or girlfriend to tell him you're having an affair with him if you aren't, or—"

"What about burning bags of dog shit on someone's porch?" she asked.

"That's a classic," I acknowledged. "But it's better to play fair and take the high ground. Taking the high ground is part of the revenge, you see."

"Interesting. But not nearly as much fun as my way," she said. "Oh look, Art Break has been here too. Looks fresh. They are so declassé. Their motto is 'Shit happens.' Watch your step."

I could barely see the big coiled pile of fake dog crap. It was then I became aware that we were walking through a very dark part of the very dark park, down a path between sloping, tree-lined banks. There was rustling in the brush. I turned to look, and reassure myself, and two men jumped out onto the pathway, one behind us and one in front of us, before Maggie and I could react. At first, I figured it was the Art Break people, but they were wearing ski masks and dark clothes, and they had guns.

I had a gun too, in my purse, as well as the fire extinguisher, and my deadly, brain-freezing shriek. Maggie had her mini-blowtorch. This might all be well and good if we were up against one armed man. But with two, one in front and one behind, we were trapped.

"Where is the girl?" asked the man in front of us, with that same weird accent that Rocky, Nadia, and the man in the bad toupee all had. He was wearing some kind of big cross around his neck.

"What girl?" I asked.

"Nadia."

"I don't know. I swear to God."

"Where is the baby?"

"What baby? I don't know anything about a baby. I don't know what the hell is going on, I swear to God," I said.

"I don't either," Maggie said.

"What about the boy, Raki?" he said, pronouncing it some-what differently than the Americanized Rocky did.

"Look, we can't help you. We don't know anything," Maggie said.

The gunman behind us started to speak in another language. The gunman in front of us looked past us to his colleague, and out of the corner of my eye, I saw that the man behind had one foot stuck in the still-cooling brown foam left by Art Break.

Beyond us all, someone yelled, "Hey, let it set!"

When the gunman in front of us turned to see who was there, I looked at Maggie, nodded slightly, and in a split second we moved. She aimed her mini-blowtorch to the man behind us to hold him at bay. His gun went flying as he dodged the fire. I smacked the one in front of us in the head with the Rollerblades in the garbage bag, then shot him in the face with the fire extinguisher. I hit him again and again. The gunman behind had taken off, half-running, half-dragging the hardening brown foam. His fellow gunman followed. They disappeared into the bushes.

"Hey, where's our shit?" asked a lanky young man in a gray T-shirt and jeans. "Maggie Mason?"

"Kip, I should have known you were involved in this," Maggie said.

"Where's our shit?"

"Some guys with guns took your shit."

Another underfed young man appeared behind him.

"They stole our shit?" he said. "Sounds like Erisian sabotage to me."

"I swear to God, they took your shit."

"Fuck." Kip turned on his flashlight and scanned the ground, the light beam crossing a gun. He bent down and looked at it. "It's a real gun, looks like."

Something else glinted on the ground. It was the cross. I slid it out of their view with my foot.

"Oh, man, what do we do?" Kip asked. "We gotta give the gun to the cops."

"And tell them what? That gunmen stole our shit?" the other guy asked. "Wipe your prints off that gun and we'll drop it on the security-station doorstep with a note, like an abandoned baby."

"We're out of here," Maggie said to me.

Before we beat a hasty retreat to Fifth Avenue to get a cab back downtown, I picked up the cross and pocketed it. In the cab, I took it out and showed it to Maggie Mason.

It was a strange silver cross with a grim-looking face in the middle. It had Cyrillic lettering around the face.

"What is it?" Maggie asked.

"I don't know. I'll ask Rocky. Or Raki, as the case may be. And there's that baby being mentioned again. What is that about?"

"I don't know. How did those men find us?"

"They must have followed us from the hotel. . . . Maybe those workmen at the elevator followed us out. . . ."

"We've got to find Nadia," Maggie said.

Why didn't I think of that? I thought facetiously.

"You probably know more of Tamayo's New York–area friends than I do these days. Maybe you could make a list and start making some calls. Someone else in this area must be part of her underground railroad," I said.

"You should talk to Edna, the switchboard operator, see if Nadia made any calls on the hotel phone system, or if she accidentally heard anything listening in to phone calls. Edna knows where most of the bodies are buried, so to speak."

"She told me her secrets die with her."

"You just need to know how to get to her. Let me work on that," Maggie said. "What are you going to do?"

"Look after Rocky," I said.

Security system or no, Rocky was not safe at the Chelsea. I could defend myself, but the manboy couldn't even microwave chili without help. He had to go.

chapter ten

The Sisters of the Wretched Souls convent sits on three bucolic, well-secured acres in one of the back settlements just south of the Hamptons, where many of the finer grocers and tonier celeb eateries stock the cakes and pastries produced by the Sisters. Well before you see the convent, you smell it. The air was full of the smell of hot sugar, vanilla, and chocolate from the bakery operation. The only thing marring this pleasant, sugary vision of peace and love was the razor wire and the electrified fence. The razor wire atop the abbey's high stone walls had gone up after several of the statues in the convent garden were stolen by crack addicts. Lewd, racist, satanic, and antinun graffiti on the stone walls had, the previous year, inspired the electrified fence. Phil and his buddies had installed that electrified fence, and he assured me that this was one of the safest places in the tristate area.

Phil had met us downstairs on Twenty-second Street in a car he'd borrowed to take us out there, so there'd be no record of the journey with a cab or a car service. Meanwhile, I'd hustled Rocky out in the dead of night. Figuring Rocky would not leave without the right incentive, despite the obvious threat, I told him Phil thought he had tracked down Nadia at a house in Long Island.

"Where is it?"

"I don't know. Phil found her. He won't tell me exactly where she is out of concern for her safety," I said.

The sweet look he got on his immature little mug when he heard about Nadia almost made me feel bad for lying to him. But, you know, it was for a higher purpose, i.e., saving his little hide. Even then, he didn't make it easy for me.

"I'm afraid to leave the apartment," he admitted. "Maybe you should bring Nadia here."

"No, we have to go there. Both of us," I said.

"Can I call my parents and tell them?" he said, picking up the telephone expertly, as if he'd been using it by himself all his life.

"Wait until we actually see her," I said. "Besides, this phone could be tapped or someone might monitor my cell phone. We have to be extra careful from here on in."

It wasn't until we drove within the convent walls that I 'fessed up.

"Nadia isn't here, Rocky. Sorry to lie to you. . . ." I began.

"But how will I find Nadia? Take me home."

"Home? And where might that be exactly?" I asked.

"I'm leaving," he said.

"You're going to walk back?" Phil asked.

It was a fair hike just to get back to the electrified gate, then a good mile to a main road and a couple of miles to public transportation.

"But—"

"You're safe here, mate," Phil said. "And all the cake you can eat."

"Rocky, I was followed and attacked by men in masks last night and they asked about you, Nadia, and a baby. You are not safe at the Chelsea."

I showed him the cross. "Does this mean anything to you?"

"Oh my Godt," he said, in the same way Nadia said "God." He got even paler, if that was possible.

"What is it?" I asked.

"Saint Michael the Martyr. He's the patron saint of a terrorist group in my homeland."

"Which is where?"

"Plotzonia."

"Give me the real name of the place, Rocky."

"Chechnya," he said after some hesitation.

"Chechnya? Are you a Muslim?"

"No."

"Member of the Christian minority? Animist? What?"

"Christian," he said. "The terrorists belong to a different Christian group."

"What do they want?" I asked.

"The terrorists want to destroy my family and Nadia's and many others," he said. "They bomb things, they kidnap people, they steal, they beat priests who disagree with them."

"Very Christian of them. What's the deal with the baby?" I asked.

"I don't know," he said.

"This baby keeps popping up. It must mean something."

"I don't know," he said again.

Looking sullen, scared, confused, and angry with me, all at the same time, Rocky slumped down in his seat.

"Okay, I will stay here," he said finally. "But when you find out where Nadia is, you must come get me so I can go see her with you. You must call me, even before you call her. Promise me."

"Rocky, when I find Nadia, you'll be the first to know, I promise. I'm developing some leads. You can call me on my cell phone, use a code name if you like. I'll come by whenever I can to see you," I said.

"Do they have TV here?" he wondered.

"Yes," Phil said.

The Mother Superior who met us at the door was younger than I would have expected, but maybe that was deceptive. Maybe it was due to that serene, godly look on her face. You rarely see that look in real life. No disrespect intended, but it is much easier to remain serene and godly when one is hidden away from the meanness and craziness of the world behind high walls and razor wire.

"Welcome," she said warmly, adding, with a little less serenity, "You weren't followed, were you?"

"No," Phil said.

"Good. Come into my study," she said, leading the way down a hallway lined with black-and-white pictures of long-dead nuns and popes.

"Is Dulcinia asleep?" Phil asked.

"Possibly, or she may be in the chapel praying," the Mother Superior said, and sighed. "I'm afraid she and some of the Sisters are getting even more competitive about praying and penance. Perhaps you could have a word with Dulcinia, Phil. At supper, she made a point of praying louder than Sisters Teresa and Marie, which provoked them to pray louder, and her a little louder still, and so on. A vicious cycle. At vespers this evening, I quoted Our Savior's exhortation not to pray loudly in public like the hypocrites but I don't think it sank in. Afterward, Dulcinia pointed out that I'd made a small grammatical error in the quotation, and when I looked in an hour ago, she was still in the chapel on her knees, looking up at the crucifix and praying madly."

We went into a large, sumptuous parlor with a huge fireplace and a lot of overstuffed chairs and sofas and rich tapestries. There was just a small fire going, to take the chill off the spring night, and by one of the chairs was an antique end table on which a half-read murder mystery lay, facedown. As the abbess and Phil made chitchat, re: "What do you do with a problem like Dulcinia?" I checked out the bookshelf, delighted to see that among the theological tomes and classics like Plato and St. Augustine were a healthy sprinkling of murder mysteries, some Iris Murdoch, and some P. G. Wodehouse.

One of the Sisters interrupted to bring us tea, cocoa, and delicious little cream cakes. (This was not an ascetic convent.) At her heels was Sister Señor, in his little habit.

"Thank you, Sister Marie," Mother Superior said. When Sister Marie was gone, Señor right behind her, Mother Superior said, "That's another problem shaping up. Señor has taken a liking to Sister Marie, and Mrs. Ramirez is very unhappy about it. I fear it is feeding her competitive instincts."

"I'll see if I can't get through to her," Phil said. "But she tends to hear what she wants to hear. I'll go look for her in the chapel. I won't be long."

The Mother Superior turned to me and Rocky and said, "Phil tells me this is a romantic mission? Your beloved ran out on an arranged marriage?"

"Yes," Rocky said.

"And her family and the groom's family are trying to find her and take her back, and you may be in some danger from them?"

"Yes," he said.

"You love her very much," she said.

"Yes," Rocky said, and his voice softened slightly, and caught in his throat, the same way Nadia's had when she was talking of love the night she arrived. Calling it a "romantic" mission had felt like a gross overstatement, as it seemed to me to be more of a mission to reunite two immature lovers so they could embark on one of the greatest mistakes of their lives. But at this moment, I was inclined to give them the benefit of the doubt. They so obviously had the same powerful, sweet feeling for each other, and maybe that would be enough to get them through the crap. Also, I hadn't seen them together. That they were quite different with each other than they were with me was within the realm of possibility.

"You must promise not to do anything to put us at risk," she said to Rocky. "We have a tradition here of helping refugees. This very convent was used to shelter runaway slaves in the last century, and our mother convent in France harbored Jewish children during the Holocaust."

Rocky nodded, and I poked him in the ribs. "Thank the nice lady for taking you in," I said.

"Thank you," he said.

"You'll have to respect our rules and traditions and defer to the Sisters and the lay workers," she said. "You don't have to come to chapel, but it would be nice. You must not leave the grounds or bring any unwanted attention our way. The back building is the Sisters' private area. You will of course respect that and not go in there."

"Yes, all right," he said.

"Sister Marie will take you to your room now and explain some of the ins and outs of the convent." She rang for Sister Marie and her Chihuahua escort, Señor.

After Rocky had left, I suggested, helpfully, "Maybe you can put Rocky to work. He's not very good in the kitchen, but I bet he can scrub floors. There's a lot he needs to learn before he gets married."

If anyone could make a husband out of this guy, it was a bunch of nuns.

"Where is he from?"

"Chechnya."

"Is he Muslim? Does he have dietary laws the kitchen needs to know about?"

"No, Christian. Let me give you my cell phone number, in case you have any problems," I said. "Just don't tell Mrs. Ramirez my cell number, or too much of Rocky's story, or—"

"Don't tell what to Mrs. Ramirez?" Mrs. Ramirez asked, shuffling into the room on Phil's arm while turning up her hearing aid with her free hand.

"Why, don't tell Mrs. Ramirez that Pius the Twelfth was the best of the Pius popes," I said. "It's Pius the Ninth, right, Mrs. R.?"

In a nutshell, Pius the Ninth stubbornly fought the Italian government's secularization in the nineteenth century, as he figured the church should run society, and he also put forward the dogma of Immaculate Conception. Mrs. Ramirez had had a portrait of him in her kitchen, until the fire.

"Pope Pius the NINTH," she corrected, sitting down in a big armchair on the right side of the Mother Superior, who shot me a less than serene look for opening this Marian Dogma can of worms.

"That's what I meant," the Mother Superior finessed. "Pius the Ninth was the best of the Pius popes."

"Perhaps Mrs. Ramirez can offer some spiritual counseling to the new guest," I said.

"What an excellent idea," the abbess said. "I'm sure our young man would benefit greatly from your wisdom, Dulcinia."

"He needs a lot of guidance," I said. "He doesn't retain information well. Best to repeat things five or six times, to make sure it sinks in."

The Mother Superior smiled at me. I was redeemed, thanks to a classic piece of nonlethal revenge, using one person who drives you nuts against another person who drives you nuts. Mrs. R. would keep an eye on Rocky, and he'd keep her out of the nuns' hair. Two birds, one stone. I love it when things work out so economically.

"THAT WAS SMOOTH, pairing Mrs. Ramirez with the boy," Phil said to me later, on the drive back to the city.

"Yeah. But I probably went too far in telling her to quote a lot of scripture and pay special attention to the subject of sexual continence. Phil, I'm turning into one of those cranky grown-ups who kicked my ass when I was young," I said. "How did that happen? I thought not being able to have kids would save me from that and I'd be cool forever."

"You will be. Like me, like Helen. Just not young cool," he said. "There's a difference. More grace, less passion."

"Grace and passion are so often incompatible, aren't they?" I said. "Oh, man, I am stumped. The girl's gone, the boy's an idiot, strange foreigners are menacing me and my equally strange neighbors, and people keep talking about a baby."

"Don't forget the dead art dealer who died right in front of you," he added.

"That's another mystery—who killed him, and why?"

"First things first," he said. "The police are investigating the murder. You concentrate on finding the girl, getting her together with the boy. Anything I can do to help, just ask."

"Thanks, Phil."

"You're going to be fine there, at the Chelsea?"

"I'm armed, the apartment is alarmed, I have a cell phone."

"I'll stay with you if you like."

"Nah, I'll be okay."

The sun was rising when Phil dropped me at the Chelsea. My hand was on that pearl-handled pistol when I got out of the car and went upstairs, my eyes darting around at every noise. As I was punching in the security code, I heard a door open behind me, and I wheeled around, gun in hand, eyes wild with instinctive fear, only to find myself staring at the panicked face of the Mary Sue convention lady.

"Sorry sorry sorry," I shouted as she withdrew to her room and slammed the door.

"I thought you were a murderer!" I shouted. "It's okay."

There was no sign or sound of other neighbors. Even the Zen-master's door was closed.

Louise Bryant was waiting right inside for me, and she was furious. In the craziness of the night before, I'd forgotten to feed her, so before I did anything else, she got a big breakfast. Maggie had called and left a message, wanting me to call her "after ten A.M. please." Sleep appealed but I ignored it, logging on to my laptop and going online. Tamayo had not yet E-mailed, but Pierre had, with just a brief note: "Very busy here. Hope all is well with you. Pierre." It wasn't much, but at the moment it seemed like a goddamned ray of sunshine, one bright note in the darkness, so much so that I read those simple sentences over a few times before turning to more urgent matters.

An Internet search for the guy on the cross, St. Michael the Martyr, turned up several different St. Michael's who were martyred, and each had to be checked for a match to the strange face on the cross. Some of the web pages had no pictures, just lists of feast days and patron saints in various Catholic and Orthodox churches.

Finally, I found a martyred St. Michael, particular to south-western Russia, whose portrait on the web page fit the face on the cross. It was St. Michael the Martyr of Mashnik, a fifteenth-century saint. Unfortunately, I found nothing specific to Chechnya, so this led nowhere, except, perhaps, to a valuable object lesson.

If St. Michael were a watch, his slogan would be "Takes a licking, keeps on ticking." According to the legend, he was expelled as a young man from his monastery due to his objections to "the cruelty and heresy" of the men who ran the joint. On his way out the door, he "liberated" some of the holy relics and icons within, later selling all but one, an icon of Jesus, to finance a pilgrimage to the Holy Land. Before he got to the Holy Land, he met up with a band of "true-thinking" but hapless Christian soldiers who were being clobbered by a stronger band of Christians in the power vacuum left by retreating pagan barbarian forces.

The ragtag rebels had several years of small victories that they attributed to Michael of Mashnik and the holy icon of Jesus carried into battle. Alas, during one battle, Michael was captured by the enemy Christians and given a choice between conversion to their "heretical" faith or death. He chose death, but when the executioner came to take him away, he fought back and escaped on foot, despite having been stabbed several times. The enemy forces caught him, and attempted to burn him at the stake, but he barely got his knees singed when a great thunderstorm erupted and put out the fire. He escaped a second time, only to fall into the hands of bandits who, after finding he had nothing to steal, staked him to the ground and left him for dead. Birds plucked his eyes out, but still, Michael of Mashnik could not be stopped. After a little rest, he pulled up the stakes and hobbled back on his burned feet, blind but following the "voice of God," until he met up with the rebel Christians. There he died, urging them in his final breath to fight on to the death and to never surrender.

Finally, I thought, a patron saint for people like me. A patron saint of damned fools. Even better, he was a patron saint of proven fools (as in Celtic mythology, in which a proven fool was killed three ways, by strangling, drowning, and stabbing with a spear).

Somewhere along the line, the icon disappeared. A legend had grown up around it, that whoever had the icon would ultimately conquer his enemies. There had been many reports of the icon surfacing and disappearing again, which could not be corroborated. The last report had it being taken during World War Two by the Nazis, who were unaware of its inherent potency and just shipped it off with a bunch of other artworks and loot to Germany.

En route, the train was stopped and commandeered by anti-Nazi partisans, who took the loot for themselves. There had been no reports of the icon since then.

The icon was painted in the fifteenth century with egg tempera on birch wood by a famous icon painter, Andrei Rublev.

It was known as "the Baby" because it depicted the baby Jesus in the arms of his mother. Now I really was worried about Nadia. Apparently, she was bringing the baby Jesus icon to Gerald to sell. She must know Gerald through Tamayo, I thought. He was dead, she was missing, and the icon was God knows where. It began to piece together, bit by bit. Nadia was going to meet someone "on business." Unable to wait any longer for Rocky, she went up alone to meet with Gerald and Miriam Grundy, an art collector. This meant that sweet elderly dame I liked and admired so much was holding out on me.

But Rocky claimed he knew nothing about a "baby." Either he was holding out on me too, or Nadia was doing this deal without him. The latter made more sense, since the kid was pretty useless. Couldn't even make his bed, let alone conduct some shady art deal.

It was almost dawn when I finally crawled into bed with Louise Bryant. At noon I was supposed to meet Maggie to track down Edna, the switchboard operator, but first I wanted to speak with Dame Grundy.

chapter eleven

M iriam is not here," Ben, her assistant, said, in an affected mo-
notonous way that masked all emotion. It had taken him almost
ten minutes to answer the door, and then he didn't invite me in,
leaving me standing in the hallway. Behind him, I saw three very
tall men, evidently auditioning for Miriam's big bash.

"Where is she?" I asked.

"She's with her spiritualist," he said. "She'll be gone most of
the day."

"Where is this spiritualist? I have got to talk to Mrs. Grundy. . . ."

"You can't interrupt her when she's with Sylvia. It's more sacred than her shrink appointment," he said dryly.

At this, he tried to excuse himself, but I wasn't about to let
him go. I wanted to know everything about Nadia's meeting with
Miriam, if she'd come to sell Miriam a valuable piece of art, and
if Miriam now had this piece of art. Nadia had come empty-
handed, he insisted, and she didn't bring up any deal.

"If she'd wanted to make a deal, she forgot to tell Miriam,"
he said.

"Are you sure? Because I think Gerald Woznik was killed because of an icon Nadia possessed."

"Grace Rouse killed Woznik. She was insanely jealous and terrified he was going to leave her," Ben said. "She's insane. Period."

"What about the icon . . ."

"The girl, Nadia, didn't have any painting with her when she came to visit Miriam. Have you seen this icon? Are you sure it exists?"

"I haven't seen it. But—"

"Miriam is a rich, generous woman, and an avid collector. Artists are always asking her for money, and many of those are scam artists."

"You think Nadia was scamming Mrs. Grundy?"

The very tall men were getting restless. Ben turned from me and said to them, "I'll be with you in a minute. I promise."

Then to me, he said, "I don't know what Nadia was up to. All I know is, I didn't like her and didn't trust her. She came alone and empty-handed. Was Gerald killed for some apocryphal painting? More likely, he was killed for betraying everyone who ever tried to help him or love him. Excuse me."

He shut the door.

According to Maggie, the one person who knew damn near everything that went on at the Chelsea was Edna the switchboard operator. "My secrets die with me," she had said, but Maggie Mason seemed to think we could coax them out under the right conditions. One of those conditions was that Maggie be present. Edna knew Maggie. I was an outsider in the Chelsea.

"It's important to schmooze Edna," Maggie Mason said when I picked her up. "Let me warm her up. I've known her awhile."

Edna the switchboard operator was married to a merchant seaman near retirement off to sea at the moment. It was her day off, and on her days off, according to Maggie, she spent her time at the movies and at the El Quijote bar.

When we got down to the bar, Edna was not there, but she

was in the restaurant. The hostess told Maggie that Edna was in
the ladies', so we sat at the bar to wait.

"White sangria, Antonio," Maggie said to the bartender, who
was, like all the men in this bar and restaurant, a proud-looking
Spanish gent in a crisp linen shirt and short black waiter's jacket.
"Robin?"

"Vodka neat . . . no, Coca-Cola," I said. It was only lunchtime
and I needed to keep my wits about me, as I had only been able
to snag a few hours sleep.

"I love this place," Maggie said, staring up at some of the hundreds of Don Quixote figurines that lined a shelf above the dark
bar. "Don Quixote—how appropriate this place ended up in the
Chelsea Hotel. There are a lot of artists in the place with that
quixotic spirit."

I couldn't quite figure out the decor of El Quijote, a well-
known Spanish seafood restaurant in the Chelsea Hotel. It was
dim, with rich red tapestries and red-fringed lamps that gave off
a rosy glow and an Ottoman brothel feeling. Backlit glass etchings
of lobsters glowed pale blue on each side of the bar. The red
leatherette banquettes in the main dining room and the wood-
work added some Rat Pack lounge flavor. Above the bar was a
narrow brick-red canopy, with rounded, red-brown tiles, looking
like a Spanish roof eave. A moving windmill rotated slowly above
the entrance to the Cervantes room, while the Dulcinea room was
flanked by a huge portrait of a flamenco dancer, whom Maggie
identified as "Carmen Amaya, flamenco legend." A sixties-style
jazz piano cover of "Black Magic Woman" played low on the
sound system.

It was eclectic but refreshing, what with the proliferation of
chain restaurants, theme restaurants, and overly designed, hip
joints. In contrast, this place looked like an accidental shrine to
the passions—crustaceans, Cervantes, and thick brocade—of its
owner.

When Edna came back out, she saw Maggie and waved her

down to the end of the bar. Edna had what looked like a man-hattan or a whiskey sour in front of her—some darkish drink with a maraschino cherry in it—and one of the local tabloids was open in front of her on the bar. It was turned to a story about Gerald Woznik and Grace Rouse. I'd read it earlier. There was nothing new in it. If you believed the *News-Journal*, Grace Rouse had already been tried and convicted.

"Hi, Edna," Maggie said, giving the woman a kiss on the cheek.

"Hi ya, Maggie," Edna said. She had a lot of silver hair, worn loose today and down her back instead of up, as she usually wore it when she was on the job.

"Do you know Robin?" Maggie said.

"Robin, Tamayo's friend, right?" Edna said.

"Yes."

"How is Tamayo?"

"Good as far as I know," I said.

"Tell Edna that story you told me about Tamayo," Maggie interrupted.

Tamayo stories are great icebreakers, so I told Edna how Tamayo had been writing a book about her adventures among the Americans for a Japanese publisher. The publisher had put Tamayo and her monkey up in the Okura Hotel, a five-star joint, sent a minder to watch her, to make sure she stayed in and got the book finished. It was really overdue. Tamayo played her music really loud while she wrote, and I guess the monkey was a real nuisance, so the management moved her into the children's wing of the hotel. With her minder.

It was a zoo. She was living in this overgrown child's room, with her monkey and her minder, who was at the end of his rope. When I got to Tokyo, I stopped by the Okura to visit. We had a very civilized light lunch in the room with the minder, who hadn't shaved in a couple of days. At the end of lunch, the minder said it was time for Tamayo to get back to work. Naturally, we locked him in the bathroom and went out drinking. There was a phone in the bathroom, but by the time he was able to call down to the concierge and get someone up to free him, we were gone, leaving just a pile of yen for him and a note from Tamayo: "For God's sake, go out and have some fun today."

Tamayo and I then hit some of her favorite bizarro spots in Tokyo, drank too much, made spectacles of ourselves. I had a dinner meeting later with some Japanese TV executives, but Tamayo reassured me: "It's okay to be drunk at Japanese dinner meetings. It's almost mandatory!" This, in fact, is a myth, though the very sober TV executives seemed to find me mildly amusing, until I made that little joke about the emperor, a noted ichthyologist, and his little red snapper. Jokes about resident royal families are frowned upon in many countries, I've learned.

I was going to leave that last part out, but Edna liked that. She warmed up.

"That Tamayo," she said, clicking her tongue and nodding. "What will she be up to next?"

"Evidently, she's running some kind of underground railroad for persecuted girls from other countries," I said, figuring Edna already knew this.

She did. "Yeah, great, ain't it? Did that girl who was staying with you meet up with her guy?"

"Nadia? Not yet."

"That's a shame." Edna waved to the waiter, holding up her glass and tapping it slightly to indicate she wanted another.

"Do you know anything about that?" Maggie asked.

"Buy me lunch, girls?" Edna said.

"Sure," Maggie said, looking at me, the woman with the expense account.

I nodded. Edna evidently needed further finessing before she'd tell us anything. We moved to a booth on the dining side of Quijote and ordered paella.

"Robin is interested in the hotel," Maggie said. "I was telling her some of the stories and I thought, Edna really needs to tell some of these tales."

"You know I'll die with my secrets," Edna said.

"Not the secrets. Just the legends. Edna lived next door to Bob Dylan for a while."

"I lived next door to Dylan Thomas," Edna corrected. "I knew Bob Dylan though. He had a baby here. I knew 'em all. Jim Hendrix once took me for coffee and cherry pie at the Horn and Hardart automat at Seventh and Twenty-third."

"The Chelsea's a magic place," Maggie said.

"How times have changed," Edna said. "Used to be hotels like this all over the circuit—"

"Circuit?"

"Burlesque circuit. I was in burlesque in its dying days in the 1950s. Do you know burlesque? We didn't take all our clothes off. We didn't need to. In burlesque, the art is in tickling the imagination." She winked and made a clicking noise, then took a sip of her drink. "We'd travel all over the country. Every city had a hotel for show people—Chicago, San Francisco, Pittsburgh. You know, a place where the touring companies would stay— actors, dancers, musicians, jazz bands. Respectable hotels wouldn't take us. The Chelsea was one of the hotels that took in show people here in New York. It's the only one left of that old breed, now that the Hotel Vincent has been turned into condos."

"Edna can recite the names of just about every artist who has ever stayed in the Chelsea," Maggie said. "Show her, Edna."

Edna took a deep breath.

"Sherwood Anderson, Nelson Algren, Jake Baker, Jean-Michel Basquiat, Brendan Behan, Sarah Bernhardt, Richard Bernstein, William Burroughs, Gerald Busby, Henri Cartier-Bresson, Edward Caswell, Henri Chopin, Christo, Arthur C. Clarke, Leonard Cohen, Gregory Corso, Hart Crane, Quentin Crisp, Robert Crumb, Arthur B. Davies, Willem de Kooning, Benicio Del Toro, Bob Dylan, James T. Farrell, Jane Fonda, Milos Forman, Herbert Gentry, Eugenie Gershoy, Maurice Girodias, Oliver Grundy, Jim Hendrix, Gaby Hoffman, John Houseman—"

She took another breath. "—Herbert Huncke, Clifford Irving,

Charles Jackson, Charles James, Jasper Johns, Janis Joplin, George Kleinsinger, Robert Mapplethorpe, Edgar Lee Masters, Joni Mitchell, Arthur Miller, Moondog, Vladimir Nabokov, R. K. Narayan, Nico, Ivan Passer, Edith Piaf, Deedee Ramone, René Ricard, Diego Rivera, Larry Rivers, Edie Sedgwick, Sam Shepard, John Sloan, Grace Slick and Jefferson Airplane, Julian Schnabel, Harry Smith, Patti Smith, Donald Sutherland, Philip Taafe, Dylan Thomas, Virgil Thomson, Mark Twain, Arnold Weinstein, Tennessee Williams, Thomas Wolfe, Sid Vicious, Viva. Did I forget anyone?" she asked, the words rushing to a breathless stop, followed by a huge intake of breath.

"Robert Flaherty, who made *Nanook of the North,*" Maggie said. "Dennis Hopper, O. Henry, Claes Oldenburg, and Robert Oppenheimer, father of the A-bomb. Though he's not an artist per se."

"Lily Langtry lived a couple doors down," Edna said. "Used to take tea here when the lobby was a dining room."

Most of these had been long-term tenants, Edna went on, some came for the durations of shows in New York, or between marriages, some for a few days, a few weeks, whenever they were in the city. A few lived elsewhere but conducted their love affairs here. Some of them I'd only heard of in passing, a few I'd never heard of at all.

"The second-class survivors of the *Titanic* stayed here," Edna added. "And European refugees were housed here during and after World War Two, just after Mr. Bard's father, his partners, and their stockholders bought the hotel."

"Impressive," I said. "How did you memorize all that?"

"I had a lot of plumbing problems one year," Edna said.

Maggie laughed. I didn't get the joke.

"Every time I complained to Mr. Bard, the manager, he'd remind me of all the luminaries who lived here," Edna explained.

"It's his way of putting our complaints in perspective," Maggie said.

"When burlesque died he put me on the switchboard and put

me to work here so I could pay my rent and have some spending money," Edna said. "Yeah, this is a great place. I used to wonder why so many creative people came here. You know why?"

"Why?" I asked.

"Privacy, tolerance, freedom, history, and magic. But this place wasn't set up to be a home for artists, it just happened."

"Happened?" I said.

"It started spontaneously attracting them, and they just kept coming, and then it attracted the late Mr. Bard, Stanley's father, and his partners, all art lovers. Some people believe it is built on a peculiar energy field or sacred burial ground."

Between bites of her food and parsimonious sips of her manhattan, Edna told more stories of the Chelsea. George Kleinsinger the composer had had an alligator he walked in the hallway. When Arthur Miller lived here, he narrowly missed running into Joltin' Joe DiMaggio in the Quijote bar one night. They were both post-Marilyn at the time. Andy Warhol made a movie called *Chelsea Girls* here and practically lived here, he visited his friends here so often. Bob Dylan had a baby here and wrote the song, "Sad-eyed Lady of the Lowlands" at the Chelsea. Clifford Irving was arrested here after the Howard Hughes autobiography hoax. Sex Pistol Sid Vicious and Nancy Spungen were "just kids. Utterly helpless and dependent on each other and on heroin, may they rest in peace." Leonard Cohen wrote a song called "Chelsea Hotel #2" for Janis Joplin here. There were stories about less-famous tenants too, a girl who had run off with Tony Bennett's piano player, an heiress who lived here, fell in love with one of the bellmen, and married him. Brendan Behan had been fished out of the drunk tank by his publisher and brought here to finish a book. He wrote two and conceived a baby here.

After a bit more to drink and eat, she got downright gossipy.

"Barry Coman, the actor, he's moving back into the hotel. His girlfriend got him off heroin!" she said. "The professor on eight? Fred. He's seeing a married woman, one of his students. They fell in love in the High German love lyrics class he teaches, and they've been doing it like Apaches ever since."

Maggie smiled. "That's not Fred. That's Gunther, the German professor on four."

"Oh, right you are, Maggie," Edna said, clicking her tongue. To me, she said, "You'll like it here."

"Oh, I'm not staying long I don't think," I said. I shot Maggie a look. We'd schmoozed Edna, most enjoyably, for a while, and she had a few manhattans in her belly. When would we get to the real purpose of our meeting?

"Tell us what you know about the murder," Maggie said.

"Just between us Chelsea girls, right? Doesn't leave here."

"Right," Maggie said. To me she said, "Code of the Chelsea— we talk among ourselves, but we don't spill to outsiders unless we have to."

"Grace Rouse called me the day Gerald was killed, wanted to know who was the woman Gerald was coming to visit. Was it you, Maggie, or someone else? She thought I might have heard something through the grapevine. I told her—"

"Your secrets die with you."

"Right you are. Grace sounded very agitated. More than agitated. Crazy."

"I met Rouse," I said. "My gut instinct was that she didn't kill Gerald."

"Maybe not. But she's pretty schizo," Edna said.

"Do you know where Nadia went from here?" I asked.

"I don't, hon," Edna said. "You girls want some café con leche with a li'l brandy?"

"No, but you go ahead," Maggie said. "The hotel keeps a log of all outgoing phone calls that go through the house phone system, doesn't it?"

"Yep."

"If you could get us a list of the calls made from Tamayo's place the day of Gerald's death, it would really help."

"I could get into a lot of trouble, Mary Margaret," Edna said.

"We're on a romantic mission to reunite Nadia and her lover, Edna. Do it for the young lovers. For Tamayo, who helped them out."

"Oh, Maggie . . ."

"How's Ernie?" Maggie asked.

Edna's eyes misted over. She smiled and clicked her tongue. "He's in Panama. He got a fever down there but he's better now."

To me, she said, "Ernie's my husband. Met him here at the Chelsea when he was in port and staying here. That was 1989. We were married in 1993."

"That was a wedding for the record books," Maggie said. "We had it on the Chelsea roof."

"This is his last year on the water. Want to see a picture? He's a sweet-looking man, ain't he?" Edna said.

"He sure is," I said.

"He sure is," she repeated. "Okay, Maggie, I'll get you the phone list. After seven, after the Bards have gone home, when I have a free moment, I'll poke around. Did I tell you about the man asking about Nadia?"

"What man? A man in a bad toupee?" I asked.

"No. But I've seen that guy here several times recently," Edna said. "Was he looking for Nadia?"

"Yes. What man are you talking about?" I asked.

"A man a few years older than me, gray hair, blue eyes," Edna said. "He was here yesterday. A foreigner."

"What did you tell him?"

"I tol' him nothin'," Edna said.

After I paid the check, Edna said, "Something else, I didn't tell you. It just occurred to me. After Grace called to talk to me, she asked to be transferred to one of the rooms. I forgot all about it. But come to think of it, I believe she asked to be transferred to 711. That's Tamayo's room."

"Yes it is," Maggie said. "What time was that?"

"Afternoon-ish," she said.

"That was the day of the murder. Where were you at that time, Robin?"

"At work," I said.

"Thanks for lunch," Edna said, getting up to go. "I gotta take a nap now."

After she had left, Maggie and I sat there silently for a while, and then went upstairs to make some calls, assuredly thinking the same thing: Grace Rouse had called Nadia the day of Gerald's death. Grace Rouse had told me she didn't know Nadia.

chapter twelve

Robin, I don't know anything about this Nadia person," Spencer Roo said to me on the phone.

Grace Rouse was not in her office and nobody would tell me where she was at the moment, giving rise to my fears that she was en route to some nasty country without an extradition treaty with the United States. She was rich enough that she could run out on a bail of two million bucks, which is what she'd coughed up to get out of jail.

"No, no, she's off dealing with some bad-boy painter," Roo said. "I'll have her call you."

I was tempted to tell him everything I knew and/or assumed about this case, but in the event she was the killer I didn't want to tip Rouse off. The new theory was, Rouse thought Gerald was meeting a lover, either pregnant or with a baby, his baby, so she went to the Chelsea, killed him, maybe killed her. Nadia's corpse hadn't turned up yet, but I wasn't reassured. If she was alive, why hadn't she called? Nadia may have fled as soon as Gerald was shot. Rouse then could have gone down the fire escape, caught up with Nadia on the street, followed her, and shot her in some dark, quiet place. Until I heard from Nadia, all bets were off.

"I told you Rouse was a psychopathic liar," Maggie said.

"She spoke well of you," I said.

"Really?"

"No. In fact, she claimed you put a personal ad on her behalf in a *Star Trek* magazine."

"*Moi?*" Maggie said. "That's ridiculous."

Now, if I didn't know so much about Maggie Mason and her history of vindictive cruelty, I would have believed her. She was scarily believable when she said that. At the same time, I figured if Maggie had known how much I knew about her she wouldn't have even attempted to protest.

"It's too bad we don't know which bad-boy artist Grace is baby-sitting," Maggie said. "We'd be able to track her down through him."

"I don't remember her saying his name, and Roo didn't know," I said. "But he's someone with a boyfriend and a psychic and fears his mother."

"That doesn't narrow it down much I'm afraid."

My cell phone rang.

It was my taxi source. He had a phone number for cabbie license BF62, who was expecting my call.

THE TAXI DRIVER of BF62 remembered the guy in the bad toupee, though he couldn't describe his facial features beyond the fact that the man had brown eyes. I remembered he had brown eyes too, when I'd seen him in Tamayo's apartment earlier. But why did I remember the man in the toupee having blue eyes at the Thai restaurant, unless it had something to do with the lighting of the place, or my own memory problems, due to age, information overload, drug experimentation, or just being metaphorically gored in the head by traumatic events a time or two in my lifetime?

BF62, whose name was Jean-Michel, took Bad Toupee uptown to Park Avenue and Thirtieth Street. After the man in the bad toupee paid the driver, he removed the hairpiece and got out. The mystery man then crossed the street, and tried unsuccessfully to hail another cab. BF62 pulled a U-ie, and picked up the mystery man again. The driver said the man with the bad toupee didn't realize he'd just been picked up by the same cab that had dropped him off. Evidently, the man was planning to take two different cabs in order not to leave a trail.

Now I understood the toupee, and the blue eyes/brown eyes thing. Come to think of it, the guy in Tamayo's apartment had had a slighter build than the one I'd seen in the Thai restaurant. The bad toupee was a disguise, one that attracted attention to a strange physical feature, distracting from other features. It had been used by criminals many times before. Most recently, in the 1980s, a league of redheaded black women posing as maids had run a theft ring up in Westchester. In that case, the victim's own prejudices helped the thieves work their scam too. Rich, lily-white Scarsdale matrons who reported thefts weren't able to describe the culprits beyond, "she was a black woman with dyed red hair."

At the end of the second cab ride, the mystery man got out on Bowery, just past Bleecker, at a place called the Bus Stop Bar & Grill. After he got out, he put the bad toupee back on.

I hung up and said, "The guy in the bad toupee went to the place on the matchbook I found in that book *Man Trap,*" I said. "The Bus Stop Bar and Grill. I'm going back there."

"I'm going with you," Maggie said.

"That's not necessary," I said.

"Grace Rouse is accusing me of murder. I want to get this cleared up," she said with that serrated edge to her voice. The rasp softened when she said, "And I want to see the lovers reunited."

"We both know, deep down, it won't work out. He's such a spoiled little princeling, his hormones are teenage hormones. How long before he's got a piece on the side? And she's a demanding, ungrateful little—"

"Now is not the time to be cynical," she said.

We crept out of the Chelsea through the basement as cautious as Mossad agents, holding close to the walls, and peering down every nook and alley of the dark Chelsea basement with a flashlight as we made our way out through the back entrance to Twenty-second Street, where we grabbed a cab. Both of us wore reversible coats and had scarves so we could quickly and economically disguise ourselves. I had Mrs. Ramirez's gun with me and Maggie had pepper spray.

"I should warn you about the owner of this place we're going to, Stinky. He smells."

"Brilliant nickname," Maggie said.

"His wife, Irene, lost her sense of smell."

"He smells and she can't smell?"

"He has enough smell for both of them. Also, he has a roving eye and she seems to be insanely jealous," I said.

"What came first, I wonder, her jealousy or his roving eye?" Maggie asked.

"I don't know."

"Did he start to smell after she lost her sense of smell?"

"I'm guessing it happened after she lost her sense of smell."

"Without his wife to tell him to clean himself, he got ripe, eh?" Maggie asked. "Just as it says in *Man Trap,* men are half-dumb animals who need to be trained and watched over."

"Yeah? That's what Grace Rouse said too," I said.

"Is that it? Ahead? Bus Stop Bar and Grill."

"That's it."

Lucky for us, Stinky was not there, having gone around the block to see his brother, who ran a garage, "or so he says," Irene added with suspicion. She was a tad curious why two women wanted to speak to Stinky so bad, and me a repeat visitor on top of that. Again, I dropped Tamayo's name, and she quizzed me on

Tamayo the same way Miriam and Edna had to make sure we really were friends.

"You're sure you're not using this as an excuse to get close to Stinky?"

"I promise you we're not," I said.

"Why? What's wrong with Stinky?" She asked this accusingly, and I got the feeling that she'd be just as upset if we weren't interested in Stinky as if we were.

"He's not our type. We only date black men and Koreans," I said. This she accepted.

After I explained again about Nadia and about the cab dropping off the guy in the bad toupee here, she said, "There were two men with bad toupees. One came in and waited, and another came in. They were looking for that girl; she wasn't here, so they stayed and had drinks, talked in another language."

"Were they wearing crosses that looked like this?" I asked, showing her the St. Michael cross.

"I don't think so. Lemme think. All I remember is they both wore bad toupees, and one had brown eyes and one had blue," she said.

"This girl is the one they were looking for?" I asked, showing her Nadia's photo again."

"Could be."

"You haven't seen her?" I said. Something about her made me think she was holding out. Except when she was glaring in anger, she was shifty-eyed.

"No."

"How would they know to come here, unless one of them had tracked Nadia?" I asked. "Look, if you know something, you have to tell me. It is urgent. Do it for Tamayo."

After staring at me hard, she finally admitted, "Nadia was here, for a coupla days. I only took her in because she was a friend of Tamayo's."

"Why didn't you tell me this before?"

"Nadia warned me not to breathe a word of this, that her life was at stake. I didn't like the girl, but I didn't want her death on my conscience."

"She was here two days. And then?"

"I asked her to leave. She was making a play for Stinky," Irene said. "I take her in, she makes a play for my husband. Is that ungrateful?"

"A lot of women make plays for Stinky?" Maggie asked.

"Yeah. It's worse than ever since he started taking Viagra. Women go for him now like bees to honey," she said.

"Where did Nadia go next?" I asked.

"I put her in a cab to go to my sister's in Queens. My sister's a widow, and believe me, she can use the company and the help around the house ever since her leg went gouty. Nadia stayed there until yesterday. Don't know where she went from there."

"Where did she stay while she was here? Did she leave anything behind?"

"Follow me," Irene said.

We went back with her, through a doorway covered by a blanket, to the back hallway, lit with one bright, naked bulb. The door was open to the staff washroom, where a tap dripped loudly, and there were peeling health department posters on the cracking white walls.

"Stinky and I, we live upstairs," Irene said. "I didn't want her up there with us, so I put her in here with the dry goods."

She opened a door to a storage room where huge bottles of pickled eggs, giant cans of ketchup, towels, and jugs of wine were stored. In the middle of the room was a small cot. There were barely two inches of space between the cot and the walls.

"It was a tight squeeze, but she was safe here. This door locks. The storefront is barred and alarmed at night," she said. "After we close up, we bring the dogs, two Dobermans, down to the bar. That's why Tamayo chose us, I guess."

"Did Nadia make any calls? Mention any names? Discuss any business?"

"She said was just staying until things were okay at the place she was staying before, then she was going to go back to pick up something," Irene said. "I don't know anything more than that."

Before we left, I asked, "How do you know Tamayo?"

"Stinky and I met her in Atlantic City. She was doing her act in one of the big hotels, and afterward we talked to her and her boyfriend at the time," Irene said.

"Did Tamayo hit on Stinky?" I asked.

"No, she never did, wonder of wonders. She joked with him that the reason he got his nickname was because he smelled bad. That always cracked me and Stinky up."

"How did Stinky get his nickname?"

"His poker buddies gave him that name because he stinks at poker," Irene said. "Don't you be going to the garage to see Stinky now."

"Okay, Irene. We won't," Maggie said.

"You promise?"

"We promise."

Irene let us out the back way. We reversed our coats and hailed a cab.

"She's a jealous bitch, Irene, but I can't help liking her," Maggie said. "She doesn't have a clue about her husband, eh?"

"No, and I was tempted to tell her. 'Your husband is not that attractive, Irene. I wouldn't worry about him stepping out on you, unless there's a whole bunch of women out there who lost their senses of smell in pesticide-plant accidents.' The problem is, nobody tells her. Everyone is too polite I guess."

"Where are these imaginary rivals of hers?"

"My theory is, Stinky flirts with women, who get a kick out of the fact that he's a smelly old bastard who still flirts, and they're nice to him because they're polite and he seems harmless, and Irene mistakes that for interest on the part of the women."

"I'm sorry I missed meeting him. Why weren't you honest with her?" Maggie asked.

"I dunno. It's kind of romantic, in a weird way; he smells, but she has no sense of smell, he thinks he's irresistible, and she thinks he's irresistible. It works for them somehow."

"Are they happy?"

"My quick impression of them together was that they were happy, in a weird way . . ."

"Of course."

"I wonder if he's a serious flirt, or if he just does it to keep Irene interested. He can't be doing it because it works," I said.

"Love is mysterious," Maggie said, sighing. "Maybe Rocky and Nadia are happy in a weird way too."

Maggie was determined to view the young lovers as romantic. She seemed so nice, so humane, that I wondered for a moment if Mike had exaggerated her viciousness. But then I remembered what he'd told me about her spring-coiled rage, how she could go along, sweet as pie, thoughtful and humane, and then suddenly shoot fire through her nostrils. I've had a few moments like that myself, but evidently Maggie had these fiery outbursts regularly, like clockwork.

The cab dropped us in Corona, Queens. Irene's sister Daisy lived in a semidetached yellow brick house with a small, weedy yard. It took her a while to come to the door, due to her "gouty leg," which she apologized for as she hobbled a few feet back to a big green vinyl recliner, patched over with brown fiber tape in several spots.

From the outside, it looked like a perfectly normal person lived here. And almost everything about the inside was pretty average, from the JC Penney oak-finish furniture and the Irish-lace doilies on the tables to the crocheted red-and-white afghan thrown over the brown houndstooth sofa. All very ordinary looking, except for all the dwarves—a hundred or so ceramic dwarves. It was kind of creepy, all those jolly, fat-cheeked dwarf faces staring at us from bookshelves, atop the TV, the mantel, end tables and corner tables. This confirmed my theory that there are no truly normal, ordinary people in the world—scratch the surface, go behind their closed doors, and everyone is an oddball in some way.

"Nice dwarves," I said.

"Thank you. I've got over seven hundred of them. I've been collecting them for three years. So you want to know about the girl?"

"Yes. She was . . ."

"She was here. Irene told me she'd help me out, get things for me. I don't get around so well anymore, and I need some help salving my sores, because I can't bend down to reach my lower leg. The nurse only comes in part-time. . . ."

"How long was she here?"

"Just a day, and then she disappeared. I asked her to go into the bathroom and get my salve and heat me a towel in the dryer. She got up, walked away, and the next thing I know the door slammed. She never came back. That was last night."

"Any idea where she might have gone next?"

"I don't know where she could go, Robin. She didn't have much money," Daisy said.

"Are you sure?" Maggie asked.

"That's what she said."

"Did she talk about her homeland or her friends here in America, anything?"

"She complained," Daisy said. "The bed was too hard, I don't have the right kind of soda, my TV programs are stupid, the dwarves scared her. The dwarves scared her! My adorable dwarves!"

"Where did Nadia stay?"

"In the back bedroom."

"Did she leave anything behind?"

"She left a canvas bag," Daisy said. "She musta transferred her stuff into the suitcase. So she could travel lighter. Go on in there."

The bedroom was even eerier. There were a few dozen more ceramic dwarves there in a much smaller space. Nadia's black canvas duffel bag was sitting on the bed.

"Bloody hell. It's empty," Maggie said.

"Take it anyway," I said.

"While you're here, would you mind going into the kitchen and getting me a celery soda? Save me a trip," Daisy called.

"I'll get it," I said.

"I'm going to check the bathroom and see if Nadia left anything there," Maggie said.

In the kitchen, dwarves sat on counters, on the refrigerator, and between pots in a cabinet.

"Thanks for your time, Daisy," I said, handing her the celery soda. "You don't have anyone to help you here?"

"A nurse comes in four days a week but the other days and evenings I'm on my own. I've tried calling neighborhood kids in to help salve me for a quarter but they all just run away."

"You ask the kids to salve your sores for a quarter and they run away?"

"Yeah. I don't think they speak English, those kids."

"I'm sure that's the problem. That's a shame though. What's the name of your nursing service?" I asked.

"Mercy Visiting Nurses of Queens. They're run out of the diocese, St. Anne's," she said.

"You have a good nurse?"

"Yeah, Consuela, there's a picture of her, over there, and her husband, Rene, and their kids. Those are good kids."

"You don't have kids, Daisy?"

"No, I married late, and then my sister and I were both hurt in an accident at the pesticide plant where we worked," she said. "We couldn't have kids."

"I can't either," I said.

"Would you like a dwarf?" she asked, brightening. "Take a dwarf with you. For good luck."

These hundreds of dwarves hadn't brought poor Daisy much good luck, though who knows, maybe the bad things that had happened had prevented something worse.

She gave Maggie a dwarf too. A dwarf for the road.

As soon as we left, I called my assistant.

"Tim, can you arrange for three days of nursing service for someone?" I said.

Sometimes, it's fun to have power. I gave him Daisy's name and all the other particulars and said, "Put it under miscellaneous promotion."

"I don't know if that's wise," Tim said. "Things are heating up here. There is a plot afoot. You don't want to do anything that might look—"

"Tim, I told you, just relax! Jack Jackson is not going to fire me. I promise you. And I promise that you won't take the rap for this."

"Okay," he said. "By the way, what did you do in Russia? Jerry's been hinting about it . . ."

"Nobody told me that you if bring someone flowers in Russia, bring an uneven number of them. The wife of a big guy in Russian TV invited me to their home for a dinner party. I brought a dozen roses for her, and it turns out you only bring even numbers of flowers to funerals. The woman was very superstitious and this freaked her out. Protocol didn't list that one on the sheet they faxed me. It wasn't my fault."

"Perhaps I should send the Russian TV wife a gourmet food hamper," Tim suggested. "And forge another apology note."

"You're the best."

After I hung up, Maggie said, "Where do we look for Nadia now?"

"I don't know. But Irene said Nadia was planning to hide out until she could go back, presumably to the Chelsea, to retrieve something, hopefully Rocky."

"So far, this has been a real romantic adventure for Nadia, hasn't it? The broker for her icon sale was murdered, her fiancé got lost, she's had to sleep with pickled eggs and dwarves and salve a widow's gouty leg," Maggie said.

"And it's been fun for Rocky too," I said. "He's now living in a convent, scrubbing floors and receiving religious instruction from a cranky laywoman who is more Catholic than the pope."

"In an odd way, these experiences might better prepare them for marriage," Maggie said.

"Have you been married?"

"No. I came close with my homeboy, my Irishman."

"Mike O'Reilly."

"Yes! Did I tell you his name? Or did Tamayo mention him to you?"

"You mentioned his name," I said.

"Until my new man, Mike was the great love of my life. He worked in television for a while. Do you know the All News Network?"

"Yes," I said.

"That's where he worked. What's your network?"

"Worldwide Women's Network, WWN."

"Michael, Michael, Michael. I still miss him. But if that had worked out, I wouldn't have met . . . the new one. Oh, I almost forgot. I have to call him. May I borrow your phone?"

"Yeah. Of course."

"It's a long-distance call," she said.

"My company pays the bills," I said.

"It's an overseas call. Are you sure that won't stand out on your bill and get you into trouble?" she asked.

"Most of my calls are overseas calls. But thanks for asking." That was very considerate of her, I thought. If it wasn't for Mad Mike, we could probably be friends. But that kind of bad blood between people, especially when one of those people holds a grudge longer than a Hutu tribesman, rarely turns into real friendship. After this Nadia business was resolved, we'd have to go our separate ways.

She turned away and punched a bunch of numbers into the phone. "Thanks," she said, while she waited for her party to pick up. *"Allo? C'est Maggie."*

She rattled off a bunch of French and though I could pick out only a few words and phrases—including *"je t'aime aussi,"*—it gave me a sick feeling in my stomach.

After she hung up, I said, "Your boyfriend is French?"

"Yes," she replied dreamily.

"Lives in Paris?"

"Yes. It is such a sappy, romantic cliché, isn't it? Falling in love in Paris. But that's the way it was."

"He a friend of Tamayo's also?"

"Of course."

Every answer intensified the sick feeling in my gut. "What does he do?"

"I vowed not to talk about him, remember? Don't discuss him with my friends, don't discuss my friends with him. That's from *Man Trap,* and it's good advice," she said. "So don't tempt me."

I tempted her. "Aw, come on, you know you want to talk about him. You miss him. What's his name?"

I wanted to ask, Is his name Pierre? Is he a genius? Is he a physicist? Does he live in a little apartment off the rue des Chats Qui Peche—the Street of Cats Who Fish? Is his favorite café the Chez Nous near rue Jacob, which is run by an old, whiskery woman named Madeline who once worked as a licensed prostitute in one of the city's famous brothels between the world wars? Did he wake you in the morning with kisses and coffee? Did he write you sweet notes about "spooky action at a distance" between "empathic photons," and the quark partners, "strange and charm," asking, "Which one of us is which?"

But naturally, to do so would give it away that I knew him. My God! What if I'd had a fling with her boyfriend? But no, it couldn't be. Maggie hardly seemed like Pierre's type, and he certainly wasn't the only Frenchman Tamayo knew.

"I can't talk about him, really. I know I'm right about this," she said. "Talking about it would violate the privacy of this developing thing. Are you okay? You look pale."

"I'm fine."

"So where do we go now?"

"I don't know."

"Let me think a moment. Grace is baby-sitting a gay artist . . ."

"With a drug counselor and a psychic . . ."

"Must be someone who has a show coming up soon at her gallery . . ."

"Drinks Dr Pepper," I remembered.

"Ruck Urkfisk!"

"He's gay?"

"Bisexual, alternating current. Sometimes he's into men, sometimes he goes for women. Never both at the same time," Maggie said. "Driver, take us to Ludlow Street."

She began humming a song by a popular French singer. I didn't know his name, but I recognized the tune. It was Pierre's favorite song.

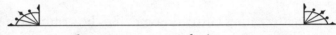

chapter   thirteen

Grace Rouse and Ruck Urkfisk were getting into a cab when we arrived at Ludlow Street, which gave us the opportunity to say "Follow that cab." We followed it all the way to Kafka's in the meat-packing district on Manhattan's Lower West Side. There was an arts fund-raiser, a "performance-artathon," going on and admission was $100 per head, which I put on my corporate credit card. Proceeds were supposedly going to an arts program for homeless kids.

Inside, it was very dark, lit only by glowing pillars of blue neon, except for an elevated, spotlit circle in the center of the room, where a performance artist was cutting some guy's hair to punk-rock music. It sounded like Richard Hell and the Voidoids. Equipped with an electric razor in one hand while dipping with the other into several pots of hair goo in glowing fluorescent colors, the "artist" improvised on the heads of three models, taking out whole chunks of hair with dramatic swoops and molding hair still on the head into colorful shapes with the fluorescent goo.

"Where did Grace and Urkfisk go?" I whispered to Maggie.

"I don't know."

"Let's get a drink," I said. "I'm parched. Then we can split up and circle the room."

The bar was pretty jammed, and it took a while to get to the front for our complimentary soda, beer, or cocktails made with Blavod, a black vodka colored with some tasteless herb. Black vodka was pretty good, and helped hide the dead cockroach embedded in the base of every Lucite glass used at Kafka's, but vodka and I are a bad combination. I got a 7-Up and began moving through the crowd looking for Grace Rouse.

Once my eyes adjusted to the weird lighting, I saw many familiar faces, a few of people I'd seen at the hotel, some friends of friends, but many more faces I recognized from celebrity news and the party pages in the back of *Paper* magazine. There was a guy there that I'd conscientiously avoided in the past, Howard Gollis, this incredibly sexy and completely insane guerrilla comic I had a brief thing with after my divorce was final and my transitional man had transited. Also, there was a guy avoiding me, Gus, an actor I'd neglected and abused emotionally while I was wrapped up in a homicide case. Between the Kafkaesque setting, the performance artists, and the old boyfriends, this was turning into a Fellini movie.

The hair artist was done and was replaced by a guy who hammered a nail in the floor. That was a quick act, and made everyone else laugh for some reason I couldn't figure out. After the nail guy came the Human Disco Ball, who wore a suit covered with tiny mirrors, rather like Tamayo's coffee table. Several other people held flashlights and/or foil reflectors, creating weird sprays and currents of lights that rotated around the room as he moved. That provided just enough light to pick out Grace Rouse in a knot of people near the back of the room.

She was standing with a tall artist who must have been Ruck Urkfisk. He was a strange-looking man, with very pale skin and rosy cheeks, and red-blond hair that had a lavender aura from the blue neon. Rouse's bright auburn hair had a deep purple glow. She was talking with Miriam Grundy. As I got closer to them, the Human Disco Ball took a bow, and Howard Gollis moved into the spotlight and began ranting loudly. His thing tonight was talking dirty in the voices of Donald Duck and Rudy Giuliani. There was no hope of speaking to Rouse or Grundy until he shut up, so I withdrew into the shadows until he had finished. When he was done, the emcee, a small, butch woman with big, round glasses, announced a fifteen-minute break before the second round of artists came up. This allowed the next performer to get his props in place and allowed me the chance to find and speak with Grace Rouse and Miriam Grundy.

But Miriam Grundy was leaving and Grace Rouse turned toward the far corner of the room. When she did, she saw me. I had to choose between Grundy and Rouse, and I chose to follow Rouse and Urkfisk. They were heading up the staircase, which lead to the VIP room.

At the foot of the stairs, a bouncer stopped me.

"I have to speak to Grace Rouse. I have an important message from Miriam Grundy," I said.

He was hesitant.

"Seriously. I have to speak with her. . . ."

"I know you from somewhere," he said. "Are you a friend of Tamayo Scheinman's?"

"Yes!"

"Robin, right?"

"Yeah."

"Go on up," he said.

I haven't been in many VIP rooms, and when I have it was always because of famous friends, either Tamayo or Claire. Every hot club in New York has a VIP room, reportedly a place where the celebs can be around other celebs without being bothered by the attention, insecurities, and gushing of us riffraff. You can't blame them, and it was a courtesy to the performers to stay out of sight as much as possible, lest the celebs distract attention from the artists.

Sometimes, the only thing that seems to unite the people in

celebrity purdah is celebrity. Claire and I were once in a VIP room with a rapper named Puffy, a reedy blond model with a weird Scandinavian name, and Salman Rushdie (who, incidentally, gets out more than I do).

This VIP room was very dark, with the same glowing-blue neon lighting. It was relatively empty. A young woman who looked a bit like that girl in the teen show about five orphans was canoodling in a corner with a boy who costarred in *American Pie*. Or was it one of the *Scream* movies? On another sofa, a guy in a suit was talking into a cell phone about "locking in that director." I had no idea who he was.

But Rouse was not there, nor was the man I assumed to be Urkfisk. Then I saw the second set of stairs. This place had a back exit for celebrity escapes, which opened up on a concrete loading dock under a black-iron canopy. Five metal steps led down to the street, which smelled of rotting meat from the meat-packing place next door.

I looked both ways down the dark cobblestone street, but Rouse and the crazy artist she was minding were gone. Maggie came out the front way and saw me.

"Where did you go? Where is Grace Rouse?"

"She and Urkfisk got away."

"They didn't stay long."

"She saw me. Maybe she left because she saw me and wanted to avoid me," I said. "Miriam Grundy didn't stay long either."

"She never stays long at these things. She shows up so the papers will mention it. She likes the attention, and the charity likes the attention she brings to them."

"Where would they go?"

"Back to Urkfisk's studio so he can paint some more."

"At night?"

"He paints best at night," Maggie said.

We hopped a cab back to Urkfisk's studio. Maggie waited inside it while I went to the big steel door in the front of the building and buzzed. A video camera in the gable above the door rotated and focused on me, but nothing happened. The intercom didn't speak and the door didn't open. I buzzed three more times, long and hard, but if anyone was there, they weren't answering.

I got back in the cab and said, "I think they're in there. The video camera turned right to me and focused. . . ."

"It's probably automatic. When someone buzzes, the camera turns to them."

"If they're not up there, where are they?"

"Maybe they went to another party. They have to come back here sooner or later. We should wait."

It was starting to rain. Waiting on the street in the shadows was out of the question, but Sunil, our cabbie, was happy to wait as long as we wanted, with the engine cut but the meter running. For him, it was an opportunity to read a chapter in his engineering textbook, and then take a nap.

"How did you like the performance-artathon?" Maggie asked.

"Some of it was interesting and provocative. But some . . . What was with the guy who hammered the nail in the floor?"

"Art joke," she said. "He was parodying Mark Kostabi, who once got two hundred people to watch him hammer a nail into the floor at a gallery."

"Why did Mark Kostabi hammer a nail in the floor originally?"

"I think the art in that was getting two hundred people to come watch him do it and call it art." She looked out the window, through the blur of rain, and laughed.

"What?"

"When I first saw the man in the bad toupee, I thought he was making an artistic statement of some kind," she said. "Challenging aesthetic prejudices."

"It's getting hard to tell the difference between what is art and what is life," I said.

"I remember more about you now," Maggie said. "You're Tamayo's friend who was involved in some other homicide cases."

"Uh-huh," I said.

"She never used your name. She always called you her friend

who got involved in murder cases. You're also her friend who works in television."

"Uh-huh," I said.

"I thought those were two different friends," she said. "But I don't follow the news much, and I don't own a TV anymore."

"You don't own a TV anymore?"

"I gave it away one day."

"Why?"

"I was recovering from a relationship, with that mad homeboy Michael O'Reilly," she said. "I was depressed, drinking too much, addicted to TV. One day, I heard the announcer say, 'This *Brady Bunch* marathon was brought to you by Cortaid Ointment and Rice-A-Roni.' And I thought, This is not how I want to be spending my time."

"That's willpower," I said. Pierre was antitelevision too.

"Yes," she said, and began to hum that French song again.

It was too much of a coincidence. Her beau and Pierre had to be the same guy. How could Pierre like Maggie better than he liked me? I'd been pretty sweet the whole time I was with him—he just brought that out in me. We seemed to be simpatico, there seemed to be a bond . . . But Maggie and Pierre could communicate. She had studied art in Paris and modeled there when younger, she knew the city, and she spoke French.

Right then, I had a Feminist Moment, where I thought of blurting out that I knew him too, that he'd seduced me and charmed me in Paris, because she deserved to know. The person we should be mad at was HIM, dammit. But that isn't the way it works when tender little hearts are involved. I was angry with him, angry with Tamayo for being his unwitting pimp, and with myself for being such a fool, but I was angriest with Maggie for falling in love with a man I just that moment realized I was in love with, and for making him fall in love with her too, through her tricks and wiles, her *Man Trap* plot. I was hurt, embarrassed, and very afraid of the wrath of Maggie Mason if she ever found this out.

What a dishonest jerk Pierre was. Or was he? For all I knew, given my lousy command of the French language, he had told me about her, right off the bat, but in French or Inspector Clouseau English. And maybe he thought I'd accepted that, because I responded in English.

Maggie kept humming that stupid song, and finally I said, "Don't you know any other songs?"

She shut up.

We waited for a long time. Maggie fell asleep, and then I fell asleep. In the morning, Sunil the cabbie awoke first, and woke us up. It was daybreak and the rain had stopped. If Rouse and Urkfisk had gone in or out of the building, it was while we were sleeping. The cab fare by now was probably more than the per capita income in the village Sunil had come from. More miscellaneous promotional expenses.

"She's dodging you," Maggie said.

"Why? Unless she killed Gerald after all."

"Brilliant! You figured it out," she said.

"That still doesn't explain where Nadia is, or why Grace called her."

"Unless . . . she thought Nadia was Gerald's lover with the 'baby,' and she came to the hotel, killed Gerald, and killed Nadia by mistake. Then she cooked up that story about me to throw you and the cops off."

"We have to get to her. I'll call Roo in about an hour when he's up. How will we get to Miriam Grundy?"

"I'll get to her through Ben," she said. "He owes me a favor. I was saving that favor for a desperate occasion but . . ."

"I must go home," Sunil said. "I could drop you here."

"Drop me," I said. "Take Maggie back to the hotel."

As they drove off, I sat down on the stoop of the building next to Urkfisk's building.

Ten minutes later, Sunil and Maggie were back. She jumped out of the cab, handed me a bag, hopped back in the cab, and they sped off. It was coffee and a raspberry cheese muffin.

Jesus, that was sweet of her, I thought. My feelings about her were all mixed up. I was afraid of her because of the stories Mike had told about her, I was jealous of her because of Pierre, but she'd been a real pal on this Nadia case.

The storm had blown in from the sea and there was a crisp salt tang left in the air. It was about six A.M. and people were starting to appear on the street. I sat on the stoop, drinking take-out coffee and watching Urkfisk's door and was about to give up and go back to the hotel when the door opened. I jumped up.

It wasn't Urkfisk or Rouse, but a pretty young Asian man.

"Is Grace Rouse up there?" I asked him.

"Yes, unfortunately," he said. "And she's making Ruck crazy."

"Who are you?"

"I'm Ruck Urkfisk's boyfriend, Daniel."

"I need to talk to Grace Rouse . . ."

"Go right on up," he said, holding the door for me. "Second floor."

GRACE ROUSE WAS SITTING in an armchair, her head propped up with one hand, watching Ruck Urkfisk paint, or rather, stand staring at a red canvas, a paintbrush in his hand. Some kind of medieval choral opera sung by a soprano and a backup choir of monks blared through the stereo system, and neither Rouse nor Urkfisk heard me come in. Paint and canvases and other painterly things were spread out on rough wooden tables. The place smelled of paints and linseed oil and the murky solvents used to soak brushes in big jars and white dairy buckets. It made me wonder if fumes weren't just as responsible for artists' crazy reputations as genius.

"Grace," I said.

She was asleep.

"Grace," I said again. She didn't awaken, but when Urkfisk stepped away from the canvas, she bolted upright.

"Don't stop!" she shouted at him. She saw me. "Robin, how did you . . ."

"I need to talk to you, privately," I shouted back.

She walked over to the stereo and turned it down. "Ruck, take a break," she said. "Fifteen minutes."

We went into the kitchen. Rouse stood by the kitchen door, watching to make sure Urkfisk didn't escape.

"What do you want, Robin?" she asked, not looking at me.

"I know that you called Nadia the day Gerald died. But when I asked you about Nadia, you denied knowing her."

"Nadia who?"

"Nadia, Tamayo's friend," I said.

"I'm not familiar with—"

"I know you called her, Grace. Don't bother denying it."

"Oh, but, well . . ."

"Why did you call her?"

"Apparently Tamayo or one of her friends had given her my home number in case she needed help."

"You're part of Tamayo's underground railroad too."

"Yes."

"Why didn't you tell me before?"

"She told me she didn't trust you. That's why she called me. She didn't trust you and wanted the name of another safe house until she and her fiancé could make it out of the city," Rouse said. Now she turned away from the door to look directly at me. "I didn't trust you either."

"That's funny," I said, "because of all the characters I've met because of this Nadia business, I am the most trustworthy one. Where is this safe house?"

Rouse was still hesitant to speak to me.

"Look, I have no selfish motive in this," I said. "Where did you send her?"

"My aunt's place, uptown. But she didn't go there. And I frankly forgot about her. I've had a few other things to think about—my dead lover, my arrest, my lazy artist . . ."

"Why didn't she go to your aunt's place?"

"How should I know? It was a quick conversation. I mentioned I was coming by the hotel later to find my lover, and if I had time, I'd stop by and check up on her at Tamayo's. I admit, some of my interest came from the fact that Nadia was at Tamayo's, next door to Maggie Mason's."

At this point, she began to weep in her abrupt, terse way. I was really tempted to tell Rouse the whole bit about Gerald coming to the Chelsea not to meet his pregnant lover, but to sell an icon people called the Baby. But I wasn't going to give it away, in case Rouse was the killer. Very quickly, she regained control and the tears stopped.

"Have you checked out Maggie Mason?" she asked me.

"Maggie has an alibi."

"Yes, yes, an online chat. That could be faked."

"She has a better alibi than that. She was with some other people."

"Friends who might lie for her?" Rouse suggested. "Maggie wanted Gerald. . . ."

"Maggie is in love with someone else," I said.

"You know this for a fact."

"Yes," I said. I did not add that the man Maggie was in love with was the man I now believed I was in love with.

chapter fourteen

Back at the Chelsea, the Zenmaster was in his doorway, lifting hand weights and staring into the hallway. He wouldn't even look me in the eye. How could one get through to this guy if he had, indeed, seen something?

Maggie had left a note taped to Tamayo's door. "Lucia and I are going over the phone records Edna dropped off. I'm waiting for Ben to call me back. Take a nap. I'll call you if we find anything."

There she was, still being sweet and considerate, making it hard for me to despise her.

If I went back to sleep now, I was afraid I'd sleep for a week. There are times when it is better to just bite the bullet and keep going. I knocked on Maggie's door.

"Who is it?" Lucia trilled.

"Robin."

It took a couple of moments before Lucia let me in.

"Would you like coffee?" Lucia asked.

"As much as possible." I followed her into the kitchen and she poured me a cup.

"Where's Maggie?"

"She had to return a call to her boyfriend."

The pink kitchen's ceiling was covered with bent silverware, the refrigerator with photos, including one I recognized. It was a photo of a road sign on the Karakoram highway in northern Pakistan that said, simply, "Relax." My ex-boyfriend Michael O'Reilly had given me the same photo during a stressful time a few years before. My copy had gone up in smoke the night of the fire.

On the door to the kitchen was a poster of Angelica Huston as Morticia Addams with the quote: *Sic gorgiamus allos subjectatos nunc*—We gladly feast on those who would subdue us. Not just pretty words . . ." Masochistically, I looked for signs of Pierre, but saw none other than a map of the Paris Metro on a bulletin board.

Maggie, still on the phone, poked her head around the corner of the kitchen and waved us into the living room/studio, where her paintings hung on the wall, paintings that seemed to be some surreal fusion between comic-book art and classical realism, very detailed in a realistic way, but with heads and muscles out of proportion and wild eyes in the faces.

"*Oui, je sais,*" Maggie said.

"Maggie has a boyfriend," Lucia said, handing me a chunk of computer printout—of phone numbers. The numbers were not sorted by room number, so we had to weed through all the calls made that day from the whole hotel.

"Have you met him?" I asked Lucia.

"She won't tell me anything about him. He must be French."

I smiled politely at this example of deductive reasoning, and tried to tune Lucia out as Maggie talked, hoping to hear her call him "Luc," or "Michel," or something else that would assure me it wasn't Pierre. Once again, I cursed the fact that I had studied Swedish in high school back in Minnesota instead of French.

When I heard her say "Sorbonne," I knew.

I had slept with her boyfriend. It was all Tamayo's fault, of course. Pierre was a friend of hers and Tamayo had arranged for him to meet Maggie, just as she had arranged for me to meet him, and Claire before me.

"You have to look for the room number on the list," Lucia said, having noticed that I was preoccupied and not going over the computer printout. "So far, the only call I've found made from the room that day was to the deli."

"Right. Let me check this list," I said, but I couldn't focus on it.

Maggie hung up with a sigh after several *je t'aimes*. "Found anything?" she asked.

God, I hated her just then.

"Not yet," Lucia said.

"Anything in the papers about Woznik?" I asked.

"Grace Rouse is still the number one suspect, that's all. All the papers have stories about the Art Break dog crap, incidentally. Not one mentioned the alien abductions," Maggie said.

"What about Nadia—have you learned anything?"

"I was just about to call Miriam's assistant. The line was busy when I called before," Maggie said. "I keep getting switched to the voice mail."

"How is Miriam involved?" Lucia asked.

"Nadia apparently had a piece of valuable art she brought here to sell, to finance her new married life," I said.

"And Gerald was brokering the deal," Maggie said, her ear to the phone. "He specialized in sub-rosa deals like that. Miriam is a collector. Nadia and Gerald were supposed to meet and go see Miriam to sell the icon, we think, but Gerald was killed before he could meet up with Nadia . . . Ben! Finally! I've been calling and calling . . . Yes, I know you're busy. Is Miriam there?"

Evidently not, because Maggie shook her head at us.

"I need to find her. It's urgent," Maggie was saying. "Don't give me that. You know where Miriam is. You owe me a favor. You know her schedule backward and forward. Ben, I know you're busy with the party . . ."

She put her hand over the phone and whispered to us, "He's having a bad day. One of the Swinging Miriams is sick and he still has to find a very tall woman for Miriam's party."

"Miriam has such good parties," Lucia said to me.

"Ben, how's your married boyfriend?" Maggie said. "Your secret is safe with me, Ben, but trust is a two-way street. Uh-huh. I thought so. Thanks, Ben."

"She's at her spa, being prettified for tonight," Maggie said, hanging up. "Lucia, can you look after these phone calls while we go speak with Miriam?"

"I think so," she said.

"Be discreet if you talk to these people Nadia called. Mention that you're a friend of Tamayo's . . ."

" ' . . . and I'm looking for another friend of hers, whose name I'd rather not mention,' " Lucia said. "Maybe I will just call you if I find anything, and you can call."

"You know the secret knock, right?" Maggie asked.

Lucia knocked on the table with the first bars of the *William Tell Overture.*

"Good. Don't let anyone in unless you hear that knock. If you don't hear that knock, don't answer the door. Be very quiet and call Victor in security downstairs."

"Yes, Maggie."

"You have Robin's cell phone number. Call as soon as you learn anything."

WE HAD TO BE ANNOUNCED at the Esther Fine spa. After Miriam Grundy had been located, an attendant in a trim uniform escorted us through the hallways to see her.

This was a tony joint, the place where old money gets its topknot tended. Not a topknot in the lot, actually. The clientele was very up-to-date and stylish. Miriam Grundy, Maggie told me, had spent 1981 with a pink streak in her white hair, though she normally wasn't quite that faddish. The Esther Fine spa seemed too "uptown" for a bohemian queen like Miriam Grundy, but Maggie explained that rich people and artists go hand in hand. At Miriam's high level in the Art World, she had to move as easily among wealthy conservative investment bankers as she did poor anarchist artists. At her age, why skimp on the creature comforts just to keep up some proletarian pose?

Mrs. Grundy was reclining in a chair with thick blue goop caking on her face. Her hair was tied back in a towel. A protective plastic sheet was tied around her neck.

"Maggie, Miss Hudson," she said to us.

"Don't talk, please," said the attendant.

"Miriam, your name has come up in connection with a delicate matter," I said, casting a quick glance at the facial person.

"Can we be alone, Vera?" Miriam said.

"It has to set. Don't talk for ten minutes," Vera said before leaving.

"How can I help you, girls?" asked Miriam, trying not to move her lips.

I was going to try to finesse Miriam a bit, see if anything accidentally slipped out, but before I could, Maggie blurted out, "Nadia sold you an icon the day she came to see you, didn't she? A legendary Rublev, called 'the Baby.' "

"No," Miriam said.

"We know it all, Miriam, with all due respect. Gerald brokered the deal for Nadia to sell you the icon. You told Robin that Nadia came alone, but Gerald came with her, didn't he? He was on his way downstairs to pay me when someone killed him . . ."

"NO!"

"No?" I said.

"Gerald didn't come, the girl came alone," Miriam said, her blue masque cracking as she talked. "I don't know anything about an icon."

"I'm sure the police would love to hear about this," Maggie said. "With all due respect, you're better off telling me, someone who is devoted to you. A girl's life is at stake."

Through her blue mask, Miriam's brown eyes studied us. "Are you wired? Either of you?"

"No," we said at the same time.

"It's sensitive," Miriam Grundy said. "It's a legendary Rublev. The Russian government, the Russian Orthodox Church, and a number of small republics would all try to claim it. It's best this goes unpublicized."

"Where is it now?"

"I don't know," she said.

As sheets of blue plaster flaked off her face onto the protective plastic sheeting, she told us how the icon had been for generations in the home of a wealthy Hungarian family who had collected art. The family was unaware of the icon's mystical properties, but from the style believed it was a Rublev. When the Nazis invaded, the family was arrested and deported to labor camps, where the father died. The mother and children survived the war, and made their way to America.

The Nazis, also unaware of the icon's miraculous protection, loaded it and a lot of other loot into a train and shipped it off to be stored until the war was over. En route, the train was commandeered by Hungarian democratic partisans, who took it east. The legend of the Baby had stopped there, until Nadia had filled in the blanks for Miriam. Nadia told Miriam that after the democratic partisans hijacked the train, it was hijacked from them and commandeered by Communist partisans, led by Nadia's grandfather, who claimed it and its contents as booty. It had been in Nadia's family ever since.

"When Nadia escaped to elope, she took the Baby with her," Miriam Grundy said.

"You know it exists. You know it's not just a legend?"

"I know it exists. I knew the family that owned it in Hungary. When my family and I fled the Nazis, that family helped us, and many other Jewish refugees, out of the country and to America," she said. "I don't know anything more about Nadia than what

I've told you. In these arrangements, sometimes it is better to have less, rather than more, information."

"Where is Nadia now?"

"I don't know. That was shortly before we heard that Gerald had been shot on seven," Miriam said.

"Where's the Baby now?"

"As I said, it is safe, and we're tracking the descendants of the family that owned it in Hungary to return it to them, quietly. With a thing like that, that people fight over and kill for, it's best for it to be in a private collection, with someone who truly loves it for what it is."

"You're sure you don't know where Nadia is?"

"Very sure."

The facial person poked her head in, and grimaced when she saw Miriam's costly mud mask all peeled off.

"Reapply the mud, will you, Vera?" Miriam asked, leaning back into the chair. We were dismissed.

"Shit," I said to Maggie in the first of our two cabs home. "We're never going to get these two brats together, Rocky is going to be stuck out at the convent for God knows how long, some crazy terrorists are after us, and Gerald Woznik's killer is walking around free."

"And your apartment burned down," Maggie added. "You know, when Tamayo gets back, you could possibly stay in my apartment."

"Where are you going?"

"To Paris for a few months."

Paris. That word just set me off. "Just like that? How long have you known this . . . what's his name?" I asked.

She smiled. "Long enough."

"You're my age. You've been around, right? How can you believe in love after all you've seen so far?" I asked meanly. "It's a madness brought on by hormones. Your biological clock is ticking."

"I don't think so, but whatever it is, it's fine with me."

"Sure, until the day you wake up from the madness and realize that this guy, whoever he is, is romancing and seducing other women behind your back, and what he feels for you isn't that special."

"Pardon me, but is my love life any of your business?" she snapped. "This is why I won't discuss him with other women. Mother of God, you've got nerve. Did the last one really burn you and sour you on men?"

Technically, the last one was Pierre, and before that an actor, Gus, who hadn't burned me, I'd burned him. Michael O'Reilly and I had burned each other.

"Hey, we're both still single. We haven't been able to find Mr. Right so far," I persisted. "What makes you think this one will be any different? I'm genuinely curious."

"Who put the pepper in your knickers? You are the anti-Cupid. You tried to discourage Nadia and Rocky, you're dumping on me now. . . ."

"Nadia and Rocky are fools, and their so-called romance has got us in a heap of trouble. As for you, you're a woman of the world. I think you can handle a reality check. Any man you can get with the deceit and manipulation outlined in that book *Man Trap* you're so high on is probably deceiving you too, and possibly himself."

"Well, I feel bad for you. You're bitter," she said, and turned away to stare out the window.

Bitter. This from Maggie Mason.

The pouting silence between us was broken by my cell phone tweetering. It was Lucia. She'd found two numbers called from Tamayo's phone the day Nadia arrived, Grace Rouse's number and an overseas number. I wrote the latter number down, and punched it in, though I had no idea where I was calling.

After a few rings, a woman answered in a strange language.

"Do you speak English?" I asked, "My name is Robin Hudson, I'm a friend of Tamayo's. . . ."

'Robin?" said the woman. "This is Tamayo's friend, Eva?"

"Eva?"

"Of Eva and Joe? I would hope you'd remember us. You stayed with us not long ago on your way through Prague."

"Eva!"

At the beginning of my two-month road trip, I'd seen Eva in Prague and stayed with her and her husband and daughter at the funky little inn and cafe they ran in Prague's Old City.

"What can I do for you, Robin?"

"I've been staying at Tamayo's, and this girl came through . . ."

"Oh yes. Juliet."

"No, different girl. . . ."

"Same girl. Only one girl came through here on her way to Tamayo's apartment. Juliet is the nickname I gave her."

"Nadia, you mean?"

"Is this phone line safe?"

"I think so."

"Yes, Nadia. Did the brat meet up with her lover man?"

"No, and she's gone missing. I wondered if you had heard from her since?"

"Yes, twice. She called me when she arrived to let me know she got there safely."

"What did she tell you?"

"There was some snag in the elopement, but she didn't tell me what it was. She was quite upset," Eva said. "She called me again a day or two ago, unhappy with the widow she was staying with."

Eva had provided another contact.

"Excuse me for being coy, but Nadia said it was a dangerous situation," Eva said. "The people you want are the ones who run the place where Tamayo showed that short film, the one involving a quarter glued to the sidewalk outside the New York Stock Exchange. Do you know the one I mean?"

I didn't, but I repeated this to Maggie, and she knew.

"That would be Tamayo's friends Caroline David and Arnold Scott, who run a multimedia performance space called The Town of Wahoo," Maggie said.

When Maggie called The Town of Wahoo, Arnold Scott told us that he did not know where Nadia was, but his wife, Caroline, did. Unfortunately, Caroline was at a funding meeting with a benefactor and wouldn't be back for an hour. He suggested we call back.

"Thank God," Maggie said. "We're almost there. We've almost got Nadia."

"Not yet we don't. I won't be happy until I see her in the flesh. Let's go to The Town of Wahoo and wait for this Caroline David person."

The phone rang again. It was Phil.

"I'm on my way out to visit Dulcinia Ramirez. Anything you want me to bring the boy or tell him?"

"How are you getting out there?"

"I'm driving. . . ."

"This is perfect timing, Phil. Want to pick us up first?" I asked. "It looks like our mission is nearly complete."

PHIL PICKED US UP where we had the cab drop us, in front of the Port Authority bus terminal on Eighth Avenue, where there was usually a huge crowd of people and we could lose ourselves in case we were being followed, though we'd taken such great pains not to be. Better safe than sorry.

Maggie hopped in the front, and I took the backseat. Once we were on our way to Brooklyn, I called Rocky at the convent.

When he heard my voice, he let loose with a litany of complaints.

"You've got to get me out of here. Mrs. Ramirez is making me insane. And I'm not the only one. . . ."

"Rocky," I said. "I think we've located the thing you were looking for. We're on our way to meet someone to take us to her, then we'll come get you."

"Get me first and take me to her!" he demanded.

"Rocky, that's out of the way. Jesus. You're so selfish. And we don't know where she is yet. We're going to meet someone who is supposed to take us to her."

"Pick me up," he said.

We were going through a tunnel and the phone sputtered and then cut off. When we came out of the tunnel, the phone tweetered.

"Come get me!" he demanded.

"We will, in due time. Sit tight," I said, and hung up. "What a brat. He wants us to go all the way to the convent, fetch him, then come all the way back to get Nadia. He's so hotheaded."

"He's anxious to see his girl," Phil said.

"All the more reason to let him chill awhile," Maggie said. "We don't want any complications now that we've come this far."

When the phone rang again, two more times, and I heard it was Rocky, I hung up and turned it off.

"This is exciting," Phil said. "The lovers are just about reunited."

He was gleeful. There is nothing that guy likes better than fixing things for other people. Unlike most fixers, Phil usually makes things better, not worse.

"Love is grand, isn't it?" Maggie said. "You have a special somebody, do you, Phil?"

"My gal, Helen. Over two years now. And you?"

"Yes," she said.

"Is he an artist?"

"No, he's a professor," she said. For someone who didn't want to talk about her boyfriend, she sure brought him up a lot.

"Oh, Robin's—" Phil began, but I caught his eyes in the rearview mirror and shook my head.

"Robin?" Maggie repeated.

"I forgot what I was going to say," Phil said.

Thank you, Phil, I thought. It was bad enough she and I were probably in love with the same guy. I didn't need to be dealing with her vengeful pranks for the next five years on top of that.

Maggie and Phil talked to each other on the drive into Brooklyn, which worked out well, as I was not feeling overly conversational. All this talk about "love"—what a laugh. I kept thinking about Pierre, and how this bitch Maggie had probably got him with her manipulative ways. And gee, I wanted him. Even though I knew it was impossible, what with the language, cultural, and etiquette barriers, not to mention a little thing I like to call "The Atlantic Ocean," I still wanted him. I harbored a hope that somehow this crazy little romance would take off between him and me. It's like Nora Ephron says, deep down all cynics are secretly hopeless romantics.

Before I met Pierre, I'd pretty much given up on feeling any kind of romantic passion again, and had been glad for its absence. The actress Jeanne Moreau said in a *60 Minutes* interview, and I'm paraphrasing here, that she didn't miss the romantic passion of her younger years, that it was a great relief to be free of it. I hear you, sister, I'd thought at the time. That's how I had felt . . . relieved, free, not an active part of the whole man–woman thing anymore, just a big, neutered ape in a tree, off to the side, scratching my head and puzzling about the strange behavior of male and female human beings.

Pierre came along and whammo—the next thing I knew, we were making out beneath the Arc de Triomphe . . . and in the Luxembourg Gardens . . . and by the old-fashioned carousel near the Eiffel Tower . . . and behind the crypt of a nineteenth-century French postmaster general in Père-Lachaise cemetery. Whoa! I remembered. I'm a heterosexual woman.

Maggie, on the other hand, had no doubt followed the Machiavellian *Man Trap* plan of playing hard to get, tempering the tyranny of her "friendly indifference" with occasional indulgence whenever he was about to give up, not giving in sexually until the man was willing to "kill to get at it," and then not enjoying it too much the first few spins between the sheets, so that the man would feel slightly inadequate and the woman would have the advantage. (When consummation comes, you see, it is then "less of a male conquest and more of a female capture," according to *Man Trap,* plus, you've convinced the man of your relative virtue, which is synonymous with lack of sexual enjoyment in women.)

It didn't help that Maggie was a few years younger than me, a glamorous artist who had once modeled in Paris. More annoying still, he was evidently calling her, but aside from a phone message left at work, he had only sent one quick E-mail to me, explaining he was busy with his experiment.

Yet, it wasn't Maggie's fault. She was an innocent party in this. She obviously didn't know about me and Mike either, so she was an innocent party in that fiasco as well. Here I was, in a stereotypical cat fight over a man. It made me feel crummy. Oh, who was I kidding, anyway? It was hopeless. What kind of relationship can two people have when the only way they can communicate clearly is in writing? Not to mention all those other ways, in which Pierre and I were grossly incompatible. If experience had taught me nothing else, it had taught me that some of us are just too crazy for love. Better I should give up this STUPID love stuff now, and set my sights on becoming a grande dame, on being an inspiration to future drag queens, like Miriam Grundy.

"You okay, luv?" Phil asked.

"Huh? Yeah, fine," I said.

"We're here."

"Oh. Great."

The Town of Wahoo was a "space" at the corner of Water and Adams Streets in DUMBO—Down Under Manhattan Bridge Overpass, an area of warehouses, buzzing electrical transformers, and industrial clutter on the Brooklyn side of the East River, between the Manhattan and Brooklyn Bridges. The area had a German Expressionist feel to it—lots of shadows, sharp silhouettes, sooty buildings, and machinery. Huge spaces at low rents had attracted a lot of artists.

Across the street from the "space," on the dingy brick wall of a boarded-up warehouse, someone had painted a big cartoon balloon that asked the question "Are We Famous Yet?"

We parked and looked around for other cars. There were none. We hadn't been followed. So far, so good.

After we explained on the intercom who we were, Arnold Scott told us to take the elevator to the second floor, and buzzed us into the old factory building.

The second floor opened to a loft apartment. A large tree branch and part of a tree trunk stuck out of a faux break in the bright red wall in the curved hallway, as if the tree had pushed its way through the wall to grow into the apartment.

"Nice tree," Maggie said.

"It's a hat rack. To preserve it, we used a specially mixed matte shellac to approximate the natural texture of the tree," Arnold explained. "The children wanted a treehouse. We have two children, Lynn and Ray."

Another, smaller branch from what looked like the same tree came out of the kitchen wall. It was hung with pots and a red mesh bag of onions. In the living area, where we all sat down, another large branch emerged near the top of the wall and snaked against the ceiling.

"I have to finish sewing Lynn's duck outfit for the spring pageant at her preschool. You don't mind if I work while we talk?" he asked.

"Not at all," I said. "Where are your kids?"

"At preschool," he said.

He told us Nadia was supposed to help out with the kids while she stayed here—she claimed to love children—for a couple of hours every night during performances.

"But it turns out Nadia does not have a way with children," he said, pinning a bill to the fuzzy yellow duck suit.

"What happened?"

"We left her with them for two hours last night. When we got back, Nadia was watching some stupid TV show, and the kids had locked themselves in the bedroom and pushed a toy chest up against it to keep her out. They were terrified!"

"Why?" Maggie asked.

"The kids wanted to watch the Rugrats video—they're both preschoolers—and Nadia wanted to watch cable. There was an argument, and Nadia threatened to smother the children with pillows while they were sleeping and throw them down the garbage chute if they didn't behave. Scared the kids so much they went into the bedroom and barricaded the door to keep her out. We asked her to leave immediately, of course."

"Caroline knows where she went next?"

"Yes, I think so," he said.

"Did Nadia say anything about her fiancé or the trouble she's been through or . . . ?"

"No, she barely talked, other than to threaten the lives of our children. She harumphed a lot. She cried a little just after she got here, but she wouldn't say why. We helped another girl and one young couple on Tamayo's railroad and had no problems. They were great kids. But this one . . ."

"Yeah, I know," I said. "You should meet her young feller. He's worse. But at this point, we just want to reunite them."

"I understand," he said.

The deadbolt on the door clicked, and a tall woman with short-cropped blond hair came in.

"Caroline, Maggie and some friends of Tamayo's are here looking for Nadia," Arnold said. "You know where she is?"

"Yes. Hi, Maggie," she said. "Nadia's in Red Hook. I'll give you the address."

chapter fifteen

Red Hook used to be one of the poorer and rougher New York neighborhoods. Located between the Brooklyn Bridge and the Atlantic Basin, it sits on a knob of land surrounded on three sides by water and known for the sprawling Red Hook housing projects and for its piers at the endpoint of the Brooklyn promenade. It had been revitalized in the last few years by the arrival of artists looking for low rents.

Phil waited downstairs in the car while Maggie and I went in. The building we were going to was downwind from a pier for garbage barges, heaped high with rotting food and diapers, big black trash bags, and scavenging seagulls. The smell was overpowering.

The "safe house" was not a house at all, but the old Brooklyn Secure Shippers, Inc. warehouse, restored by the New York Council for Artists' Housing to studios and apartments for poor artists. The freight elevator we rode up in was bigger than my office at WWN. Kyra, the woman who was now sheltering Nadia, had a huge studio and not much furniture. Amid the fabric pieces, quilts, and tapestries she was working on were about three dozen air fresheners.

"Sorry about the odor," Kyra said. "It's the garbage barges. They're closing that pier next month. Usually it's not that noticeable."

She nodded toward a door to her left, and said, "Nadia's in the back room. Is she really leaving now?"

"Yes," I said.

"Thank God. She's a real pain. If she's not bitching, she's weeping," she said, going into a kitchen area, leaving Maggie and me to give Nadia the news.

We went in without knocking.

Nadia was now in weeping mode, and looked pretty pathetic sitting in the middle of a pile of tissues, chocolate bars, empty soda cans, air fresheners, and newspapers, on a futon covered with a quilt. A soap opera was on a fuzzy TV with rabbit-ear antennae. I was tempted to ask her if she was crying because of Rocky, because of something on the soap opera, because of the way the wind was blowing from the garbage pier, or because she didn't have cable. But then I remembered my human duty, and gave her the good news.

"Nadia, we've found Rocky. You can get married, if you really, really want to," I said.

She looked up and said, "Rocky?"

"Yeah. He showed up at the Chelsea and we stashed him somewhere safe. Grab your stuff, we'll take you to him, and you can tell us all about the Baby and Plotzonia."

"I don't want to go to Rocky," she said.

"Why not?" Maggie asked.

"Does he know I'm here? Oh my Godt."

"No, but he knows we were coming to get you," I said.

"You idiot!" she screamed. "Rocky is the boy I ran away from! He's the one my parents wanted me to marry. He's why I didn't come back to the Chelsea—because I saw one of his henchmen lurking about, and when I called Tamayo's apartment, Rocky answered. I've got to get out of here. Are all Tamayo's friends ID-IOTS?"

"Rocky is the boy you ran away from? He's not the guy you came here to marry?" Maggie asked, ignoring Nadia's rude question.

"No!" She got angry, red-faced, spitting angry. "I came here to marry Gerald. That lying bastard!"

"How did you know Gerald?"

"I met him through Tamayo when I was visiting her last year."

"You didn't know he was living with Grace Rouse?"

"Not until I called her about a safe house, and she mentioned him," Nadia said.

"Who are the guys with the bad toupees?" I asked. "One of them wasn't the man you were supposed to marry?"

"No, you idiot," she said. "Those are Rocky's bodyguards."

"You thought you were going to marry Gerald?" Maggie said.

"He promised to marry me," she said. "I brought the icon, as I promised, and he was supposed to run off with me after we got the money, to get married."

"Who killed him?"

"I don't know. My family, Rocky's family, his crazy girl-friend . . ."

"Or maybe the terrorists of Saint Michael the Martyr?" I asked.

"You know about the Knights of Saint Michael?" she asked.

"Had a run-in with them, me and Maggie, the other night. They were looking for you, for Rocky, and for an icon called the Baby. You've got some explaining to do. . . ."

"Were you followed?"

"No. Why—"

"Where's Rocky?"

"At a convent with a bunch of nuns," I said. "Shit. By now he must know that we know that he's not your groom. I'd better call the Mother Superior and let her know there's a problem."

I turned my cell phone back on and as soon as I did, it tweet-ered.

It was Rocky, calling me.

"Bring Nadia here. Tell no one. If you do not do as I say, I will start killing nuns. I will kill Mrs. Ramirez first," he said, and hung up.

After I relayed this to Maggie and Nadia, I said, "I'm calling the cops."

"If you call the cops, it will make all sorts of trouble for me. It will cause an international incident, and the nuns will die," Nadia said. "I need to get back to the Chelsea to pick up some-thing from Miriam."

"The icon you sold to Miriam Grundy?" I asked.

"If you sold the icon to Miriam Grundy, how come you couldn't just take off with the big bag of unmarked bills?" Maggie asked.

"I have no money! Miriam insisted on having the icon ap-praised before she paid me, and Gerald had said she was trust-worthy. I had no choice but to leave it with her and trust her, stay an extra day at the Chelsea. I was to go back the next day with Gerald to pick up the money."

"Miriam told us she didn't have it," I said. "Her assistant told me you didn't have anything with you . . ."

"He didn't see it. I hid it under my sweater when I went in to meet Miriam. It isn't very big, I must go back to the Chelsea Hotel . . ."

"No, first we have to go free the nuns," I said. "Jesus, Nadia. You can go back to the Chelsea later."

"All right," she snapped. "I can go talk to Rocky. I'll get him to free the nuns."

"Then we call the cops and turn him in, right?" I said.

"Yes," she said.

"You're sure you can convince him?"

"Yes. Rocky is mad for me. I'll . . . What will I do, Maggie?" Nadia asked.

"Yes, what would *Man Trap* advise?" I asked. "I don't think this is covered."

"It isn't covered, but I expect he's going to want to think that you've seen the error of your ways, and you realize you love him," Maggie said.

"He's very much in love with you," I added.

"Vomit," Nadia said. "How could you believe I'd want to run off with him?"

"He's the boy who showed up before you did the night you arrived," I said. "He's the one I sent away. He had pictures of you two together. How was I to know? If you'd been more forthcoming with information, maybe I could have called it. But all you were willing to tell me was that you were escaping an arranged wedding and running off with some dreamy guy. Now you're going to have to make things right."

"I'll play the part. I'll pretend I love him," she said, flashing what looked like a sincere look of love and contrition. The girl was good.

"Grab your stuff, Nadia, and let's go down to Phil," I said.

"WHEN WE GET TO THE CONVENT, drop me outside the electrified fence," Phil said, "and drive in without me. I'll break in and—"

"That's awfully risky, Phil," I said.

"Remember, luv, I helped put in that security system; I know how to disable it, I know the layout of the convent, and I have my gun with me."

"I have Dulcinia's gun," I said.

"The lad's outgunned then. We can take him," he said, pulling away from the curb. "Robin, you spoke to Rocky, so you go in with Nadia, but leave the cell phone with Maggie. Maggie, you'll stand guard outside the main gate."

He talked for a while about the layout of the convent. After he disabled the security system, he would enter through the back, where a small hill made it easy to climb the wall. Nadia and I were to keep Rocky talking, and loudly, so Phil could follow our voices and find us in the convent complex. He would try to sneak up behind Rocky and disarm him and anyone else with him.

In the backseat, Maggie sat with Nadia, who hugged her suitcase to her chest.

"Start talking, Nadia," I said. "First, where is Plotzonia? Rocky said it is Chechnya but he probably lied about that too."

(She said the name of the country, and it wasn't Chechnya—that little pisher Rocky had lied to me—but another smallish republic nearby. To prevent hard feelings, it shall be known by Nadia's nickname, Plotzonia, as I have offended enough people in the world and don't want native Plotzonians and Plotzonian-Americans mad at me for my comments about their country. I'm sure many of them are decent, free-thinking, good-hearted people who are simply powerless in the face of their dictatorial government. Most Americans haven't even heard of the place and couldn't find it on a map, I expect, but some may know it in connection with the Vlada, that terrible little subcompact car that had enjoyed a certain détentish vogue in the United States in the 1980s, until it was discovered that the cars wouldn't run in heavy rain.)

"How do you know Rocky?"

"We've known each other since we were children," she said.

Though Nadia was not in love with Rocky now, she admitted she had been in love with him. Rocky and Nadia had been childhood sweethearts, when their fathers were both members of the Plotzonia delegation to the United Nations. Plotzonia wasn't really a separate country at the time—it was firmly under the Soviet thumb. The Soviets just called it a sovereign country to give it another vote in the United Nations General Assembly. When the Soviet bloc broke up, Plotzonia declared its true independence and the reigning Communist puppet, Nadia's grandfather, quickly consolidated control through the army and became a "savage capitalist," though not a democrat. Things were relatively calm for that part of the world, until grandpa died. Nadia's father and Rocky's father both returned to Plotzonia, where a power struggle broke out between Nadia's father, the North Plotzonian clan chief, and the South Plotzonian clan chief.

A year of civil war ensued, putting a crimp in Plotzonia's economy, which is largely based on the vices of others—drugs, guns, other smuggled goods. The civil war drove Nadia and Rocky apart. A third faction, which had split off from the North Plotzonian forces, the Knights of St. Michael the Martyr, went to war with North and South Plotzonia, vowing to return the country to the One True Church. The South Plotzonians—Rocky's clan— were winning the civil war when the Knights came in and mucked things up for both the North and the South.

In order to fight the Knights of St. Michael, the forces of the North and the South decided to make peace. As part of the peace deal, it was agreed that Nadia and Rocky would marry, formally uniting the two clans and the country. Nadia wasn't sure if she still loved Rocky—their year apart had given her time to reconsider—and she knew she hated Plotzonia, but she was resigned to her fate as an overmedicated consort of a dictator-to-be. In exchange for marrying the boy, she demanded a trip to New York to buy her wedding dress and see Tamayo.

"That was about six months ago," Nadia said.

A chaperone went with her, but Nadia ditched her and went to stay with Tamayo at the Chelsea, and there she met Gerald Woznik and fell under his spell. They talked about art, and Nadia mentioned that her family had quite a lot of art, including a legendary icon believed to have been painted by Andrei Rublev.

"You were in love with Gerald," Maggie said, shaking her head. "Did you sleep with him?"

"No. I'm still a virgin," Nadia said with pride. "We kissed though."

"And when you went home to Plotzonia?"

"We E-mailed. I told him I loved him, and wanted to come back to him. He had a plan. I'd run away, bring the icon, we'd sell it, and use the money to start a new life in South America."

"He was conning you," Maggie said. "He would have dumped

you as soon as he got his share of the cash. Gerald would never leave New York."

"I didn't know. He told me not to tell anyone about us. It was a secret romance, until my father's secret police intercepted our E-mail. After that, we wrote in code."

On her way down from Miriam Grundy's apartment, she'd heard that Gerald had been killed, and she'd gone straight to the basement and sneaked out. She hopped a cab to the Bus Stop Bar & Grill. It wasn't until the next day, when she saw the newspapers, that she learned what kind of boyfriend Gerald Woznik was.

"I was fooled," Nadia said bitterly.

"Aw, luv, we've all been fooled," Phil said. He'd been quietly thinking up until now. "You'll be wiser next time."

"Yes, next time maybe you'll see through the bad man, and past him to a good man," Maggie said. "I did."

"Tamayo didn't know it was Gerald? Or about the icon?" I asked.

"No. She just knew I was in love and running off to elope. I saw her about a week before I left, in Plotzonia. She was on her way to Kazakhstan with her boyfriend, Buzzer."

"I've never been to Plotzonia," Phil said. "What's it like?"

"The most boring place on the planet," Nadia said. "And the people there are really stupid."

In the next half hour, we learned more about Plotzonia than you ever wanted to know, our heads filling with facts that no doubt displaced important things like poetry, fond memories, and the names of friends' children. Plotzonia has a population of seven million, less than New York City, with slightly more than half the population residing south of the Malo River, in North Plotzonia. Here's an interesting tidbit: Some of the earliest known condoms had been made with the bladders of a large river fish, the blue-speckled carp that had lived in that river. The blue-speckled carp, alas, was long extinct.

The main industrial products were tractors and the Vlada automobile; the main agricultural products were potatoes, turnips, and pork; the main natural resources iron ore and salt. But since the breakup of the Soviet Union, Plotzonia's location, between Central Asia, the Middle East, and Eastern Europe, made it a popular transit point for guns, drugs, and the white-slave trade, bringing a great deal of money into the region. The people of North and South Plotzonia were ethnically almost identical— Caucasian Christians of the Eastern Orthodox variety. Due to the Great Schism of 1304, they'd belonged to two different sects of the Plotzonian Orthodox Church. They squabbled constantly and only knew peace under the iron hand of foreigners—the Ottoman Turks, Napoleon, the Russian czars, and after World War Two, the U.S.S.R.

"The most popular Plotzonian singer is Irina Illyishum, known as Plotzonia's Celine Dion. She blends pop music with the balalaika and a local wind instrument known as the fimpin. It's torture to listen to it, and they play it everywhere, from loudspeakers, in the tea houses, in the bazaars, at parties, in music videos on TV. TV! The government, my father, controls the television and radio, and we only have two old American TV programs, *Highway to Heaven*, and *Little House on the Prairie*. Michael Landon is almost a god in my country. The most popular Plotzonian TV show is called *Nation and Destiny* . . ."

"An uplifting drama about a family of smelters," I said.

"You know it?" Nadia said.

"Plotzonia TV tried to sell it to my network, and that's how they promo'd it—an uplifting drama about a family of smelters. It was one of the most depressing shows I've ever seen in my life."

Funny, all I would have had to ask to know the country she and Rocky were from was "What is the most popular TV program made in your country?" One simple question, and I hadn't thought to ask it.

"I had satellite TV, but the common people do not, and so they are very stupid," Nadia said.

We could smell the convent now. Phil stopped the car and insisted we go over the plan. When he was satisfied we were all in sync, he handed the wheel over to me. I dropped him and Maggie off outside the range of the main gate's video cameras, Nadia put her suitcase into the trunk of the car, and she and I proceeded to the gate.

After pushing the buzzer, Rocky's voice said, "Nadia?"

"Yes, I'm here, Rocky," she shouted out the window.

"Who else is with you?"

"Just Robin."

The gates opened, and we drove up the curved driveway to the front of the convent. Before leaving the car, I took the safety off Mrs. Ramirez's pearl-handled pistol, and slipped it into my blazer pocket.

When Rocky opened the door, he was standing there with Mrs. Ramirez, who was gagged with duct tape, a gun to her head.

"Nadia," he said, softly, when he saw her. But the softness didn't last long. "Go into the parlor—that way. Move!"

In the parlor, some of the Sisters were leaning against one wall, their arms linked, their hands cuffed behind their backs in a human chain. Where did he get handcuffs? I wondered. They were all gagged with duct tape as well, and their legs were bound. On the floor by the nuns, I saw Señor, his feet tied calf-roping style with red cake-box ribbons, his mouth muzzled with a rubber band. He was growling through his muzzle. Rocky had shown the dog enough mercy to remove his little habit and throw it onto a chair, thus restoring a modicum of dignity to him.

"Where are the other Sisters?" I asked.

"I locked them in the chapel," he said with a bit of pride. "Throw down your gun."

"What gun?" I asked.

"The pearl-handled pistol," he said.

"I left it at home."

"Throw down your gun or I'm shooting Mrs. Ramirez."

In a situation like this, you have to stop and think like a NATO general, weigh the potential collateral damage against the greater, utilitarian benefits. Mrs. Ramirez was very old, she'd lived a long life and was looking forward to going to Jesus. If it would save the lives of the five nuns, a Plotzonian princess, a chihuahua, and me. . . .

But I couldn't do it. I took the gun out of my pocket and put it on the floor.

"Kick it away," he said, and I did.

"Nadia, cuff Robin with the nuns," he said.

"Rocky, this isn't going to help," Nadia said. "Let's just go."

"Tie her up, woman!" He then said something in Plotzonian, she said something back in the same tongue, and then she complied and cuffed me. I was arm in arm with the nun chain, right next to the Mother Superior, Nadia cuffing my hands while Rocky supervised.

"Gag her," he said, throwing Nadia a roll of silver duct tape.

Nadia complied with this request a little too quickly, in my opinion.

Well, smart girl, I asked myself, how are you going to get out of this one? I was chained to five nuns, my hands tied, a gun to Mrs. Ramirez's head. My feet were tied too, so I couldn't kick anything at Rocky to distract him so Nadia could grab the gun. In any event, the nearest kickable object was the trussed-up Señor.

"Okay, Rocky, let's go now," Nadia said.

"Not until you get on your knees and beg my forgiveness for running out on me," he said.

"On my knees?" she said with a snort.

"On your knees, woman."

Where was Phil, I wondered, and tried to send a telepathic message to him—"Hurry!"—then tried to send a longer one to Nadia—"Use those damned feminine wiles and tricks of yours, girl! Bat those eyes at him, lick your lower lip, invite him to kiss you, and when he does, grab his gun and knee him in the balls at the same time! If that doesn't work, turn on the waterworks and soften him with tears!" But she did not pick up the signal.

As Nadia knelt, Rocky said, "Did you have sexual intercourse with that man?"

"Rocky, this is insane . . ."

"Did you?" he asked, jamming the gun hard into Mrs. Ramirez's head.

Nadia hesitated before answering, and there was a glint of defiance in her face. But she said, "No."

"Why not?"

"Because I still love you, Rocky," she said. "Deep down, I always loved you."

"You swear?"

"I swear. There wasn't time for anything to happen. I found out what a devil he was in time. He put me under a spell, that man," she said, and added something in Plotzonian. They moved back and forth between English and Plotzonian, as if they weren't even aware they were doing it. It made it hard to know what was being decided.

"Beg for my forgiveness."

"Forgive me, Rocky. Forgive me. Forgive me."

He said something in Plotzonian. It sounded like "vizhee co tebya" something something something . . .

Nadia caught my eye, looked back at Rocky, and said in English, "I don't know how to get the Baby back. I sold it."

"You sold it? Who to?"

"A woman."

"Where is she?"

"I don't know."

He walked over to me, dragging Mrs. Ramirez by the scruff of her dress. "Do you know?"

I shook my head.

Behind Rocky, Phil appeared in the doorway, and my spirits lifted, until Phil lurched forward and I saw his hands were cuffed behind his back and he was being pushed by the brown-eyed man with the bad toupee, now sans the AstroTurf. Behind them came a heavier-set man with blue eyes, pushing Maggie.

Bad Toupee spoke in Plotzonian, gesturing to his prisoners with a gun. Rocky barked out something, and the two men took Phil and Maggie away at gunpoint.

"You're locking them in the chapel?" Nadia said. "You're not going to hurt them, are you?"

"No," Rocky said, though he was probably lying. "Not if we have no more trouble."

He and Nadia argued in Plotzonian about the Baby.

Finally, Nadia blurted out in English, "All right, all right. I sold it to Miriam Grundy. She has it. Talk to her."

"We must go get the icon," Rocky said. "If she won't give it back, we'll force her to give it to us. Where is she?"

"At the Chelsea Hotel," Nadia said.

chapter sixteen

There's always that point, in the middle of a jam, when the usually dormant voice in the back of my head suddenly awakens and asks, "Where the hell are we and how did we get ourselves into this one, Robin?"

You probably know that voice. It's the voice of reason. Sometimes events carry a person away, and the resulting clamor drowns out that voice until it's almost too late.

In the past, I've heard it ask, "Robin, why are we beating that woman with her own comatose grandmother?" "Why are we locked in a cage like a lab animal?" "Why are we in black leather slave outfits and why are we being chased by a man with a sofa glued to his back?"

Now it was asking, "Robin, why are we chained to a bunch of nuns in the back of a cake-delivery van speeding its way into Manhattan to try to recover a legendary holy icon, and how the hell did we get here?"

Rocky and his two Plotzonian henchmen had this bright idea. They took me and the five nuns and joined us in a circle, with Rocky and Nadia in the center. On the upside, they untied our legs so we could walk in this awkward knot of nuns as one, like the crew of WJM in the group hug scene on the last episode of *The Mary Tyler Moore Show* except that we were facing outward, not inward.

We formed a human shield around Rocky and Nadia. We were Rocky's insurance policy. Bad Toupee—whose name, I gathered, was Pavli—was driving. The guy with the blue eyes had been left behind to watch Phil, Maggie, Mrs. Ramirez, and the nuns who were locked in the chapel. I'd managed to talk Rocky out of taking Mrs. Ramirez with us, pointing out that as a frail old woman (ha!) she would only slow him down. Nadia then pointed out that with five nuns, me, and a smattering of firearms, what more protection did they need?

Now that I was in the jam, the question was, How do I get out of it with minimum loss of life? Clearly, we knew too much and there would be considerable incentive to kill all of us once we were no longer needed, all except Nadia, who would either escape again, or get dragged back to Plotzonia to marry Rocky. Did Plotzonia have an extradition agreement with the United States, I wondered? As a haven for criminals and gunrunners, it was unlikely. If we all died, who would be able to tell this story, implicate the future dictator of Plotzonia, and see justice done? Lucia? She didn't have much of the story, and wasn't all that credible, being a scandalous exile who drank cocktails for lunch. Miriam Grundy knew about Nadia and the icon, but she didn't know Nadia's country or anything that didn't seem to pertain to the icon itself. The Zenmaster wouldn't get involved. Carlos the bullfighter had been gored in the head and had a short-term memory problem. The others who had come in contact with Nadia had only the tiniest pieces of the puzzle. With no witnesses left, what would the police think when they found a bunch of dead Sisters and a few dead laypeople in a convent on Long Island? What possible motive would they find for the mass murder of cake-baking nuns? Would a link be made to the profane and satanic graffiti on the convent walls the year before?

It wasn't hard to see how this would play out. The public out-cry would force a massive police investigation. With no witnesses or real clues, a witch hunt for satanists, wiccans, and New Age flakes would ensue, until some grandiose, recently released mental patient was arrested and either railroaded or induced into con-fessing to a crime he didn't commit. A crime like that can't remain "unsolved."

Six months later, someone would find a dog chewing on my femur in the Brooklyn dunes, and police dogs would sniff out the handcuffed remains of the other dead nuns. A mental patient would confess to these crimes too, and issue a manifesto talking about his regular visits preceding the crime, from the Archangel Gabriel, who appeared in the form of a mild-mannered hardware clerk talking in code at the local ServiStar.

Pavli of the bad toupee said something sharply in Plotzonian.

"You think we're being followed? Who is following us?" Nadia asked, thoughtfully translating into English for the benefit of the rest of us.

More Plotzonian jangled through the air.

"The Knights of St. Michael the Martyr!" Nadia said. "How did they find us?"

Pavli said something, including, in English, "Long Island Ex-pressway."

"You thought you lost them on the Long Island Expressway on your way to the convent to meet Rocky?" Nadia repeated. "You fool. You know what will happen if they get their hands on me and Rocky? And the icon? Lose them!"

Pavli stepped on the gas, and Nadia screamed, "You fool! You want to attract the police and get a speeding ticket?"

Pavli began switching lanes, cutting from one into another, throwing us from side to side with every swerve, and taking a hard left onto a very bumpy road, so that the nuns and I bounced up and down on our bums. Three more hard lefts followed, until we were back on smooth highway. Pavli chuckled. We must have lost the Knights.

We rumbled over some kind of metal bridge, and slowed down. Through the back window of the van, which the Mother Superior, another nun, and I were facing, it looked like we were in Manhattan. Within ten minutes, we had pulled to a stop.

"Now what, Rocky?" Nadia asked.

"We'll go inside, and try to convince this woman to return the icon. Pavli will stay here. When we have the icon, we'll—" And he slipped back into Plotzonian again.

"Using the nuns as protection is a good idea, Rocky, in case we run into the Knights or the police. But why do we have to take a boat AND a ship AND an airplane to get home?" Nadia asked.

"Because that is what is decided," Rocky said.

Yeah, with a gun you can control your woman, I thought. Even with a gun, he wasn't manly. He was sullen and childish. If he succeeded in dragging Nadia back to Plotzonia, and marrying her, I gave the whole thing six months. If Nadia held on, it would only be until such time as her husband actually took power, and then he'd be found poisoned in the john while his wife engineered a coup Catherine the Great style. Or the common people she disparaged would overthrow them and display their dismembered heads on pikes high atop the palace walls.

Nadia would, I hoped, say something to Miriam Grundy that would tip her off that something was amiss, and Miriam Grundy would call the cops.

Next to me, the Mother Superior gave me a look. I wasn't sure what it meant, just that it was supposed to mean something. She looked down at her feet, and I noticed she had wiggled her foot half out of her shoe, which was really more of a slipper.

When Rocky and Nadia crawled out between our linked arms and jumped out of the van, the Mother Superior's foot pushed forward, so the toe of her slipper was caught between the van doors, preventing the latch from fully catching. Quietly, and with as little movement as possible, she pushed the shoe upward and wiggled it until the latch loosened and the van door, with a soft click, opened the barest smidgen. She pulled the slipper back.

The Mother Superior tugged lightly on my arm, and at the arm of the woman next to her, who spread the tug around the circle until it came back to me and we inched ever so slightly toward the door, then stopped. We waited a moment—had to do this carefully so as not to alarm Pavli—and then moved forward another half inch or so.

We were mere inches from the door when Pavli erupted in what sounded like some pretty ripe Plotzonian cussing. He turned the engine back on and shifted into gear. As he did this, we bumped quickly toward the door, but were not able to get out until he suddenly pulled out, the van doors flew open, and we went tumbling in a pile on the pavement.

It took a moment to hoist ourselves to our feet, and there was no time to get untied, so with Mother Superior in the lead, and me at her right hand, the nuns and I began moving as one down the block, toward the Chelsea Hotel about fifty feet away. Pavli was in traffic now, and behind him was the car that had followed us on the way in, which slammed into the space Pavli had just vacated. Out of the corner of my eye, I saw Pavli jump out of the van in the middle of traffic and head our way on foot.

Remember, we were still gagged, so we couldn't shout out anything such as "Call the cops" when we went into the Chelsea Hotel, a knot of gagged nuns. Here, where a scene from *Aida* was once filmed with live lions and the composer George Kleinsinger used to walk his alligator in the hallway, where Sarah Bernhardt had slept in a coffin and William Burroughs wrote *Naked Lunch,* where Robert Oppenheimer pondered the implications of his bomb, and painters of every major school of the twentieth century had worked, lived, loved, and passed out in the hallways, it was natural to assume five nuns and an incongruous redhead, tied together in a circle and gagged, were some sort of performance art or surrealist statement.

I tried to mime "Take the gags off" to our fellow elevator

passengers, who unfortunately were three Mary Sue women, including the uptight one who looked like Marilyn Quayle, back presumably from a day learning how to rip off windows, orphans, and unemployed homeowners. Frantically, I waved my face at them, trying to communicate with my eyes that I wanted the gag off, but they just backed into a corner, forming their own little knot, while one pushed the seventh-floor button repeatedly, as if this might make the elevator go faster or make us vanish. The nun knot jumped over so I could lean down to the panel and punch 10 with my nose. As soon as I pressed it, the uptight woman who kind of looked like Marilyn Quayle screamed and sprayed me with pepper spray, missing my eyes and nose, but getting my cheek.

It stung like a sonofabitch. Unable to scream or gesticulate, I started writhing and twitching in pain, causing the nuns in the circle to bump awkwardly against each other, like buoys tied together in rough waters. This was the last straw for the uptight woman, who fainted just moments before the elevator stopped on seven. The other two pastel women each grabbed an arm of their fainted friend. They didn't even take the time to try to help her to her feet. They half-ran out, dragging her down the hallway behind them.

The elevator doors closed and we lurched upward. Half my face stung and one eye was watering. At ten, we got off and, with me in the lead, shuffled quickly toward Miriam Grundy's apartment.

Mother Superior pushed the doorbell with her nose, my face being a tad tender, and a butler, painted all blue and naked except for a blue loincloth, answered. We shoved past him, into the apartment, through the hallway to the spiral staircase up to her studio. The spiral staircase was a challenge for the six of us, but we managed to get up it. All the while, I was listening for the next doorbell, the one that might be Pavli, or the Knights of St. Michael the Martyr.

There was a real variety of humanity in this room, from men

in black tie and women in formal dress to men with pompadours and zoot suits and women in pink leopard print and feather boas. That was in addition to several "living statues," actors painted chalk white, posing very still in various positions, the Swinging Miriams female impersonators, some very, very short waiters, and a couple of tall people here just to mingle. Miriam was nowhere in sight.

As the gagged nuns and I moved as one among the guests, some man shouted, "Bravo! Bravo!" and started clapping, inciting others to applaud and cheer for us. The applause brought Miriam out from a room off the studio.

"What is going on?" she asked.

Behind her, Rocky appeared. When he saw us, he pulled out his gun and put it to Miriam's head.

"Nobody move," he said.

The guests laughed and clapped some more.

"I want the icon now," he demanded.

"I told you I don't have it," Miriam said. To her guests, she screamed, "This is not art!"

"Where is it?" Rocky asked.

"I don't know. This is not art!" said Miriam.

"Shut up," said Rocky.

"This is a challenging piece," said a woman behind me.

At this point, Pavli appeared, waving his gun in the air as he made his way through the crowd. I looked at the Mother Superior, trying to catch some hint that she knew what to do. But she looked as baffled as me. She shrugged. I shrugged. We began to shuffle toward Pavli, pushing some of the crowd ahead of us toward him, when the latest complication arrived, the Knights of St. Michael the Martyr, one of whom shot his gun into the air, silencing the crowd at last.

But the guests were only quiet for a moment, and then spontaneously burst into more laughter and applause.

When the Knights saw Rocky with his gun, they each grabbed

a hostage, a Living Statue and a Swinging Miriam. There was some shouting in Plotzonian, and Ben appeared, holding up the icon.

"Ben, no," Miriam said.

Rocky let go of Miriam and grabbed the icon. Pavli grabbed Miriam Grundy. One of the Knights pointed his gun at Rocky, and Rocky then pointed his gun at the icon of the baby Jesus and yelled something in Plotzonian.

The Knights dropped their guns and released their hostages.

"Nadia?" Rocky called. "Nadia? NADIA?"

Nadia had vanished.

Holding the icon hostage, Rocky stormed across the room, fell to the floor, and crawled between me and the nuns, reemerging in the center of the nun knot. With the icon in one hand, and a gun in the other—pointed at my head—he pushed us out of the studio and down the spiral staircase. I could hear Miriam Grundy behind us—"This is not art! This is not art!" and "Stop pulling my hair."

When we got out the door, Pavli let Miriam go, and ran ahead of us to push the elevator button. There was no time to wait for it. We were pushed toward the wrought-iron stairwell that runs up the center of the building. It was just a matter of time before one of us tripped and we went rolling down.

That's when I thought, I might as well take the bullet. It's a far, far better thing I do, etc. etc., and it could prevent something worse, the deaths of all the nuns. What did I have to live for after all, now that I knew Pierre loved another? But first I needed to cripple Rocky to help give the other nuns the advantage, and so I could get a little revenge before I left this vale of tears.

My hands were cuffed, but my fingers were free. Suddenly, I reached back and grabbed the little gangster where he lived, yanking hard, really hard. I had a lot of pent-up anger. I grabbed him so hard that instead of shooting me, he shot above my head, into a painting on the wall. The nun knot bounced against the wall, and the gun flew out of Rocky's hand and rattled down the stairs. Now he was unarmed, surrounded by six really pissed-off women with cuffed hands but free fingers.

What we had here was a Man Trap.

Pavli went to retrieve the gun. Behind us, the Knights, having retrieved their weapons and their living statue hostages, were shouting in their harsh language. We were caught between them, Rocky and the icon between us. At the tenth-floor stairwell railing, Miriam's guests were watching, amused, a couple taking pictures, still not getting the message that this was not art. Below us, other residents had come out to see what was going on, including Lucia and Carlos, and were staring up the stairwell.

It was a stand-off, and we were in the crossfire if anyone started shooting.

Someone did, one of the Knights, but he missed us and hit Pavli in the chest. Pavli crumpled onto the delicate and beautiful wrought-iron railing, and fell over it, plunging all the way down to the first floor.

The party guests oohed and ahed as he was falling down, and stopped, and stared, as it dawned on them that this was not all part of the performance. Then they started screaming.

Amid the loud, Plotzonian shouting and the screaming of the party guests came a clear New York voice. It was Detective Burns of the NYPD.

"Put down your guns," he shouted. "Police. You're surrounded."

He was standing on the tenth floor. Behind him, blue uniforms spilled out of the elevator, while other cops ran up the stairs toward us. The cavalry had arrived.

chapter seventeen

I knew a little about the icon," Ben admitted. "And I knew I hadn't hired nuns and gunmen for Miriam's party, so naturally, when I saw them, I did the logical thing. I called the police."

We'd all of us been taken to Manhattan South to give formal statements, and Ben and his lawyer were with a cop at the desk next to me. That cop got the logical explanation.

Detective Burns, who was interviewing me, asked, "The Knights of St. Michael the Martyr grabbed the Living Statue and the Swinging Miriam before or after the Plotzonian princess escaped?"

"I don't know," I said. "In all the commotion I didn't see Nadia leave."

"And the gagged nuns were—" The phone rang, and he stopped to pick it up.

My face hurt like hell. In addition to the residual sting of the pepper spray, the duct tape hurt when it was ripped off, leaving a big red rectangle of irritated skin behind. Nuns, Living Statues, Swinging Miriams, the real Miriam Grundy, selected party guests, and a few of their lawyers were giving statements at other desks.

The nuns all had red marks from the duct tape and were all rapidly fingering their rosaries.

After Burns got off the phone, he said, "That was the police station in Fowler, Long Island. Everyone at the convent is alive and well."

Across the room, another detective called out, "State Department is here about the Plotzonians."

"This one is going to put diplomatic immunity to the test," Burns said. "You think one of these guys killed Woznik? I'd sure like a murder rap to help fight State on this one."

"One of them probably, but I don't know which one," I said.

"We'll be able to put the cohorts away, and the Knights, but the young man, this Rocky, he's the son of a big guy in his homeland. The State Department wants him. Apparently, some USAID workers are being held hostage in South Plotzonia, and they want to trade for them."

"So he'll go unpunished?"

"We'll see. Let's go over what we have so far. Rocky showed up at the apartment where you were staying. You sent him away. Nadia showed up and you let her in . . ."

We went over it twice before he thanked me and said I could go.

"So when will I get my rifle back?"

"I'll get it to you as soon as I clear up a few other things," he said.

At the next desk, Ben was saying, "Unfortunately, Miriam gave the girl the money for the icon tonight, at gunpoint, so she's out quite a lot of money. A million, maybe more. Cash."

Ah, good old Nadia. Still looking out for number one, even at the height of a crisis. She got the money from Miriam and now she was on her way to God knows where. What the hell. The rest of us were safe and sound now, and not inclined to worry about her welfare any longer.

On my way out, I ran into the Mother Superior, who had just finished up with the cops.

"I know this great after-hours joint. What do you say we grab the girls and go for a few belts," I said to her. "It's Miller time."

She laughed and said, "Some other time, perhaps for lunch, if not for . . . belts. We come into the city every now and then to see shows and go to museums. Perhaps you can join us."

"Yeah, that'd be fun. Hey, I'm sorry I got you into this."

"Oh, it worked out all right," she said. "It certainly won't hurt the Sisters of the Wretched Souls."

"It's good publicity."

"It is indeed, especially with Him." She looked upward. "Do let us know if we can help again on the underground railroad."

"Seriously? Even after all this?"

"Yes, of course. Though, perhaps next time you could do some research and make sure the people we're helping deserve our help."

"You are one cool nun."

One of the younger nuns came to say a car was there to return them to Long Island. I grabbed a cab back to the Chelsea, dragging my beleaguered, weathered old ass past the Zenmaster, past Lucia, who patted my arm on the way to Tamayo's door. I barely had the strength to punch in the security numbers. When I got inside, Louise Bryant jumped me, claws out.

She wanted to be fed.

Before I went to bed, I unplugged Tamayo's phone. In the morning, I plugged it in again and called Maggie, to see if she'd made it home all right and wanted to swap escape stories. Phil, Maggie, and the nuns imprisoned in the chapel had simply waited until the man with the bushy mustache fell asleep. Then they took his gun, woke him up, and drove into Fowler, Long Island, and the cop shop. They got there shortly after events went down at Miriam Grundy's party.

"Our escape wasn't nearly as dramatic as yours," Maggie said. "We got less than an inch in the newspapers. But there's a huge picture of you and the nuns, tied up and gagged. Have you seen it?"

"I'll read all the papers later," I said.

"The *News-Journal* is calling the murders of Woznik and the Plotzonian man . . ."

"Pavli," I provided. "Mr. Bad Toupee number one."

". . . the 'Chelsea Girl Murders,' because we were all involved, and it happened in the Chelsea Hotel. We helped solve the case," Maggie said.

"Well, except for the murder of Gerald Woznik. We still don't know who pulled the trigger on him," I said.

"We may never know," Maggie said.

"I hate it when murderers get away," I said.

"Come by for coffee later," Maggie said. "I have to go now. I have to call Paris."

I didn't bother to say good-bye. At that, I hung up the phone. I felt sick and sad, because now I didn't believe in love anymore, not at all. Pierre had been the last chance for that misty-pink romance stuff. My instincts about love could no longer be trusted. I'd never been able to trust those instincts, but now I was aware of it. Even the few examples of true love I'd observed weren't enough to give me faith, because if you look at them in the long term, all great love affairs end badly, if not in heartbreak, then in death.

After a shot of vodka—I earned it, dammit—I went online to see if there was any E-mail.

Someone was knocking on the door and shouting, "Miss Hudson? This is Belinda Jacobs from the All News Network. Will you come out and speak to us please?"

ANN is my alma mater, in a way, but there was no way I was going out there, even if I hadn't looked through the peephole and seen two other news crews standing in the hallway.

Tamayo still hadn't E-mailed. Pierre had, as had assorted friends and coworkers who had heard the news. I didn't read his E-mail right away. I wrote Tamayo a long note with a link to an online news story about the latest adventure.

"If you see Nadia in your travels, have her give me a call," I wrote.

Before I opened Pierre's message, I poured myself a cup of coffee, and read through a few messages from other friends, my "real" friends.

"Robin, Robin, Robin. What am I going to do with you?" asked Louis Levin. "Did anyone videotape that by any chance? There's a picture of you from the Fotofax this morning, up on Democracy Wall. You're gagged with a bunch of nuns, and there's a sheet underneath for a caption contest. When you've got your sea legs again, get in touch. There's a lot brewing here."

"CALL ME!" wrote Claire Thibodeaux.

"Your aunt Minnie and I dropped off the old oven at the Eco-center today and then we went to Duluth to do some shopping. We had lunch with Marianne Hallett, who used to be Marianne Presslee when you went to school together. She sent her regards," wrote my mother, who is now online but mercifully lives in a news-free zone of her own creation.

I left Jerry's E-mail, and Solange's, and a few others unopened, and opened Pierre's.

He hadn't heard the news either.

"Dear Robin," he wrote. "Very busy here at the lab. Have hardly had a moment for anything but the experiment, but during those few moments I've had to myself, I've thought about our time in Paris. I hope all is well. When are you coming back to Paris? With a kiss, Pierre."

It was painful. I hadn't felt this much pain about a lover in a long, long time. How could he have written those sweet notes he'd left on my pillow each morning in Paris, those notes about rogue planets, empathic photons, astronomically inspired strange attractors? Or looked at me the way he did, kissed me the way he did? Heartless bastard! In a flash, my pain turned to raw anger.

Furious, I wrote back: "You have a lot of nerve sending me a kiss when you're having an affair with Maggie Mason. Nice try, bud. Fool me once, shame on you. Fool me twice, shame on me. You can kiss my hairy white derriere, you phony French fuck."

I hesitated for a moment before I sent it. I couldn't help imagining how crummy he'd feel when he found out that I knew Maggie Mason. How would it be, next time he and Maggie got together, with her not knowing about him and me? It kind of irritated me to think he might compensate by being extra sweet and loving to her. And as she did not know about Pierre and me, she would eventually bring up my name despite her rule about not discussing her girlfriends with her boyfriend and vice versa. If she couldn't keep to the part about not discussing her beau, she was bound to mention me, maybe in connection with this adventure. How would that make him feel? Would he feel guilty? Would he bristle? Would Maggie wonder why he was reacting so? Unable to get an explanation that didn't blow his cover, would she think it was because of something wrong with her, or with him? Would this toxic secret fester and explode and bring them both heartbreak?

That should have given me a little schadenfreude rush, but it didn't. I was too sad and sick about it to enjoy even a moment of hard-earned shameful joy.

I hit the Send button and watched the message vanish into the ether before I logged off.

As soon as I did, a key turned in the lock, the door opened, and the alarm went off with a shriek.

Tamayo was standing there, news crews behind her trying to see in.

After I turned off the alarm, she said, "Robin, what the hell is going on?"

"GEE, NADIA WAS ALWAYS a riot when I was with her," Tamayo said after I filled her in. "Spoiled, but fun."

"I guess I missed her fun side," I said.

"But, Robin, I don't understand. Why were you staying here in the first place?"

"My apartment burned down," I said.

"Wow. You've had a bad week."

"No shit. What are you doing back in America?"

"Buzzer and I broke up," she said. "I felt like coming home to recuperate. Also, I was running out of money."

"Sorry about you and Buzzer," I said. "Oh, and by the way, thanks for telling me to look up your pal Pierre in Paris."

"Oh, you saw Pierre! Isn't he wonderful? I knew you'd like each other."

"Wonderful? Tamayo, you are far too liberal in your friendships. He's a jerk! Didn't you also introduce him to Maggie Mason?"

"Oh. Maggie. I forgot to tell you about Maggie . . ."

"You forgot to tell me about Maggie and Pierre?"

"No, about Maggie and Mike O'Reilly. They had an on-and-off thing for quite a while and . . . Maggie and Pierre?"

"Her boyfriend, who happens to be my last fling, Pierre."

"Pierre is not her boyfriend. Pierre only met Maggie a few times. He didn't like her, and she didn't like him. She's involved with some actor who is off on location somewhere."

As tired as I was, it took a full ten seconds to put this together.

"That bitch!" I said. "I just sent Pierre an E-mail asking him to kiss my hairy white derriere for having an affair with me and with her at the same time."

"Oh, she's wicked," Tamayo said, somewhere between sympathy for me and admiration for Maggie's revenge. "Unfortunately, Maggie knew about you and Mike. I should have warned you."

"She didn't let on that she knew," I said. "That bitch."

The next sound Tamayo heard was me slamming the balcony doors. Furiously, I pounded on Maggie's balcony doors, and when she opened them, I stormed in screaming.

"How did you know about Pierre?"

Maggie turned and looked at me coolly. "When I spoke with Nadia, just after she arrived, I asked her all about you. In retrospect, I should have been trying to get more information about her but I was more interested in getting something on you. I picked up a little more information eavesdropping on you and Phil when you were on the balcony one evening."

The nerve of this woman. She was proud of herself.

"Who did you call when you were supposedly calling Paris?"

"Who knows? Some bewildered stranger in a foreign country speaking a language I didn't understand. Check your phone bill when it comes in. It should say."

I let loose with a blizzard of cussing. When I was done, she said, very calmly, "Well, that's what you get for sleeping with Michael O'Reilly. I loved that rat bastard and he dumped me to start going out with you."

"You know, I was unaware that you were involved with Mike while I was. I didn't hurt you on purpose," I said. "You hurt me on purpose."

"You must have known. How could you not know? Didn't you wonder who had listed you in the pen pal pages of *Prison Life Magazine*?" she asked.

"That was you too?" I asked.

"Now we're even," she said. "Now we can be friends."

"Friends?" I said, heading to the balcony doors to leave. "We can never be friends, Maggie."

I slammed the balcony doors behind me, and went back into Tamayo's to write an apologetic, explanatory note to Pierre. I had a feeling that if he accepted my apology and gave me another chance, I'd be kissing his hairy white derriere for some time to come.

chapter eighteen

There are always some unanswered questions in these matters, but there was one that I just couldn't let go of. Who had actually fired the gun that killed Gerald Woznik?

There was only one way to find out. I went back to the Zenmaster and asked him if he wouldn't like to give up his enlightened isolation and rejoin the human race, if he wouldn't like to dance with someone, or share stories, or maybe even hug someone again. He didn't respond. I said, "Think about this: Your efforts not to have an effect have had an effect. You've had a damaging effect by trying not to have an effect. You can't escape it." At the time, he'd stepped backward into his room and slammed the door again. But that must have got him thinking.

The next day I actually saw him leave his apartment, go down to the deli, and come back with newspapers. He looked as if he had tears in his eyes. For a few days he didn't leave his apartment and didn't stand in his doorway. Then, one day, I was walking by in the hallway and he stopped me and very quietly told me who it was.

Rocky.

Rocky had fired the gun that killed Gerald.

Later that day, the Zenmaster gave his statement to Detective Burns.

Bit by bit, other gaps were filled. Rocky and his henchmen had tracked Nadia to the Chelsea and planned to spring a surprise on her and drag her back to Plotzonia. Rocky thought the manly thing to do was to go to New York himself, knock off his rival, and take Nadia and the baby Jesus icon back to Plotzonia. And the cynics say romance is dead.

FOR SEVERAL DAYS, I avoided Maggie Mason. On one of the last mornings of my vacation, Tamayo woke me up, shouting, "Rise and shine," while kicking the sofa bed to make sure I rattled awake.

"Come to class with me. I already fed your cat. Just throw on some crappy clothes and let's go," she said.

"What class?" I asked.

"Nude male figure drawing. It's a drop-in class. You can use my supplies. But hurry, we have to get there early or the pensioners will get the good seats."

"I don't want to go to a class," I said. "I want to enjoy the rest of my vacation."

"You must come to class with me," she said. "I insist."

I don't know why I'm so weak in the face of Tamayo's whims, but she has a way of convincing me and legions of other people to do things they might not normally do, like shelter runaway brides. After I threw on some clothes, she handed me a pair of binoculars.

"What are these for?"

"In case the pensioners get all the good seats," she said. "So we can see the model."

The class was drop-in for Art League members, who were allowed to bring one guest with the payment of the guest fee, supplies extra. The model wasn't there yet. As Tamayo had predicted, most of the seats were taken by elderly women.

"What did I tell you?" she said. "Back of the class."

We took seats at easels beside each other. Tamayo gave me some charcoal, and put her bag on the empty seat on the other side.

"Who are you saving that seat for?" I asked.

"Another friend," she said.

Far at the front of the room, the model appeared, dropped his towel, and took his place reclining on a mat. He was a chiseled, Chippendale type, not my type personally but who seemed the ideal for drawing musculature and so forth.

That's when Tamayo's friend, Mary Margaret Mason, came rushing in.

"Sorry I'm late, Tamayo," she said, stopping short when she saw me. "What are you . . ."

"I'm leaving," I said, standing up.

"Sit down," Tamayo said. "I've been thinking that if peace can't be made between Maggie Mason and Robin Hudson, what hope is there for the Middle East, or the Balkans? I'm having a big . . . party soon, and I want you both to be there, and I don't want you bringing this hatred and tension to my big event."

"Ssssh!" hissed the instructor.

We sat down, slowly, warily, not wanting to be the first to sit. Just as Maggie's "bum" touched the seat, I held back, squeezing a childish victory from the fact that she sat down first. Then I sat down.

"Okay, this is the deal," Tamayo said. "Maggie was wrong to pretend she was sleeping with Pierre. Very wrong. Right, Maggie?"

Maggie hesitated.

"Maggie, this is very important to me. You know that was wrong," Tamayo said. "Unnecessarily mean. Right?"

Neither Maggie nor I would give any quarter.

The instructor came by and made a disapproving noise when she saw my sketch. I'd made a stab at something vaguely resembling the naked man far at the front of the room, then tried a stick figure, then gave up and drew a horse head, the only thing I can draw with any skill. No doubt she thought I was some kind of perv who took this class just to stare at naked men.

"You're in a benevolent mood," I said to Tamayo. "If she'd played this childish girl game with you, you'd feel differently. Why is it so damned important Maggie and I—"

"Buzzer called me last night, to make up. He wants to get married."

"Are you going to marry him?" Maggie and I asked in unison.

"Maybe. And if I do, I want both of you to be my witnesses. My best women. So you have to get along, for me and Buzzer," Tamayo said. "Maggie, Robin didn't know about you and Mike. I know she didn't. You should apologize for getting revenge."

"She didn't? Are you sure . . ."

"She didn't. I swear. Apologize."

"I apologize."

"And you promise not to play any more mean jokes."

"I promise not to play mean jokes on Robin," she said, adding a nice little qualifier there. That still left the rest of the free world for her to victimize.

"Good. Robin, now you accept Maggie's apology. Please? It's so important to me."

It took every last residual drib of Christian goodness left in the cracks of my hard heart to do it, but I said, "I accept your apology."

"Now, Robin, you have to admit that Maggie's prank was brilliant. Wrong, but brilliant."

"It was brilliant," I said. "EVIL genius."

"Really brilliant," Tamayo repeated. "We give you points for creativity, Maggie. Okay? Shake hands."

We shook hands, but very quickly.

"Peace, between two of my friends," Tamayo said happily. "I am SO good."

Peace maybe, but friendship, never. I'd be watching my back for . . . forever.

Tamayo? Married? These were two words I never thought I'd see side by side in a sentence. Jesus, love was breaking out all around, like a virus or something. Will people never learn?

A COUPLE OF WEEKS AFTER the big Plotzonian caper, Phil and Helen picked me up at the Chelsea and we walked together back to the old neighborhood for a tenants' meeting at the community center on East Tenth Street.

"Have you been back to the building since the fire?" Helen asked.

"Not yet. Have you?"

"It's grim," she warned.

We rounded Tenth Street from Avenue B. Even from the corner, the damage was obvious. Up close, it was heartbreaking. My windows, the windows of the apartments on both sides of me, those directly above and both stories below, looked gutted. Black soot rimmed the windows. It made me think of mascara around the eyes of a weeping woman. Bits of half-burned things still lay on the ground beside the stoop—charred photos, letters, clothing, the remains of Mr. O'Brien's mail-order-bride magazine.

Man oh man. That was the apartment I moved into not long after college. I'd been a young reporter in that apartment, a married woman, a divorced woman, a murder suspect, a crime fighter, an executive. Hundreds of scenes flashed before me in a slide show of memories—the day I moved in, numerous fights with Mrs. Ramirez in the hallways, the night my ex-husband proposed and the night he left me . . . All that history, up in smoke.

I lingered and looked until Helen Fitkis gently tugged me away.

The meeting was just starting when we walked into the community center. The Greek guy who owns the building and his lawyer told us they had decided to rebuild, but it was going to take time. We were given several options. We could move back in when it was done, we could break our leases, or we could move into a building he'd just bought in Brooklyn. Some insurance stuff was discussed, and Mr. Burpus asked when it would be safe to go into his old apartment just to get his things. A guy from the fire department said that "determination" would be made soon.

After the meeting, a few of us went to a neighborhood beanery and had a bite, some beers, and reminisced about the building and the tenants who had lived there. Mrs. Ramirez was sans Señor, her Chihuahua, who had remained behind at the convent. Dulcinia Ramirez intended to return to our building and had asked all the nuns to pray for its quick restoration. It was a safe bet the nuns had been praying for that since the day she arrived.

Mr. O'Brien and his housekeeper were hoping to return to the building too. Sally, my witchy neighbor, was going to the American Southwest to commune with spirits for a while, and didn't think she'd be coming back. She looked tired and seemed to need a rest.

But it was Phil, our super, and his friend Helen Fitkis who dropped the big bombshell.

"Time to move on," he said. We were all expecting him to announce he was going off to some refugee camp clinic somewhere, as Phil did that for a few months every year.

But instead he said, "We're going to retire," Phil said. "In Liverpool."

"Liverpool?"

"It's me home, luv," he said. "I'm seventy-five now. It's time to go home."

"And you're going too, Helen?"

She smiled and said, "Of course."

"Wow. Without you guys . . . the building won't be the same."

We all got quiet, kind of blown away by how much things were going to change for all of us. Then we hugged and said good-bye, promised we'd see each other again and keep in touch, and tried to believe it. But you know how that goes.

e p i l o g u e

Rocky's fate is under negotiation. The DA wants to keep him here and prosecute him for murder and a bunch of other stuff, and the State Department wants to trade him for hostages. Public opinion is leaning toward the hostage trade. Meanwhile, Rocky's been in jail for several weeks, and it's a safe bet he doesn't feel like such a big man now. For some weird reason though, I feel a bit bad for him. He got his heart broken and it made him crazy. Love makes people crazy.

But if he gets off, if he goes home scot-free, I am going to make him pay, one way or another. I don't know how yet. Maybe I'll consult with Maggie Mason, see what wicked ideas she has, because I'm fairly sure it's okay in this instance to wreak a wicked revenge, and why not put Maggie's dark powers to use for good instead of evil?

No charges were brought against anyone else, not Miriam or Ben, Grace or me or Nadia, thanks to our canny lawyers and our cooperation with law enforcement.

The baby Jesus icon, which the police recovered when they arrested Rocky, is now evidence and the object of dispute between

various Plotzonian sects, Russian museums, the Russian Orthodox Church, and Andrei Rublev lovers. Miriam Grundy is out
more than a million bucks for the icon. It's one of those things
like the ark in *Raiders of the Lost Ark,* or the spear of destiny
Hitler was so keen on, that is believed to have magical powers.
Seems like the damned thing has caused more trouble than it has
prevented, despite its legendary power to bring victory to those
who possess it. But people believe what they want to believe,
sometimes in defiance of all evidence.

When Grace Rouse learned that Nadia had betrayed her and
indirectly cost Gerald Woznik his life, she had a small breakdown.
After weeping, in a messy, red-nosed, rat-haired way for a week,
she pulled herself together and took off for a German spa to soak
her worries away and meditate, stopping at JFK to tell reporters
she was giving up on romance for good. From now on, she was
going to be a "Whore Queen," a rich woman who bestows her
various favors on young men willing to perform heroic deeds and
create great works of art to please her. Love was not a part of
this transaction.

Who knows where Nadia is? I haven't heard from the ungrateful brat since she went back to the Chelsea to collect the money
for the icon the night of Miriam's ill-fated party, though Tamayo
got an anonymized E-mail, dateline unknown, saying "Thanks"
and mentioning a new boyfriend, who "really is my true love this
time."

The Mary Sue women returned to their sweet-smelling home-
towns, no doubt happier and more appreciative of home than
they'd ever been before, which is a blessing in disguise for them.
I'm sure they'll all appreciate it more fully in a few years, with
the right combination of family support, talk therapy, and prescription medicine.

It'd be another month before I left the Chelsea Hotel, and I
have to say, the place really grew on me in that time. Along with
a healthy assortment of nutty artists, there were some fairly nor-
malish artists and other people, and a steady stream of travelers

from other places. There were a lot of children who lived in the hotel with their parents. I figured they must be warped, growing up in such a bohemian place, exposed to so much art, but I met some of them and they were pretty regular kids, preternaturally smart yet somehow more innocent than most kids you meet.

I can't explain what it is about the Chelsea that makes it the Chelsea, beyond the idiosyncratic architecture and the residents.

Maggie Mason, once we were back on civil (if not friendly) speaking terms, came closest to nailing the heart of the joint when I suggested over coffee at Tamayo's that the Chelsea was "hip."

"Hip? Hip? It's been on the downside of hip, it's been on the upside of hip, it's been 'in the gutter looking up at the stars,' " she said. "The Chelsea isn't hip. What the Chelsea is, is humane, through all times and fashions. It's the most humane place I've ever lived. It is a place that loves art, and artists, and, in a very broad way, all of humanity."

Not long before I left the Chelsea, I came in late one night. Right behind me came a woman, in her thirties, a coat over her nightclothes, carrying five big shopping bags in each hand. The bags were overflowing with personal belongings. She had obviously left somewhere in a hurry. She dropped the bags at the desk without saying a word, not even thinking to ask the bellman to help her, and ran back out to a waiting taxi to ferry in ten more shopping bags. One of them had a toaster sticking out of it, another a box of Eggo frozen waffles and a whip. She made one more trip to the taxi, and came back with three more bags and a dog. The staff didn't bat an eye at this and neither did I.

ONE LAST THING: The Holy Woman Empire.

While I was busy with the Plotzonian business, a major shakeup was brewing at the Worldwide Women's Network. The stockholders and advertisers were not happy with our very modest success and were demanding changes, big changes, and they were getting them.

Solange and Jerry had hired the executive producer of an

hour-long women's show on one of the broadcast networks to replace me. Jack Jackson and his new wife, Shonny Cobbs, met this woman at the Emmy Awards and were impressed with her success and her ideas, and asked Solange and Jerry to see if they couldn't use her at the network. This woman had won Emmys, had been a big mucky-muck editor at a major women's magazine, dated moguls. When Jerry and Solange suggested replacing me with her, Jack had to listen to them, and take into account that on top of the awards and other kudos, she had a proven track record in marketing and business leadership, whereas I, er, do not have those same credentials. Hey, I got street cred and that counts for something, but in the world of Big Media, her cred wins out.

Jack told me this himself, because that's the kind of guy he is, and because I am one of his "pets," along with Norma, the cafeteria lady, and Dr. Larry, a philosophy Ph.D. Jack met on a plane and later hired as his "official ethicist."

"We've got another job for you," he said. "It's a good job. We want you to set up a programming office overseas to develop new programming and repackage existing programming. The office would be set up within an existing news bureau for the All News Network, to keep overhead down and enable resources sharing. . . ."

"Where overseas?"

"You have a choice, Robin. London and Berlin are both big bureaus with good international broadcasting contacts, but my wife, Shonny, is convinced Paris would be the best choice. Shonny says the French raised all those girly things—perfume, fashion, cosmetics—to an art, but it's also a place with a tradition of women intellectuals. It's the city of love. Great all-round Chick City. You speak French?"

"I'll learn," I said.

I know a job in Paris is nothing to sneer at, but all the same, it was hard to go back to work, demoted, and face Jerry and Solange. When I got back from lunch, Jerry Spurdle was waiting for me in his office, sitting in his Italian leather executive chair with his back to the door, talking on the phone. He pretended he didn't see me, though my reflection was clearly visible in the glass wall behind him.

"Yeah, I'm the head fox in this henhouse," he said on the phone. "They brought me and my nine inches of alpha manhood in to dilute the estrogen quotient and provide some real leadership for these moody girls, to make sure they don't fill up the schedule with man-bashing and wife-beater movies."

The line light on his phone was not lit up. He was taking to nobody. This was for my benefit.

Suddenly, he feigned discovery of my presence, and said, "Gotta go."

"So what do you want, Jerry?" I said. "I gotta message to see you ASAP."

"Hey, Robin. I meant to tell you earlier, you're carrying those extra pounds well."

"Thanks."

"I so admire how as you age, you become more and more defiant of those western beauty ideals. You've become a handsome woman, in your way."

It was funny. The more blatantly offensive he became, the less offended and more amused I was. The less offended I was, the more offended and offensive he became. Kick me when I'm down, Jerry. Why not?

"Was there something else, Jerry?"

"Yeah. Too bad about your demotion. You should have listened to me," he said. "I know advertisers and I know programming that sells. Now look what's happened."

Not a word about the ordeal I'd been through. I know he was expecting me to just absolutely lose it, and tell him what a putrid pile of sallow skin he really was.

"Well, it's a blessing in disguise," I said, because saying that instead really pissed him off, and because, yeah, it was a blessing in disguise.

It's a demotion, sure, which normally would be kind of humiliating, and would inspire much mirth among my enemies. But it's a demotion that will take me to Paris for six months, which is, not coincidentally, when my contract is up, and when my old apartment building will be rebuilt. It's a demotion that prevents something worse—having to work around Jerry and Solange in the ulcer-inducing Holy Woman Empire. I won't have to travel as much or as far either.

As W. C. Fields said, "Don't cry over spilt milk, it might have been poisoned," which is another way of saying something bad can prevent something worse.

And how cosmic can you get? I have a thing for a guy in Paris, and I'm being sent to Paris. This would be enough to restore a girl's faith in the universe, provided she didn't find out later that her friend Louis Levin had called up Shonny Cobbs after learning about the shakeup, that her friend Louis had made the case for Paris, and that Shonny then put a few sweet words in her husband's ear about it.

So, here I am, six weeks later, packing my cat and my few remaining belongings to go to Paris. Who knows what will be found there? Romance? Maybe, though Pierre now suspects I'm completely insane. Even though he knows a bit about Maggie's reputation, he thinks I should have trusted him, and that it is a bad sign that I didn't. Evidently, he doesn't know how insidious and convincing Maggie's revenge can be.

Whatever awaits, I know it's going to be great. I don't speak the language, so how much trouble can my big mouth get me into there? I checked the stats on homicide in Paris, and they're very low. They average fewer homicides in all of France than we do in New York City. The odds of having a pleasant, untroubled time during my stay in Paris are very good indeed.

ACKNOWLEDGMENTS

Thanks to my long-suffering editor, Claire Wachtel. In addition to taming my prose and soothing my jangled nerves, she keeps the sticklers for time at bay with her big pitchfork, which she sharpens daily on the backbone of a long-dead *Kirkus Reviews* critic.

Danny Baror, my foreign rights agent and a former Israeli tank commander, leads our underdog battle for World Domination, bringing much foreign booty into our queenly coffers, and we think we owe him many blue drinks, but for now, thanks a million.

I've taken liberties with the characters and layout of the Chelsea Hotel in order to protect the privacy and security of the real residents and, er, serve my story and own nefarious purposes. I thank the Chelsea for indulging me in this, and for so many other things, including a great deal of help with research, much of which didn't make it into this book. To Stanley Bard, who walks the razor's edge between business concerns and his love of artists—I could not have done it without you. Thanks to Michelle, and special thanks to David Bard, who gave me a great deal of his time to show me all the ins and outs of the hotel and share some of the better legends of the place. Jerry Weinstein, you IS the Last Manly Man, man. Bonnie Kendall, **xoxo**. Other Chelsea staff were also helpful and kind: Amy, Jerome, Kevon, Vincent, Pete, Damon, Timur, Steve. My neighbors and friends: Scott Griffin, Tim Moran, Jan Reddy, David and Caroline Remfry, John Wells, Arnold Weinstein, Richard Bernstein, Herbert Gentry, Jan Reddy, Paul Ramiro and Annalee Simpson, Blair and Jennifer, Tony, the Transcendent Turk, Lena, Hiroya, DeeDee, Tony on six—many thanks.

Though the Chelsea makes an appearance in a lot of songs and literature, there is only one comprehensive history of the hotel that I know of, *At the Chelsea*, by Florence Turner, a wonderful book about the hotel in the 1960s. I relied heavily on this book for historical information. I also obtained information from the Chelsea Hotel web site: http://www.chelseahotel.com.

AND THANKS TO:

Sandi Bill, for sharing the philosophy that a bad thing could prevent something worse, which I attributed in this book to Phil. Phil himself was inspired by a guy named Bill who worked for a relief group, IMC, in a refugee camp in Peshawar, Pakistan. I lost his last name. Great guy. Too silly to die.

Noel Behn.

Pat Tracy

Caroline White—no longer my editor, forever an ace dame.

Jennifer Gould.

Diana "My creed is wonder" Greene.

The much-tuckerized Maggie Mason, who lends her name to a character within. Unlike the Maggie Mason in this book, the real Mary Margaret Mason hardly ever steals other women's men—when she can help it.

Nancy Lane.

Lisa and Matthew Quier.

Tamayo Otsuki.

The lovely lady Sammy, her husband, Mohammed; Robby; Hanny; Rene Fitz; and all the other fine-looking gentlemen at the Aristocrat Deli, for many kindnesses and credit above and beyond.

The Reverend Rhoda Sweet Boots.

Nadja Dee.

Cathy Criscuolo, who sent me the Mr. Chicken update.

Joelle Tati, Tania Capron, David Torrence at No Alibis in Belfast, Ion Mills and Pam Smith at No Exit in London, Filthy McNasty's, Lawrence and Lynn, Nevin Hayter, EvaJessie, Ian Simmons, Katrina Onstad, and my accountant, Martin Watkins.